The Reluctant Mother

Hemmie Martin

Winter Goose
PUBLISHING
where words take flight

Winter Goose Publishing
45 Lafayette Road #114
North Hampton, NH 03862

www.wintergoosepublishing.com
Contact Information: info@wintergoosepublishing.com

The Reluctant Mother

COPYRIGHT © 2017 by Hemmie Martin

First Edition, May 2017

Cover Design by Winter Goose Publishing
Typesetting by Odyssey Publishing

ISBN: 978-1-941058-63-3

Published in the United States of America

Also by Hemmie Martin

The Divine Pumpkin
Attic of the Mind
In the Light of Madness
Rightful Owner
Shadows in the Mind
Garlic & Gauloises
What Happens After

For Rosie Woo
Happy 20th birthday, sweetie

To Vicky

Best wishes

Jennie x

Colette

I don't know how I've ended up here; I didn't mean for this to happen. It's supposed to be the start of a new life as a family, but now I barely know or care who I am.

I detest these insipid beige walls, and the lemony light filtering through the window that only partially opens. I need more air. Why are they depriving me?

A scream from another room jolts me, sending a spasm of unabated terror coursing up my spine, before it splays across my shoulder blades like fireworks.

"How are you this morning?" asks a nurse, in a willow-green shirt and faded jeans, carrying a small plastic pot in her hand.

I can't respond, so I cast a fleeting glance towards her eyes and hope she understands me. She hands me a plastic beaker of dusty water before giving me the pot containing tablets of various colours, like jelly beans. I notice the clean white bandages on both of my wrists. She waits for me to swallow the tablets before walking away. *Thank God.*

The isolation gives me space to visit the macabre theatre in my head, only my mind feels like a thick pea-and-ham soup. Nothing makes sense, and I haven't the energy to sift through the swill.

I know one thing for sure: Finn played a part in me being here.

I barely recognize my body. Under my nightdress I detect a squishy, marshmallow-like mound over my stomach. My breasts are engorged, hard, and leaking.

Then, in a moment of clarity, I think about Dylan and wonder how he's doing. Does he miss me? Is he even aware of my existence?

Through the mullioned window, grey clouds are scudding across the sky. They mimic and mock my mood, throwing it back in my face.

I wonder how long they'll keep me here.

Finn

Dylan is crying *again*. My God, is this what parenthood's all about?

"Is my little grandson hungry?"

"That or he needs a nappy change, who knows?" I sigh.

Diana walks over to the Moses basket and picks up a bundle of blankets. A tiny arm stretches out from within, reaching for an invisible thread he hopes is connected to some milk.

"Oh, we have a dirty nappy," she says, wrinkling up her nose. "Over to you, Daddy."

I ease myself off the bed and stroll over to the changing table where I grapple with his squidgy legs. I remove the offending item that's full of a yellow tinged substance, reminiscent of melted toffee ice cream. The smell makes my eyes fur-over.

"It's a shame Colette's missing this," I say, breathing through my mouth.

"You're doing what's best for your son, he's defenceless. Colette's old enough to fend for herself."

"You've never really liked her, have you?"

"Don't be ridiculous; she's nice enough."

I don't want to argue with her. I need her to be around to care for Dylan whilst I ferry between the hospital and home; and she knows it.

"Can we leave our differences to one side for now? I'm just trying to keep things together."

She shrugs and leaves the room.

"So, little fella, are you feeling better now?" I say, picking him up and placing him over my shoulder. Feeling his heavy head lolling against my neck makes me realise how fragile he is. Maybe my mother's right, I need to focus on him; Colette has a whole psychiatric team supporting her.

With Dylan asleep, I take the opportunity to jump in the shower. I need to feel human.

Diana's in the kitchen when I descend. Placing the baby monitor on the Welsh dresser, I sit at the table and butter a slice of cold toast from the rack.

"I should visit Colette today."

"What about Dylan?"

"I can hardly take him with me. I thought you could look after him for a bit," I reply, showering toast crumbs across the table.

She makes an audible sigh I can't fail to notice, but choose not to rise to.

"I can only stay for a couple of hours. I've got Weight Watchers later," she says, patting her hips.

"I'll be back in time."

Seemingly satisfied, she pours freshly percolated coffee and places it in front of me.

"Aren't you afraid when you go there? I mean, all those mad people cooped up together."

"They're not running around naked and screaming. Most are doped up to the eyeballs and sitting around quietly."

"Is Colette like that?"

"Yes. And if you let Dad babysit, you could see for yourself."

"George isn't competent enough to be left alone with a baby; he can barely look after himself."

"I'm sure he'd cope; you worry too much."

"That's what *mothers* do."

I feel the hairs on the back of my neck stand to attention. I avoid eye contact, not wanting to see the I-told-you-so look in her eyes.

I down the dregs of coffee and dust the crumbs from my mouth and lap. Kissing her on the cheek, I leave promptly before Dylan wakes up; I need to conserve my energy for Colette.

Sliding into the driver's seat, I spy Dylan's car seat, reinforcing the fact that I'm a father, yet also highlighting the reason I'm without my wife. Both sentiments collide in my mind, and the discomfort is too unbearable to dwell on.

Without further analysis, I head for the hospital; but not just any hospital, oh no, the one where mentally deranged people reside until they are deemed sane enough to re-enter into society.

Having parked the car, I turn up my collar and march towards the large red-bricked building. I'm thankful for the time alone in the biting wind; it refreshes my mind and helps me focus on what's important. I need Colette to get better.

Crisp brown leaves litter the ground, leaving naked trees shivering in the wind. The high wall around the hospital sends out the message that it's containing the madness within, saving us all from seeing or hearing it, lest it contaminate and whither the human race.

Warm air hits my face as I step inside to sign the dog-eared visitor's book; declaring to the world I have a mad wife, and I'm now unworthy of circulating in civilisation until she's been fully cleansed and cured.

I look through the window in the door and see Colette lying on her bed, with only a sagging belly and uncharacteristically large breasts to indicate she'd had a baby two days ago. She complained to me on my last visit that her nipples leaked milk. I hate the sadness in her eyes.

Tapping on the door, I watch as she turns her head slowly without a smile gracing her lips; I miss that smile. Taking a deep breath, I enter the room.

"Hello darling, how are you today?" I ask, bending down to kiss her on her forehead; her dry lips look too sore and cracked to touch.

She remains silent, but her burnt chocolate eyes scream at me to help her. *How do I do that?*

I pull a chair closer to the side of her bed and sit down. Taking her hand in mine, I give it a squeeze, trying to avert my gaze from the bandages.

Her ebony hair looks stark against the white pillow, and unkempt without the usual gel to tame the elfin cut into neat little points. She'll hate it if she catches sight of herself in a mirror.

"Dylan's doing fine. Mum's looking after him whilst I'm here. I'm not getting much sleep though."

"I don't have an easy time sleeping here either, Finn," she scowls, pulling her hand away.

"I'm sorry. I didn't mean anything by that."

I watch a bulbous tear edge down the side of her nose and settle in the corner of her mouth, as though attempting to moisten her parched lips. It doesn't help.

"Have you seen the doctor today?"

"No, just a nurse asking me if I want to join a therapy group doing God-knows-what. I'm new so they're letting me off, but soon it'll be compulsory to come out of my room and join in. I'm not sure I'll cope."

"You'll cope, you're strong enough. You'll be home soon." I hope my lack of conviction isn't betrayed by my voice. She returns to gazing out the window.

Rain is pelting against the window, casting rivulets of water zigzagging down the glass. For a moment I wish I was standing out there, letting the rain wash away my pain and confusion.

"What happens if I don't get better?"

"You will. This is a passing phase after giving birth."

"I didn't think the baby blues meant a stay in hospital."

"You've got more than the blues, darling. Haven't they explained it?"

I wait for her to reply, but I see her eyelids drooping and her mouth dipping into a down-turned crescent moon.

"I'm tired now," she whispers.

I watch her drift silently into the abyss before quietly creeping out.

A different nurse is now sitting at the nurses' station. I wander over to her but she doesn't look up; a cough gets her attention.

"My wife, Colette Forbes, doesn't seem to know why she's in here, and she's very sleepy. Is that normal?" The last word seems ridiculously out of place.

"She only came in yesterday, so the side effects of the meds are kicking in. She'll get more accustomed to them. The psychiatrist did chat with her about postpartum psychosis but I don't think she's taken it in yet."

The sound of the door buzzer takes her attention away from me. I want to continue talking but I sense her reticence; perhaps working here has chipped away at her humanity? I wonder if nurses are more cautious when socialising and meeting potential partners? Perhaps they assess every person they come into contact with to see whether they're worth the risk.

Feeling defeated, I leave the ward and wander down the unadorned, cold stone corridor towards the freedom outside; somewhere Colette won't be seeing for a few days more.

I leave the ward feeling defeated and wander down the unadorned, cold stone corridor towards the freedom outside; somewhere Colette won't be seeing for a few days more.

I meander towards the car as I'm relishing this fleeting moment, free from responsibility; a notion that is so far removed from reality, I fear some of Colette's madness has rubbed off on me. I set the car in motion and drive home guided more by luck than by judgement. Upon putting my key in the front door, I hear Dylan exercising his lungs. The key slips in my grip.

"Ah, just in time, Daddy. Your son won't settle. I've been carrying him around but nothing's working. Your turn now, I've got to dash off." And with that, Diana rushes out the front door.

"I bet Grandma doesn't tell her friends where your mummy is. What do you think?" I thought talking to him would be soothing but he continues crying. I rock him gently until at last he falls asleep.

I tiptoe upstairs and place him quietly in his basket, his rosebud mouth suckling on an invisible teat, whilst his tiny fingers wrap themselves around the corner of the blanket. He looks a vision of peace and innocence. *Aren't you a lucky boy.*

My body shudders with loneliness. The house is still and the air is void of tempting cooking aromas. The radio is silent, missing its avid listener. I wonder if she misses Woman's Hour?

I flick the kettle on and tip some coffee granules into a mug, which

I notice is chipped; Colette will undoubtedly throw it away once she returns home.

The kitchen was always a cluttered room, but with the bulky sterilizer and array of feeding bottles and tins of powdered formula scattered along the worktops, the claustrophobic feel is more intense. I'm struggling with it, and I know Colette will hate it.

I want to sit in the garden, but the inclement weather dictates otherwise; the sofa in the lounge will have to do. I rest my head against the back of the sofa and stare at the ceiling, where cobweb hammocks hang from the dusty light fitting to the cracked cornices.

Finally, I have the headspace to reflect on the previous couple of days, from when Colette's changes were no longer manageable.

Dylan was born at ten in the morning, so after the obligatory checks, the midwife said mother and baby could be taken home. I was bolstered by mental concrete pillars of dread; momentous responsibility thrust upon me, whilst Colette wept silently. The midwife said the baby blues were normal and that they would soon pass.

But Colette became agitated and less engaged with Dylan. I took over the role of nappy changer and pacifier—the latter for both of them. Colette found breastfeeding too stressful and painful, so I rushed out to acquire bottles and formula.

The midwife kept popping in, a concerned look brushed across her face. She quelled my quiet concerns, placating me by saying men couldn't possibly comprehend what a woman has to go through during the process of giving birth. There was a lot of adjusting to do and I should be supportive and patient. But I could tell something was wrong by the uneasy quality of the atmosphere during the visits.

I watched as my wife morphed from a charismatic, enthusiastic woman, into a shadow of blackness interspersed with mood changes that defied understanding. If Dylan cried or whimpered, she snapped at him and anyone around her.

When I told her my parents wanted to visit their first grandchild, she said she believed my parents were going to take Dylan away from her.

When I told her that was ridiculous, she burst into tears and said that of course I was on their side and hobbled out of bed and locked herself in the bathroom, refusing to come out.

I called the midwife to seek advice, and she lambasted me as though I'd shut her in there myself. Then before I knew it, Colette was transported to hospital, and I was handed Dylan to look after.

As though piqued by my thoughts, Dylan wakes, announcing his displeasure at being left alone. I dash up the stairs two by two, scooping him up before placing him over my shoulder. He begins suckling on my neck.

He hollers throughout the whole process of preparing a bottle; if there was a time when I wished I had lactating breasts, it's now.

The evening ahead stretches out like the night before Christmas does for a child. The interminable time seems doubly worse as I only have Dylan to punctuate the time by his feeding and nappy changing routine. It means I can't even drown my sorrows in a few pints of beer at the pub, or even in the house, come to that.

I only become aware of the doorbell ringing when someone leans on it persistently. With Dylan cradled in my arms and a bottle lodged in his mouth, I move to the door and negotiate opening it.

"Oh my, don't you look the doting daddy," declares Lois, Colette's best friend.

"Hi, um . . . I've rather got my hands full . . ."

"Don't fret, why don't I come in and make a cup of coffee. Or I can hold the little one whilst you open a bottle of wine."

Looking at her, I think if I pass him over, he'll chomp at her breasts believing they're full of milk. I've often wondered if they're full of silicon. But I digress. Standing back, I let her in. As she sashays by, her heavy oriental perfume mixes with the baby sick on my shoulder, resulting in a nauseating odour. I'm sure Colette would tell me off for not using one of the special positing cloths she's bought.

Dylan finishes his bottle as Lois fills the kettle. She then turns around and leans against the worktop.

"So when's Colette coming home?"

I look at her blankly. How does she know?

As if reading my mind, she explains. "Diana told me what happened. I'm really sorry. Anyway, she thought you could do with some adult company."

"She was quick in telling you."

"I met her in the deli and I asked if I could visit the new family. She said I could but I wouldn't find Colette at home. She told me everything in a very hushed, theatrical tone. She's so funny."

I'd forgotten how much my mother likes Lois. We were all friends who grew up together and attended the same sixth form. She appeared disappointed when I started dating Colette and not Lois. But it was not for her to choose.

"So, how's she doing and when can I visit her?"

"I don't think visiting her there is a good idea. She'll be home soon in any case."

Lois spoons coffee granules into two mugs before pouring the water in. "What's it like in there?"

"Just like a normal hospital."

"Really?"

I don't want to talk about it. Why doesn't Dylan cry when I need him to?

As I lay him down in his Moses basket on the table, I feel Lois's eyes bore into me.

"So how are you doing?" she asks, handing me a mug.

"Bearing up, I suppose. I have to for Dylan's sake."

"It must be a shock though. I mean, Colette's never had mental problems in the past, has she?"

"She gets moody and stroppy once a month like you all do." She throws a damp tea towel at me. "See what I mean," I smile.

It feels good to smile, and yet so wrong.

A sliver of weak sun breaks through the cloud and catches Lois's honey-coloured hair. The blunt fringe always made her Delphinium-blue eyes stand out, much like the eyes on a porcelain doll.

"I can come 'round and keep you company in the evenings if you like. I'll bring wine." She says it as though we were seventeen again, drinking whilst the parents were out.

"The wine won't be necessary, but adult interaction would be good. I can't promise to be scintillating company, though."

Dylan stirs, making a meowing sound like a kitten before settling down again.

"I bet you haven't eaten properly since kiddo was born. Why don't I whip us up something? I'll see what's in your fridge," she says, pulling the door open. "You have wine and champagne."

"That was to celebrate with Colette when we all got home."

"You'll be sharing it with her soon enough. Here, pour a couple of glasses. I'll throw something together."

It's nice to have someone looking after me. Picking up the Moses basket, I gently move Dylan upstairs. My mother says he looks like I did as a baby, but all I see is Colette, with his fine features and tiny button-nose.

By the time I return downstairs, the kitchen is alive with the aroma of garlic.

"I've made a mushroom, cream, and garlic sauce to go with pasta. Hope that's okay?"

"Sounds great."

I devour the food, caring not that it's burning the roof of my mouth; a few gulps of chilled white wine dampens the fire.

"I'm sorry I haven't asked. How are things with you?" I mumble.

"I'm cool. I mean, William's dumped me, but hey, I can cope with rejection."

"He's a fool. I thought you were both getting along so well."

"All it took was a few differences here and there for it to implode." She takes a sip of wine. "I want to find what you and Colette have. You know; deep friendship as well as love."

"You'll find it, and usually when you're not looking for it."

"I hear you. Anyway, cheers to your new family," she says as she holds her glass aloft.

She holds my gaze a second too long.

Colette

I can't even pronounce what the psychiatrist has just told me I'm suffering from. I ask for a clearer explanation in a voice I don't recognize as my own.

"Postpartum psychosis. It's a psychotic episode sometimes experienced after giving birth. It's different from postpartum depression, although you can still feel depressed . . ."

"But why am I feeling this way?" I have to interrupt him before he overwhelms me with more big words, and mechanical drivel.

"We believe it's linked to the hormonal changes during pregnancy and the birth."

"How long will I be here?"

"We'll keep monitoring you, but it could be up to eight weeks."

I can't hide the shock on my face.

"You've no history of mental illness prior to this episode, have you?"

I shake my head.

"This may just be a one-off episode. Let's take this one day at a time, Mrs Forbes."

I suspect he doesn't want to spend time allaying my fears. To him, I'm just another woman unable to hold on to my sanity. Another woman destined to be an inadequate mother.

I watch him walk out of the room followed by a posse of medical students, like ducklings following their mother.

I wait for the nurse to return, who will undoubtedly force me to leave my room and engage in one of the therapeutic groups. I can't be bothered with myself, let alone strangers.

A distant memory of my baby surfaces through the quagmire. I realize I don't even remember what he looks like, or what his cry sounds like. I don't know how heavy he is, or whether he has that powdered baby scent. Does that make me an awful mother?

There's that scream again. I wish whoever it is would give us all a rest and kill themselves. The cut under the bandage on my left wrist is itching, so I rub it against the bed frame making the wound hurt, but it feels good at the same time.

Flashing images against the backdrop of my eyelids show me smashing a mirror from my handbag and slicing my wrist with a jagged edge. I miss Finn.

"Right then, Mrs Forbes, the doctor thinks you should participate in a group this morning. There's an art session in the day room in ten minutes. That should give you enough time to get ready."

The nurse vanishes before I have time to protest, so I drag my heavy body off the bed and put a cardigan on. It is an oversized garment, allowing me to wrap it around myself, forming a woolly shield against the world.

It's my first journey down the corridor since my arrival. I'm surprised to find only a few private rooms and then two long wards, one for men and the other for women. I wonder whether I'll be moved to the ward eventually. I hope not.

The day room is easy to find thanks to the large bright sign on the door. The walls are a disgusting banana yellow, with posters offering mission statements and proverbs focusing on mental wellbeing and serenity.

"Welcome, I'm Hannah," says the young woman who is putting out coloured crayons and chalk.

I give her a brief smile and wait for her to tell me what to do. I'm tempted to leave when the arrival of another patient forces me further into the room.

"Good morning, Holly. How about you take . . ."

"Colette," I say quietly.

". . . Colette to sit next to you."

So here I am, sitting in the dayroom next to a woman who is clearly younger, and by the look of her matted hair and gregarious makeup, madder than me.

Five more people arrive, including two men; they both look roughly my age. There's another young woman, and I wonder if she's had a baby too?

The art therapist hands out paper and requests that we all draw what our mental health issue looks like to us; like Winston Churchill's proverbial black dog, she says.

I have no idea what mental health looks like. *What is she talking about?*

I'm feeling wildly uncomfortable in the group, as though I've cheated my way in. I watch their nervous tics and twitches, coughs and mutterings, and I wonder if I'm displaying my demons as they are theirs.

Holly introduces me to the group, but everyone appears in their own world, reluctant to let anyone in. I suppose that's just how I'm feeling; it's like looking through a mirror, and it's disturbing.

Holly moves around the large table and sidles up to me.

"How are you getting on?" she says, looking at the blank sheet. "Try not to think about it too much. Let your thoughts flow into your crayon. It doesn't have to be perfect or clever or even artistic. Just open your mind and allow your thoughts to be translated onto the page."

I keep my eyes shielded from hers. *What is she talking about?*

I glance around to see what others are drawing. Some are drawing houses with black roofs; others are drawing bolts of lightning, or just doodling. The girl next to me appears to be drawing herself as she's drawing her plaited hair.

I really try to let my emotions flow, but they're gripping tightly to the shell of my mind. The only thing I want to draw is a baby covered with black lines, but I don't want her to see my baby. Instead, I draw a black ball of scribbles, like a child does before understanding the meaning of outlines.

I sense pity emanating from the girl next to me, so I shield my paper with my arm. Her breath feels hot on my flesh as she exhales forcefully.

Holly continues moving around the room, speaking to individuals about their work. I hope to God she doesn't come back to me. But eventually she does.

"It means nothing really. I couldn't think what to draw," I lie. Her breath smells of tobacco, thinly veiled by peppermint.

"Maybe this is exactly how you're feeling at this moment in time. It's early days and you're probably confused and suffering with the side effects of the meds."

I nod in agreement to appease her. But I know what's wrong with me, having a baby has made me mad. Could I possibly turn the clock back?

After an hour, we all shuffle out of the room, leaving Holly to put our drawings into our folders. The two men stand outside the door discussing football, but the rest of us move silently away; we're floating in our own soundproof bubbles.

The corridor stinks of food, reminiscent of primary school dinners. Deep vats of minced beef slopped over small pasta shapes, or greasy sausage rolls and fatty chips. The scent is making my stomach fold over, so I'm going to hide in my room until the feeding of the mad dogs is over.

Finn

Dylan attempts to grab my earlobe as I bend down to kiss him before leaving. He smells of baby powder with a faint hint of formula. Surprisingly, neither is unpleasant. I catch Diana looking at me with grave concern in her eyes, as my father's head is buried in the newspaper.

"You're not going to bring her home before she's fixed, are you?"

"I don't think 'fixed' is the right term, Mum. And I doubt I'll be able to do anything without the doctor's say so."

"I wish you'd get involved more, George," she snipes.

"Finn knows what he's doing. Everything will be fine in the end."

"What do you know? You hardly join in with our discussions."

"I watch from afar, like an omniscient being. I can see things more clearly that way."

Diana's broken vessels on her cheeks almost give off a florescent glow. I decide to step in to stop things escalating.

"I think Dylan would appreciate a soothing atmosphere. Why don't you two take him out for a stroll? There are blankets in the buggy."

Diana looks outside as the weak winter sun peeks through the soft grey clouds. George puts down his paper and rubs his hands together.

"Good idea, Son. It will do us all good to get out for a bit. Send my love to Colette."

He always says the right thing.

"Did Lois pop 'round yesterday?" Diane asks nonchalantly.

"She did." I don't want to discuss the matter further, and I can't put the visit off any longer.

It's a pleasant morning to be strolling around, and I hope my parents and Dylan are having a good time. As I reflect on the morning's conversation, it occurs to me that Diana never sent her love to Colette. Perhaps she's struggling with this whole mental issue more than I thought.

Once on the ward, a nurse directs me to the courtyard outside, saying Colette is enjoying some fresh air. The change in situation gives me hope she's on the mend. My hope is punctured as I see her face.

"Hello darling. It's peaceful out here, isn't it?" I say.

She turns slightly towards me as though not recognizing my voice. Her eyes are glossy and glazed, like American doughnuts.

I sit down next to her on the bench, but she shuffles a few inches away. I contain the pinched feeling on my heart.

"I've brought your favourite sea salt chocolate. Would you like me to open it?"

She doesn't seem to register what I'm saying, so I place the bar on her lap. My hand brushes over hers and I'm sorely tempted to hold it, but I sense her tense-up, so I withdraw.

"I've brought a few photos of Dylan. I thought you might like to keep them with you." I pull an envelope from my jacket pocket and take out the first photo. It's the one of Dylan sleeping in his basket.

She doesn't take it from me. Doesn't she love our son? I resist the urge to ask her the potentially explosive question.

We sit here in silence for ten minutes, with only the occasional blackbird landing on a bare tree branch to break the monotony with its beautiful song. Then something snaps inside of me. I need to talk to someone about her, she's no longer the woman I married, and I'm scared.

She remains impassive as I stand and hurry inside to find a nurse. I need answers.

"Excuse me; can I speak to you about my wife?"

She looks up and frowns. "Yes, Mr Forbes."

"I'm not sure she recognizes me, and she's not interested in the photos of our new baby. What's happening to her?"

"It can be common for a woman to feel detached from her baby as a result of the symptoms of postpartum psychosis. Unfortunately, we don't have a mother and baby unit here, and the nearest one is full."

"That isn't necessary; I wouldn't let her keep our son with her in any case."

She just stares at me then searches under the desk for something, before presenting me with a leaflet.

"Hopefully you'll find all the answers to your queries in this."

I take it and glance over the front cover. The words are jumbled and incomprehensible so I fold it in half and shove it in my jacket pocket. I hover in front of the desk unsure of what to do next.

Out of the corner of my eye, I spot Colette making her way back to her room. I don't know how to react. Should I press her to offer me more interaction, or should I let her work at her own pace? Heavy heartedly, I leave.

With a deep breath, I put my key in the front door; seeing Diana daily is posing more of a challenge than I expected.

I find her sitting at the kitchen table opposite Lois who's cradling Dylan in her arms. They both look at me as I hover in the doorway. Why are women making me feel uncomfortable today?

"Look who's popped by," Diana says, pointing out the obvious.

Lois peers at me from under her eyelash-teasing fringe and smiles. "Thought I'd see how Daddy is doing. But as you weren't here, Diana offered me a coffee."

"You've always been such a good friend to Finn. Anyway, I think I'll leave you young ones to talk. George and I are having lunch with some friends." She stands, removing her jacket from the back of the chair. Bizarrely, I don't want her to leave.

I watch her kiss Dylan and Lois before I accompany her to the front door.

"If you'd like an evening off, your father and I could babysit whilst you take Lois out for a meal. The change would do you good."

"Thanks for the offer, but I don't think I'd be much company."

Diana shakes her head slightly, kissing me on the cheek. "Think about it."

On returning to the kitchen, I find Lois washing out the coffee mugs; I see her watching me in the reflection of the window.

"Thanks for coming over, but I'm okay now," I say, hoping she'll take the hint.

"I'm your friend; of course I want to check on you. I can't imagine how you're managing to cope."

"Surprising well, actually. Dylan's a leveller."

"Yes, but Dylan also needs a strong and calm daddy. You don't want to be passing all this stress onto him. You need to lean on someone too."

"I've got my parents."

"Oh please, you're not talking to a stranger. I *know* your parents, remember."

I laugh; she's right. My mother's a cantankerous and pompous Women's Institute Chair, and my father's like a garden gnome; jolly to look at, but pretty useless.

The lightness of mood draws me in, and before I know it, Lois and I are reminiscing about our youth over a strong mug of coffee. When she throws her head back and laughs, I'm transported back to the halcyon days when worries were for others and fun was the only goal of the day.

"Colette isn't the same person, I think you'd be shocked," I finally say.

"Why don't you let me go with you next time? It might do her good to see me, and I'll be a support for you."

I know what she's saying makes sense. And the drive there and back would be less onerous.

"Okay, come with me this evening. We could go for a meal afterwards. Mum said they'd babysit."

Lois agrees, and I actually feel like I can get through the day alone with my son.

"I'll be off then. These could do with a polish," she says, holding out her hands and wiggling her fingers.

There it is again, that intoxicating smell of her perfume as she bends down to kiss me. It lingers in the air long after she's gone.

A few hours later, the doorbell rings announcing my parent's arrival, laden with shopping bags.

"I didn't think you'd have much in for us to eat," Diana says, handing me a carrier bag.

George just nods, raising his eyebrows as he enters. I'm about to follow them when the bell rings again, and my mouth slackens as Lois stands before me, in what can only be described as an all-in-one Lycra cat suit, as worn by a Russian gymnast.

"Are you ready to go?" she asks.

"Um . . . come in a minute, I need to grab some things."

Diana peeks around the kitchen door and greets Lois.

"You look stunning. Hope you have a lovely evening."

I cringe at her choice of words, has she forgotten we're visiting Colette first?

I dash upstairs and grab a bag of clothes to take to Colette, then run back down before Diana can say anything else inappropriate.

Lois's perfume swamps the atmosphere in the closed confines of the car, so I crack open the window and set off.

We drive in silence, my heartbeat pulsating behind my eyes as I think about sharing Colette's temporary lunacy with someone else. It will make everything real, and I'm not sure I'm ready for that.

The nurse at reception looks wide-eyed as Lois signs the visitor's book after me. I wonder whether Colette will give the same reaction; although any reaction from her would be good right now.

Colette

I recognise Finn's knock on the door. I wish I had more joy in my heart to share with him.

Instead of turning to see him, I watch him in the reflection of the window, thanks to the ebony gloom outside. But my lungs involuntarily seize-up as I see another figure behind him; a figure with a glowing halo.

I'm determined not to turn my head, but then I hear her voice.

"Colette, I'm so happy to see you," Lois says as she flits around my bed to face me. Her hand feels soft and cold on my arm.

I feel the corners of my mouth twitch, but the smile doesn't materialise.

"Your baby boy is gorgeous; he looks just like his daddy. Diana's helping out and I'm supporting Finn so he can care for you and Dylan." She pats the back of my hand. "How are you doing?"

"I'm not sure," is all I can reply.

Finn drags a chair over so they're both in my vision. He looks rugged with stubble on his chin, and his hair slightly grown out of his normally cropped style. There are more flecks of premature white hair on his head and chin; he's looking distinguished.

As he reaches for my hand, I don't want to flinch, but it's like an automatic reflex, I can no more stop that than keep my eyes open when I sneeze.

I see the hurt in his eyes as he slides his hand back. I want to tell him not to blame me, it's his fault I'm in here.

My eyelids begin closing involuntarily, but not before I notice how beautiful Lois is looking. She's not changed over the years; time has done her no harm. I always knew I couldn't compete with her in the looks department, but I never needed to, as I got Finn.

Through my half-closed eyes I see them looking comfortable together.

He deserves someone as beautiful as her, not the emotionally wrecked average-looking me. I close my eyes, willing them to leave.

My eyes are closed, but my ears remain receptive to their whispers. Much as I try, I can't help hearing the odd word. Tired; distant; depression; recovering; an array of words that mean nothing. *Are they talking about me?*

Distorted images bombard my mind. I imagine them holding hands, with Lois resting her head on his shoulder; her blond hair rippling over his body. He looks content. I haven't seen him looking like that for a long time.

I mentally glue my eyelids shut to encourage them to go. *Please let me be.*

Finn

The atmosphere in the restaurant is in sharp contrast to the hospital. The sage-green walls glow softly in the flickering light from candles placed on every table and grouped together on the mantelpiece. Orange and tangerine flames glimmer in the fireplace, rippling warmth over the convivial environment. I can finally breathe.

I'm aware of people looking in our direction as we're shown to our table, then I realize they're looking at Lois, not me. I suppose I would be checking her out discreetly in their position as well.

"I've never been here before. It got rave reviews in the local paper," she says.

"It's fairly close to the hospital so I booked it out of convenience, really."

"And there's me thinking you'd booked it because of the romantic ambiance."

I look at her blankly.

"All the candles, silly."

"I'm a man. I don't notice subtleties like that."

The waiter arrives and hands us a menu and the wine list. It's more haute cuisine than I'd realized, but Lois seems enamoured with the place, so who am I to complain?

I finally find something bland enough to eat to match my withered appetite. To be honest, I don't want to be here, I want to be at home with my son, holding him asleep in my arms.

"You look a million miles away. What's bothering you?" she asks.

"When we first discovered Colette was pregnant we were so excited. We had no idea it would end up this way, and I'm not sure if I'll ever get the true Colette back."

"Of course you will. The nurse said this was just a psychotic episode.

That doesn't mean forever. You'll have the vibrant Colette back before you know it."

"I hope you're right. It's just so damn hard having sleepless nights with Dylan, then hospital visits on top of working."

"I could always stay over and do the night duty for a while to give you a rest."

My eyes widen.

"In the spare room, silly. Anyway, the offer's there."

When our food finally arrives, I find the lamb shank succulent, but my stomach can't cope with the richness. A burning bubble pumps up my oesophagus and explodes in my mouth.

I excuse myself and dash to the men's room to rinse out my mouth and splash my face with cold water. My reflection looks pale and haunted. Fatherhood is truly taking its toll on me.

I return to the table feeling sheepish, and Lois graciously lulls me back into conversation.

"You need it more than me, so why don't you drink and I'll drive us back afterwards."

Without hesitating, she fills up my glass then requests a bottle of sparkling water from the waiter. I don't have the strength to object, my brain is clicking over at minimal speed.

The wine tastes good; in fact, everything seem brighter, and Lois looks stunning. A heavy ache in my heart periodically drags me down; reminding me that life isn't so sweet outside of here, but I bat those thoughts away.

"Colette's a very lucky lady."

"I don't think she'd agree with you currently."

"I guess not."

She pours the remainder of sparkling water into her glass and toys with the floating slice of lemon with her middle finger.

"When did you fall in love with her?"

"I think it was the first time we met. She was so complex and I knew it would take me a lifetime to get to know her. I knew she'd keep me interested."

"That sounds clichéd. Perhaps her complexity was hiding this from you."

"What do you mean?"

"I've been reading up on postpartum psychosis. This could happen again if she has another baby." She pauses to sip some water. "It's also possible that this is the first episode of bipolar disorder. She could remain mentally ill and need medication all her life."

I swallow a piece of lamb I've barely chewed and it lodges in my throat, only to descend slowly towards my stomach in uncomfortable spasms. I swig large mouthfuls of wine.

"The doctor never mentioned that." It feels wrong to use the word psychiatrist at this moment in time. "Where did you read this?"

"On the Internet. I thought I should warn you. How would you cope?"

My eyes scan the room in a daze. I see table after table of normal couples. If Colette's mad, would we still be able to dine out? I feel my skin prickle with sweat underneath my shirt. The lamb chunk has finally reached my stomach, only to sit there like a brick on a lily pad.

"That won't happen to Colette. The doctor said it was a one-off episode."

"What does he know?"

"And what do *you* know? You seem to want her to be ill." My voice notches up a couple of levels, and the people next to us stare.

"Don't be silly, she's my best friend. But I'm also your friend, and now you're a father I want what's best for you all."

I can see I've upset her. Her head's bent forward so her fringe forms a shield, although the candlelight still catches a bead of moisture in the corner of her eye.

"I'm sorry, Lois. That was totally uncalled for. I'm just under a lot of strain at the moment." I reach across the white linen tablecloth and touch her fingertips. "Let's not fall out, you're a good friend and I need you right now."

Her shoulders drop as she lifts her eyes to meet mine. She moves her fingers beneath mine, and for a fleeting moment, I'm once again transported back to a time when life was simple.

Lois begs me to share some cheesecake with her and I reluctantly capitulate. Occasionally, our spoons clash.

"Do you fancy a coffee?" I ask.

"How about we have one back at yours? We need to relieve your parents from baby duty."

She's right. I'd momentarily forgotten about my parents. And Dylan. I'm a terrible father.

Lois is a less cautious driver than me, and I feel myself sobering up on the journey back as I grip my seat with my sweaty hands. By the time she finally parks outside my house, my neck is knotted and my stomach feels queasy.

I brace myself to hear Dylan crying as I put the key in the door, only to be welcomed by a serene atmosphere, with my parents sitting in the lounge watching TV.

"You're back early," Diana says.

"We thought we'd relieve you," replies Lois.

"Oh there was no need to. Dylan had a feed and a change an hour ago. He's been a poppet all evening."

"Thanks to you two," I utter.

"Your father did nothing as per usual."

"There was no call for my expertise, your mother had everything under control," pipes up George, winking at Lois.

"I'm going to make a coffee. Would you like one?" she offers.

My parents decline then Diana decides they should go and leave us in peace.

"Hope you have a lovely evening," says Diana.

"That all rather depends on Dylan," I say, hugging her. I find a moment of comfort within her corpulent arms.

Lois puts the kettle on as I see them off. On my return, I find her leaning against the Welsh dresser, looking lost in thought.

"Seeing Colette earlier upset me. She didn't seem the same person."

"She's not at the moment, I did warn you. She's ill and needs help to regain her normality."

"How long will she be in there?"

"Up to eight weeks. It really depends on her progress."

The kettle boils, sending plumes of steam circulating around the kitchen cupboards and spiralling towards the hideous Artex ceiling. I pour a couple of whiskeys, deciding against coffee all of a sudden, and take them into the lounge with Lois following behind.

We sit on either end of the sofa. The whiskey coats my throat, soothing the passage to my stomach and urging my eyes to close as my head lolls on the back of the sofa.

I'm not sure if I've fallen asleep, but I'm suddenly disturbed by Lois moving from the sofa.

"I think Dylan's stirring; I'll check on him. Don't forget your drink."

She glides upstairs before I'm privy to hear her chattering away to him through the baby monitor. It's funny hearing her use a sing-song voice, a voice she's never used before. Dylan sounds as though he's settling again, so I pick up my glass and drain the last of the amber liquid.

By the time she returns, my body is swamped with fatigue and I can barely string two words together; the past few days have battered me like a gale lashing against open shutters on a house. She pulls me to my feet then guides me up to bed.

Colette

I wake up feeling irritable, so when the nurse arrives with my meds, I'm horribly rude to her before throwing the tiny pot of tablets across the room. Then out of nowhere I burst into tears.

She returns with more tablets which I toss into my mouth and swallow with a gulp of water.

"How about getting washed and dressed. You've an appointment with your psychiatrist later this morning," she cajoles.

Her words punch me in the stomach, draining me of air and the ability to talk. I turn away and wait for her to leave. I'm not going to another session of anything; the art therapy was abysmal, and I harbour such anger towards the psychiatrist who's keeping me here, I fear I may harm him and make matters worse.

It's early morning and only darkness filters through the crack in the curtains. The corridor and my room are bathed in a crude fluorescent light which burns bright orange on my retinas. I swear I'm acquiring more frown lines since my admission. There's a constant smell of antiseptic and fear lingering in the air, intermingled with stale sweat and rank trainers and slippers, standing regimented next to beds.

I spy the bag Finn brought in, and I'm curious to see what he's packed for me. I get up and drag it off the chair, heaving it onto the bed with a thump. The teeth of the zip snag as I rip it open before pushing my hand in and yanking the contents out.

Fragments of my life spill over the rough hospital blanket. Jeans which I doubt I'll fit, a jumper I barely remember; two t-shirts and another nightie. A miss-matched selection of underwear which has obviously been bundled into a corner of the bag as an afterthought.

Tucked inside the jumper is a photo of a baby I take to be Dylan, why else would it be there? I stare at his face; round like a cherub's with a shock of black hair on top of his head. His eyes are like chocolate buttons, and his nose is like a mini marshmallow pushed into the centre of his face.

I'm disturbed by the fact that my heart doesn't leap at the sight of him. A mother's whole heart should surely lurch towards her baby instinctively?

I put the photo face down on the bedside table and drop back on the bed. A blanket of black smoke engulfs me, squeezing me so tightly I can't breathe. I want it to suffocate me, so I can leave this miserable world I now inhabit.

But is it the world's fault, or is it Dylan's?

My shallow breaths make my heart spin. Is Finn the devil who tricked me into marriage and deceived me into having his child, whom he knew would make me ill? Maybe they both want me out of the way?

I'm drowning in wave after wave of fluctuating emotions when the nurse returns and coaxes me into getting washed and dressed. I want to resist her, but I don't have the energy.

I pull on the pair of jeans and encourage them over my thighs, but there's no way they're going to fasten over the ripples of flab rolling over the top of my knickers. I fling them across the room narrowly missing the vase of flowers on the table. The nurse stands by the door, refraining from picking them up.

I scrabble around for something else to wear, but end up wearing the maternity trousers I came in, with a fresh t-shirt that crushes my lactating breasts.

Avoiding the mirror, I run my fingers through my hair as I follow the nurse down the corridor to the psychiatrist's office. Once in the room, she sits at the back, hovering like a bodyguard ready to protect her master.

I don't know if I've seen the psychiatrist before, as I don't recognize him. He is neither handsome nor ugly, but rather non-descript. With his shaved head it's impossible to tell whether he's losing his hair or has the style out of choice. He wears John Lennon glasses perched on the tip of his beak-like nose, and a thin moustache ripples along his top lip rather like a spiky caterpillar.

He introduces himself as Doctor Holland before asking me how I am.

I'm sure he can read my mind, so I stay mute, focusing on his forehead, willing him to hear my thoughts so I don't have to bother talking.

He waits for several minutes, tapping his pen on his front teeth. "How are you feeling right now, Colette?"

I'm surprised and annoyed he doesn't know the answer. He's peering intently at me, invading my aura.

"I think my husband and son have conspired against me to make me feel this way."

"How have they done that?"

"I don't bloody know." I feel myself blushing.

"What makes you think that?"

"I don't know, I can't think straight, but I keep hearing Dylan telling me that I'm worthless and he doesn't want me as his mummy."

Dr Holland jots down a few words on the pad resting on his lap.

"Have you ever felt like this prior to giving birth? Any bouts of depression?"

"No."

"Any family history of mental health issues?"

"My mum was depressed at times," I whisper before putting my hands on either side of my head to stop his questions drilling into my mind. He's my enemy too.

"Your questions are painful and confusing. I'd like to go back to my room, please." I stand up and turn towards the door. I notice the nurse also stands.

They don't stop me as I open the door and head for my room, but I hear the nurse's footsteps close behind me.

Entering my room, I fling myself face down on my bed and burst into tears. The nurse asks if I need anything, but I tell her to piss off, which she does very, very quietly.

Finn

I wake up to the smell of coffee and bacon. But what startles me the most is the silence that floats in the atmosphere; something feels wrong.

I push myself up on my elbows, allowing my foggy head to clear before climbing out of bed and grabbing my dressing gown from the back of the door.

I follow the mouth-watering aroma and find myself standing in the kitchen doorway looking at Lois grilling bacon and holding Dylan over her shoulder. He's fast asleep, his face nestled into the nape of her neck.

"I don't know whether health and safety would allow cooking bacon whilst holding a baby," I whisper, smiling at her.

"I'm coping very well, thank you very much. Come in and grab a coffee, and stop worrying."

Instead of taking Dylan from her, I pour myself a coffee and sit down just as she puts a plate before me. The bacon roll smells divine.

"I can't believe I slept all through the night, and so did Dylan."

"Actually, he didn't. He woke up at two, four, and six, but you slept through them all."

"Hell, I must have had a lot to drink. I'm so sorry to have put upon you like that."

"No worries, I said I could help out. I'll take a nap later whilst you play Daddy."

I bite into the soft roll and the fat is crispy and heavenly in contrast to the doughy, flour-topped bread. I watch her lay Dylan down in his basket before grabbing a coffee and sitting opposite me.

"I've never given motherhood a thought, but last night I had a taste of it and I like it." She takes a sip of coffee, fixing me with her china blue eyes.

"You've tasted one sleepless night, but wait until you've a whole week or a month of it. I doubt you'd feel so sweet about it then."

"That depends on who the daddy is I'm sharing the sleepless nights with."

I shrug, biting into the roll once more; remembering Lois was always the optimistic go-getter of the group.

Dylan stirs, wriggling his bottom and stretching his arms out as though begging to be lifted up.

"I'll get him," I say, as we both stand.

His nappy feels bulky, so I take him upstairs to unpeel it, revealing a sticky beige substance. I breathe through my mouth but my eyes are still watering.

He lies on the mat as I wrap him up like a parcel. He's got Colette's eyes, and staring at him makes me feel connected to her, so scooping him up, I hug him tightly before returning downstairs.

Lois is now in the lounge browsing through one of Colette's old Cosmopolitan magazines. I sit down at the other end of the sofa with Dylan.

"Why isn't Colette in a mother and baby unit?" she asks, closing the magazine.

"They don't have a unit here and they couldn't find a space elsewhere. Besides, I don't think she's well enough to take care of him; she barely takes care of herself properly."

"Are you going to take him to visit her?"

"Not just yet. The doctor wants her to stabilise more first. Besides, Mum is fiercely guarding him here, and you know how she can be. I've given her the day off today."

"Aren't you going to visit her today?"

A lump forms in my throat, causing me to cough. I don't want to face the prospect of seeing her today. It's too damn hard. I want solutions, I want to make things right for her, but I'm impotent and I hate it. I don't answer her question and she doesn't push me.

A while later, when Dylan starts grumbling for a feed again, Lois has anticipated his needs and has a bottle already prepared.

"I wouldn't have taken you for the mothering type," I say as she tests the milk's temperature on her pale wrist.

"I've not had the opportunity before. You two are the first of the group to venture into this world," she replies, handing me the bottle.

Dylan's lips purse to accommodate the teat, and he quickly settles to feed. He looks up at me, locking eyes. *Hello, Colette.*

"Why don't we take him out today? We could pop to a café later and have a cream tea. I really fancy some clotted cream." A smile parts her lips slightly so I catch a glimpse of her white teeth.

"I'm not sure I'm ready for that. Parenting seems too scary outside of the house."

"Nonsense, I'm here to help you. We'll pack one of those bags mums always have hanging on the back of the buggy. We'll feed and change him before we go. What can go wrong?"

What indeed? I reflect on her words and come to the conclusion that it's worth a shot. Through the window, the rain has dissipated to a fine drizzle.

"That's settled then, I'm going to lie down. Wake me up in an hour, Finn."

As she walks past me, I smell her scent mixed in with Colette's mint shower gel. I close my eyes briefly to envisage a woman concocted of both of them; the quirkiness and love of the former, with the sexy beauty and sanity of the latter. What a perfect woman she would be.

I cradle Dylan with his bottle in the crook of my arm and phone the hospital.

"I'm enquiring after my wife, Colette Forbes. How is she this morning?"

I listen as a nurse tells me of Colette's fractious night, lack of appetite, and unwillingness to care for herself or engage with others. It all sounds so hopeless. And then I lie.

"I'm afraid I won't be able to visit her today. I've got an urgent matter to deal with."

The nurse's tone of voice remains neutral; I suppose they're trained to respond that way. I say I'll visit tomorrow. Replacing the receiver, I quash the rising shame within me.

Stepping outside with a buggy feels nerve-racking. Lois offers to push but I feel I should get used to it; I need to be a father not just a lying husband.

I turn my collar up and tuck Dylan's blanket around his tiny form, before raising the hood up to protect him as we walk towards the town.

Women smile at us, occasionally peeking inside the buggy, as though they have an in-built radar seeking out new-borns.

"Let's go in here," Lois says as we reach Violet's, a Victorian tea shop.

I peer through the leaded bay window and see small round tables decorated with white lace tablecloths and a posy of undoubtedly fake violets in a miniature white vase.

Lois opens the door for me and I bump the buggy up the small step, jolting Dylan but not waking him. Once inside, I feel overwhelmed with choice of tables, just like I am with spaces in an empty car park.

"Let's sit here," she says, standing by the table in the window.

I navigate between the tables, minding people's bags on the floor, before finally sitting down. Women at the table next to us are craning to see the treasure beneath the blanket.

"How old?" asks a portly woman.

"Five days," replies Lois.

"You look amazing for having such a young one."

I'm about to speak when Lois reaches out and grabs me.

"Thank you," she replies, squeezing my hand.

When the focus of attention is diverted from us by the waitress, Lois leans forward and whispers in my ear.

"Isn't it amusing they think we're a family unit? It's fun to pretend, right?"

I smile. I can't fathom women out at times, although Colette is less complicated in her sane moments and that was one of the things that attracted me to her. I suddenly feel a pang of guilt about sitting here whilst she's locked away.

"If I change my mind and visit her today, would you look after Dylan for me? It would only be for a couple of hours, tops."

"Sure, anything to help."

The waitress brings over our order as Dylan wakes up and demands attention. Everyone turns to look our way, then coos as I lift him out of the buggy. He exerts his power by wailing as loudly as his little lungs can manage, so I try rocking and bouncing him, but nothing's working.

"Come here, let me try," Lois says with outstretched arms.

Cradling him, he nestles into her breast searching for milk. "Have them warm the bottle up, will you?"

Whilst she feeds him, I spread strawberry jam and clotted cream on her scone, and leave the plate within her reach to prepare my own.

"I'm famished. Would you mind holding the scone so I can take a bite? I daren't stop feeding him just yet."

I pick up the scone and hold it in front of her mouth for her to take a bite. A blob of cream rests on the corner of her mouth, which I automatically wipe away with my finger, before blushing.

"Oh do relax, Finn. We've known each other for so long we're almost siblings."

I try to laugh but it comes out as a squeak. Dylan seems to appreciate the jovial atmosphere as he turns his head to look at me.

When my mobile rings I automatically think it's the hospital chastising me. *Do they actually do that?* Grabbing it from my pocket, I glance at the screen. Diana.

"Darling, where are you, I was worried. I phoned your home but you weren't there. You're not at the hospital with Dylan, are you?"

"No, Mum, I'm in a tea shop with Dylan and Lois." I roll my eyes at Lois who's grinning at me.

"Thank God. I didn't think you'd be that stupid."

"He's going to have to see her, just as soon as the doctor says it's okay. They need to bond, and he needs to be with her as soon as possible."

"Really, Finn, we have to discuss that as a family before that happens."

"I don't want to talk about it now."

"No, enjoy your time with Lois and Dylan. Speak later."

I shove the mobile back in my pocket and take Dylan.

"Mum's concerned about germs and him coming to harm if I take him to the hospital."

"I heard you say she'll need contact with him soon otherwise there'll be no bond between them."

"I'm not sure that's true, I just said that. After all, adopted kids still form a bond with someone they didn't meet at the birth. Dylan will love Colette no matter what."

"Maybe you're right. I'm no expert in child rearing."

The mood dips and Dylan is beginning to smell, so I pay the waitress as Lois places him back in his buggy.

The wind's driving rain towards us. Dylan's shielded from the elements, but Lois and I are stippled with hard raindrops stinging our faces. The joy is over.

I jiggle the key in the front door and Lois charges in with the buggy, as Dylan is now complaining hard about his dirty nappy. Suddenly, I'm hit by resentment that my time's constrained by him; I can't do anything without putting his needs first, and for a fleeting moment I want to run away, believing Colette's in a better place than me. *Now that's absurd.*

Dylan wriggles so much he squishes the mess up his back and down his chubby thighs. I start to heave at the sight and stench.

"I think a bath would be an easier way to clean him," Lois says from the doorway.

"I can't do that alone. Mum normally helps me."

"Good job I'm here then."

Together we bathe him; I hold him whilst Lois washes him. He looks so fragile in the water; I'm scared I might break him.

"We make a good team," she says, rubbing his domed tummy.

"You definitely need two people to do this. God knows how single parents cope."

"People manage; you'd manage if you had to. You have little faith in yourself."

"Fathers aren't meant to be the primary caregivers. We provide the financial support, not this." I let go of Dylan with one hand to point at the bath and almost let him slip under the bubbles.

Lois laughs as the colour drains from my face.

"You can be such a clumsy misogynist at times."

Once clean, she scoops him up and wraps him in a fluffy towel before taking him into the nursery to get him dressed. I lean against the door-frame and watch her deftly manipulate his arms and legs into a sleep suit, talking to him in a baby voice which still seems at odds coming from her.

On picking him up, he grabs a handful of her hair and won't let go, and for a split second, I wonder whether he's forming a bond with her.

Colette

Someone's shouting in the corridor and footsteps are running towards the noise. An element of me is curious and frightened, yet apathetic. I know I'm not responding to life as I should, but I can't help myself, or should I say I don't want to help myself. I don't like myself like this.

Scuffling sounds ensue from the corridor, and I see flailing arms through the tiny window in the door as they're trying to calm her down. That's what happens in here; we are contained and kept away from society, for its own sake, not ours. We are the weeds in a perfectly manicured lawn, and need to be eradicated.

Gradually the corridor quietens and I turn to face the window, only to see smoky grey flat-bottomed clouds that signify rain scudding across the sky. It's a day to remain indoors, which is all I can do anyway.

A tap at my door forces me to turn over to see who's there.

"Good morning, Colette. I thought you and I could have a chat in my office in about an hour. Do you think you can get yourself ready for then?" says a nurse.

I just stare. Her auburn hair is scraped back into a severe ponytail which brushes along her shoulders as she moves. Her curvaceous figure is enhanced by the cut of her shirt and trousers. Somewhere deep inside me, I feel the echo of jealousy.

As I wash, the face in the mirror seems alien to me. It has no memories of childhood or adolescence. It is devoid of all feelings and emotions. It's not me, whoever I am.

I knock on the office door and the nurse beckons me in.

"How are you feeling today?"

"Overwhelmed with the pressure to perform in here."

She frowns and repeats the word *perform*.

"I'm obviously supposed to be different from who I am currently, but I don't know what or how to change."

"Who do you think is asking you to change?"

"Everyone in here, everyone out there," I indicate through the window. "I feel on display, like an exhibit in a show, only people don't need to pay to see me."

"Talking of seeing people, how do you feel about not seeing your husband yesterday?"

"I hardly noticed until you asked me about it. He was probably busy."

"Too busy to see you?"

"He's looking after the baby."

"Do you think you'll be ready to see Dylan soon?"

I shrug. What do I know? I think on some level I realize I'm not ready to be a mother. It was foisted upon me by an impatient mother-in-law, and Finn eager to please her.

"What thoughts are running through your mind right now?"

"Diana, my mother-in-law."

"What about her?"

"Finn always does as she says. She wanted a grandchild and Finn obliged."

"You didn't have to get pregnant if you didn't want to."

"I love Finn, and I wanted a child with him eventually. I just think it all happened too soon."

"What are your feelings towards Finn now?"

"They haven't changed. Look, I hate all this questioning. I haven't committed a crime." I know I should remain seated, but I can't prevent my legs from pushing me upwards and pacing around the room. I know she's watching me.

"Am I mad?"

"That's not a term we use. The doctor has diagnosed you with post-partum psychosis. This isn't your fault and you will get better."

"Will I? Will this happen again if I have another baby?"

"That's a distinct possibility."

"Is that a fancy way of saying yes?"

The nurse smiles gently and nods. "I'm sorry, but forewarned is forearmed. We can prepare for this next time."

"I'm not sure I want a next time."

"That's understandable, but you don't need to make that decision right now."

"Too damn right I don't, but I bet mother-in-law will want a granddaughter. She's a witch."

"I think we need to discuss your feelings towards her a bit more next time. I would like you, though, to think about seeing Dylan. Finn could bring him in for a short while. You wouldn't have to cope alone."

I can't answer her. The whole concept feels like I'm being pushed underwater, unable to breathe or think clearly. I want to go back to my room, so I leave her office without saying another word.

I walk up to my bed and lie on it, waiting for the next wave of inexplicable emotions to hit me.

A gentle tap on my arm drags me from my slumber, catapulting me back to life; a life I've grown to hate.

"Sorry to wake you, but if I didn't, you wouldn't know I was here."

Finn is sitting on the chair next to my bed. I've no idea how long he's been here. Pushing myself up on my elbows, I wait for my head to become less fuzzy.

"I've just had a dream. You and I ran away to another country to live where no one knows us. I felt so happy and free." I pause as my mouth's dry. Grabbing the plastic beaker from the bedside table, I take a large mouthful. "Let's do it, let's run away. You can pack up everything we need, then get me out of here, tell them I'm well, tell them you need me, say you—"

"Slow down, Colette, you're gabbling. I can't just get you out of here."

"Can't or won't? Don't you want me back home with you? Don't you see, this is what the baby wants? He wants you all to himself." I know I'm shouting, but I can't stop myself.

He looks alarmed as I spring off the bed, launching myself at him. I can see the whites of his eyes and his forehead glistening with sweat. I'm lashing out at him as he's pinned to the chair. Suddenly the room's swamped with people rushing towards me. I feel them pulling me back towards the bed, holding my arms and ankles tightly. I'm screaming at Finn even though I can't see him.

Suddenly I'm rolled onto my side and a needle jabs my left buttock. Shadows fall before my eyes, and I'm quietly numb.

Finn

Diana looks at me with a pained expression on her face, the palm of her hand pressed against her heart.

"Thank God you didn't have Dylan with you," is all she can say. There's no concern for Colette or what she is going through.

"Can't you understand how upsetting it was seeing her like that?"

"I'm sure it was, darling, but you have to remain strong for your son, my grandchild. Things will work out in the end."

"How so? What do you envisage happening in the near future?"

She sits down and slowly picks up the teacup. Her nose wrinkles at the smell of cold tea.

"I see you and Dylan doing well. I see him as a bright boy, eager to learn, just like you at that age."

"And," I gesture with a sweeping hand.

"And I see you happy in your family unit . . ."

"With Colette," I interject.

"One hopes."

"Does one?" I reply sarcastically.

"Don't speak to your mother like that, it only winds her up."

I've forgotten my father's in the room. He shakes the newspaper he's holding, before folding it in half. "We're all a bit stressed, this is putting a strain on everyone. One can only hope Dylan isn't suffering too much."

"I'm sure he's fine." I want to say more but I'm emotionally crushed.

"I don't think you should be alone this evening. Why don't you call Lois and ask her visit?" suggests Diana.

"I'm in no mood for social niceties."

"And in no mood to cook, no doubt. Leave it to me." She bustles out of the room, closing the door behind her.

"She means well," says my father. "She was so looking forward to being a grandmother, but this has taken a lot of the kudos away for her. She can't brag much about the little one for fear of raising the issue of Colette. She doesn't know what to say."

"That's unusual for her."

I can see he's about to reprimand me, but his face softens and he gives me a wry smile before returning to his newspaper.

Diana returns and taps the paper he is holding.

"Come on, George, we've got to get going," she announces, removing the paper from his grip. "I've made you a cheese and pickle sandwich, you've not much in. You could always boil an egg if you're still hungry."

He groans, pushing himself up from the chair, rubbing his knee before straightening it.

I'm sinking further and further into a dark place, so I am relieved when they go. The solitude hits me once again, but this time I'm ready for it. Just about.

I'm asleep on the bed with Dylan curled up next to me when the doorbell rings. Shifting my weight around, Dylan stirs but remains asleep. I, however, feel as though I've run a marathon; with aches and pains in places I didn't know could hurt.

I stagger downstairs to find Lois at the door with a bag of shopping.

"God, have I woken you? Diana said it'd be okay to come over."

Nothing is making sense, until I realize Diana's done exactly what she wants, regardless of my wishes.

"You don't look too pleased to see me. I can go if you want me to."

"No, it's all right. I'm just not very good when I first wake up."

"Me neither. I always need two cups of strong coffee before I can be civil. Can I come in?"

I move to the side, letting her in just as Dylan starts crying. Exhaling loudly, I trundle upstairs with Lois on my heels.

As I sit at the kitchen table with a beer, Lois prepares steak and chips. Dylan's been fed and bathed, and is now asleep in his basket upstairs.

"You look pensive," she comments before turning over the steak. The kitchen echoes with sizzling sounds.

"I'm thinking about everything and nothing."

"That's such a male copout. Seriously, what's making you look so serious?"

"I suppose I imagined family life with Colette to be like this; sharing the care of Dylan, and eating meals later in the evening over a bottle of wine, or beer," I reply, hoisting the bottle in the air. "It seems so natural with you." *Hell, what am I saying?*

I notice her back straighten as she flips the steaks onto the plates before serving the chips. When she turns around I see a faint rosy hue on her cheeks.

"Sorry, I didn't mean anything by that," I say as calmly as possible.

"Don't worry; I know you and Colette are a solid item."

The blushing pink steak is succulent, but my appetite's poor, and after the first bite, I push my plate to one side.

Dylan occasionally whimpers and snuffles through the monitor. Periodically, I glance at Lois to see her hair glowing like a halo, but the black smudges under her eyes are new.

"Perhaps you should go home after dinner, I'll cope tonight."

"That's thoughtful of you, but I'm on my third glass of wine, so I couldn't possibly drive now."

I can't drive her home either, unless I'm prepared to bundle Dylan into his travel seat.

"Okay, stay here, but you sleep; I'll do the night duties."

She seems satisfied with that and resumes eating. I grab another beer from the fridge.

"What did you think of me when we were at college?"

Her question knocks me sideways into the past we shared.

"You were difficult to fathom out. I don't think I ever got to know the real you. You were like an actress playing many different roles. I admired you for that." I pour some beer down my throat. "My mother adored you because your family were rich." I smile at that, wondering if she knew Diana still feels the same today.

"Am I still difficult to work out?"

"Well, you've taken to being a hands-on aunty to Dylan. Never in a million years would I have thought you'd handle a dirty nappy."

"I'm not some aloof princess. I'm offended." She pushes her empty plate to one side and picks up her wine glass.

"I'm sorry, no harm intended. Look you've been brilliant; I couldn't have coped without you."

"Or Diana."

"Yes, but for different reasons. I couldn't have a relaxing meal and a few beers in her company," I laugh.

My laughter shatters the sombre mood, but before we settle in the lounge, Dylan wakes up for a feed. We both troupe upstairs together, giggling like the students we once were.

With Dylan settled once more, we return to the lounge and sit side by side on the sofa, our arms pressing into one another. With the remote I put the stereo on, and the melodic tones of Pink Floyd inch their way across the room. The words dance around my mind and transport me to a linear reality where I'm in control; where I'm loved and take pride in loving back.

The combination of music and Lois's scent is hypnotic, and before I realize what I'm doing, our lips are pressed firmly together. The tip of my tongue explores her mouth until I'm consumed by passion; a raw, desperate emotion that makes me grab her hand and pull her upstairs, as though we are fleeing the jaws of a raging fire.

Colette

I stayed awake all night; pacing the room before writing a letter to Finn asking him for us to start over. And by that I mean without Dylan. I know deep down he'd be better off without me.

I tour my room holding a photograph of him in my left hand, trying to feel some form of emotion that doesn't end up in me feeling angry, sick, or numb. I feel I'm a battered miniscule vessel on the open sea; knocked this way and that, not knowing when the rocking will stop.

I want to see Finn, but I know he's planning to bring Dylan in too, and I don't want that. I'm not prepared to share my time with Finn with a baby. Seeing the baby will remind me I'm no longer just Colette Forbes; I'm now a mother, a failing mother at that.

"I'm going to put you on a drug regime of Lithium. We need to stabilize your mood before we can move further forward. How do you feel about that?" asks Doctor Holland.

My leg bounces up and down rapidly. I'm drumming my fingers on the arms of the chair; my eyes darting around the room searching for a quick escape. He waits a few minutes for my answer before continuing.

"There are possible side effects to the medication, including hair loss, mild hand tremor, loss of appetite, tiredness, and mild nausea, especially at the beginning of the treatment. Does that worry you?"

I shrug. "I have to do as you say. It's the only way, right?"

"It's a good start, but it isn't forever. This is your mental health we're dealing with; you have a say. You'll continue to get emotional and practical support regarding your relationship and care of Dylan, even when you return home. I'll update your notes on the computer so the nurses can get you started."

He dismisses me by diverting his eyes to his computer screen, and the nurse sitting to my left touches my arm and stands up.

She encourages me to sit in the dayroom, but I refuse and make a bee-line for my room. I'm hoping the new medication will release me from the hell I am trapped in. Otherwise, what other options are left to me? I glance at my bandaged wrists, and bang them on the bedside table, letting the pain reverberate up my arms.

It's visiting time. I wonder if Finn will turn up. Panic rises within me, has he abandoned me here? Is the baby still controlling him?

Emotions are ricocheting around my mind when a knock at the door jolts me. Finn is peering at me through the window in the door. He isn't smiling.

I wave him in.

"Good to see you out of bed. How have you been?" he asks.

"Where were you yesterday?"

"I couldn't get anyone to look after Dylan, and the nurse said to wait a couple more days before bringing him in. Didn't you get my message?"

"No." *The staff are my enemy.*

"Well I'm sorry."

I know I'm not well which distorts my perception—according to the nurse—but he looks distant and dare I say it, troubled?

"You're hiding something from me, aren't you?" I take long strides towards him, but he backs away like a frightened puppy. "Tell me what's wrong. Has the baby died because I don't love him? Has he?" My raised voice is even frightening me, but I need to know.

"Dylan's fine." He pauses. "You don't love him?" His voice echoes bewilderment, his eyes widen.

"I can't talk about how I feel. In here, emotions are magnified and twisted. The outside world feels like I'm Alice peering through the looking-glass."

"I don't understand you, I wish I did, but I don't. I feel you're on an island and I don't know how to swim."

"Perhaps you should find a boat."

He half-smiles with bitter mirth.

"How's Lois? She hasn't been back to see me."

"It's a hard place to visit, but she sends her love."

"How do you know that? Are you making it up?"

"She's my friend too. She calls 'round occasionally to see how I'm doing."

"She's seeing more of you and the baby than I am. Perhaps he'll think she's his mother?"

"Don't be ridiculous; she's not breastfeeding him." His cheeks and the tips of his ears glow bright red.

"Why did you mention her breasts?"

"Good God, Colette, you're doing my head in. I love you. You're my wife and Dylan's our son. Nothing's going on with Lois."

A film of sweat clings to his face, and miniscule globules magnify the redness beneath. I'm not going to speak anymore; I want him to leave.

The suffocating silence rushes loudly in my ears and before long, Finn's moving towards the door.

"I'm hoping to bring Dylan next time."

"Will he be safe?"

"I won't leave you alone with him."

"I didn't mean from me, I meant from the other patients," I snap, incensed at his suggestion, albeit knowing darkness lurks within me.

"Yes of course."

I can tell he doesn't mean it, but I don't have the strength to challenge him. I'm suddenly awash with fatigue and I want him to go, but instead of saying it, I climb onto my bed and roll my back to him.

A few seconds later, I hear the door open then softly close.

Finn

"Is Lois coming 'round this evening?" Diana asks.

"Not that I'm aware. Why?" I snap, regretting it straight away.

"I'm only asking. No need to be so rude, Finn." She looks down her nose at me, reverting me to the seven-year-old boy who feared such a look. Would I be sent to bed without dinner?

"Are you tired?"

"I'm fine; please can we talk about something else?"

"So that's Lois and your wellbeing off limits. Can we discuss my grandson, or is that likely to set you off too?"

"Don't be facetious," I mutter under my breath, low enough for her not to hear.

Right on cue, gurgling noises emanate through the monitor, so the doting grandmother dashes upstairs to retrieve him, whilst I hover in the background downstairs.

"He's looking more like you every day," she says proudly, entering the lounge and moving to the sofa with Dylan in her arms.

"I think he's looking like Colette at the moment. He's got her button nose."

"He's got the Forbes regal nose, actually. He'll grow into a mini you in his public-school uniform."

"I think Colette wants him to go to the local comprehensive."

She expels a lung full of air. "We'll pay the fees if it's the money."

"He's not yet out of nappies, how about we wait a few years to have this debate, Mum, *please*."

"We need to get him on the list ASAP, otherwise—"

"I can't do this now," I interject rather loudly, setting off Dylan's reflexes.

Diana chastises me whilst rocking him to and fro. I really want her to leave so I can hold Dylan, and be reassured that everything's going to be okay. But everything isn't okay, is it? *What have I done?*

"Your father and I have been talking," she begins in her authoritarian tone, "and we think Dylan shouldn't be exposed to the madness in that hospital. We are ready to employ a solicitor if necessary."

I am not expecting this. Words bounce around my mind disabling my ability to string a sentence together. I focus hard.

"I don't think that would be necessary. Colette has a private room and I'd be there constantly. He'd come to no harm; besides, Colette wouldn't hurt him, she . . ." I know it is wrong to stop mid-sentence. I know she'll pick up on it.

"She what, exactly? Loves him, loathes him? Come on, Finn, you can't keep secrets from your mother. Spit it out."

"Of course she loves him; she's just having a hard time at the moment. Please let the doctors and me deal with this."

I watch her gaze lovingly at Dylan's face as he squirms under the blanket, rocking gently on her sea of flesh as she inhales deeply.

"I'm not convinced, but don't you dare let anything happen to him or—"

"Or what, you'll get custody and raise him yourself with the help of a nanny agency?"

"There's no talking to you today. Much as it chagrins me, I'll leave and return when you have a more civil tongue in your head." She hands me Dylan, stroking his head gently.

"Maybe that's wise. I'm rather stressed out today."

"Well you need to sort yourself out; Dylan needs at least one sane parent." She leans forward and kisses his forehead before looking at me reproachfully.

I accompany her to the door with Dylan in my arms and watch with relief as she gets in her car. Shutting the door behind me allows the flood gates to open, and soon bulbous, salty tears run down my face and drip from my jawline onto his tiny face.

I'm struggling to get Dylan out of the bath when the doorbell rings. Hoisting his wet body over my shoulder and placing a towel over him, I step gingerly downstairs to see the outline of Lois through the stained-glass panel in the front door.

My hand slips on the handle as I twist it, and in a moment of panic, I almost drop Dylan.

"Bloody hell," I curse, opening the door.

"That's one hell of a greeting," she says, stepping inside and picking up the towel from the floor.

"I wasn't talking to you; I was talking to myself." I'm aware of Dylan's surprising weight on my shoulder, so I slip him into the crook of my arm as Lois places the towel over his wriggling, squidgy body.

"See, you have managed to bathe him alone, clever you. We should get him dressed now though, it's a very cold day to be naked," Lois says as she begins mounting the stairs.

"I can manage, you know. All you women think I'm incapable of caring for him."

"Who's 'all you women' meant to be?"

"You and my mother."

"Hell, don't lump me in with her. I'm only trying to help. But okay," she says, returning downstairs, "you get him ready for bed and I'll open a bottle of wine."

I obey her, knowing full well that I'm playing with fire, but the warmth from the flames is tempting and comforting.

I switch on the baby monitor in his room before tiptoeing downstairs, where I find Lois in the lounge with a bottle of wine and two glasses.

"Come and sit here," she says, patting the seat next to her on the sofa.

I acquiesce and collapse next to her, letting her put a wine glass in my hand. The tannins coat my teeth and the back of my throat.

"So where do we go from here?" she asks, sitting back and tucking her legs under her.

"We?"

"Please don't play coy, Finn, it doesn't suit you. Yes, we, *us*. What happens now?"

I clear my throat and run my hand over the top of my head.

"Look, Lois, please don't get me wrong. I appreciate your friendship and support, but—"

"But sleeping with me was a mistake, was it?" Her voice is surprisingly soft, and the lack of potential aggression weakens me.

"I wouldn't call it a mistake as such. You were there when I needed the comfort of another human being, and we've known each other for years. It felt comfortable and right at the time."

"I've always had a soft spot for you."

"Really?"

"I liked you before you began dating Colette, but I couldn't get you to notice me. You were dazzled by her and I lost you forever."

"Colette is still around."

"But not the Colette you married. She was a stranger when we visited, I can't imagine how you feel."

"I have good days and bad, but I have to stay strong for Dylan."

"I still want to support you. How about I visit Colette on days you can't, just so she knows she's not alone?"

I can't believe what she's suggesting. Does she really think I'd let her see Colette alone now?

"If you're worried I'll tell Colette about our little indiscretion you needn't trouble yourself. I'd never do anything to harm you, ever."

Her sincerity shines out, calling me to trust her. I'd love nothing more than to share the visits; it's torturous doing it daily.

"I can't do this all alone, but I won't hurt Colette. She's a kind and gentle person, and finding out about us would destroy her."

Lois puts her manicured hand on my knee and drums her fingers.

"I promise I won't do anything to hurt you or Colette. I realize that the only way I can stay close to you is if I remain a friend and ally to you both. Trust me, Mon Cher." Leaning forward, she touches my cheek with the tip of her cold nose.

I turn towards her, inhaling the scent of her vanilla lip gloss. I sense emotions burgeoning within me, but I quell them fast; I must stay true to Colette, no matter what I've already done.

Her lips are now pressed against my cheek, and if I don't summon up super-human strength, I know where we'll end up. So I gently put my hand to her face and pull my head away.

"We have to start behaving from now on, Lois, otherwise it's going to be too hard."

"It's already too hard," she whispers back to me, turning her head in order to kiss the palm of my hand.

I say her name louder to break the spell, and she stops mid-kiss.

"I'm sorry. I'll stop being naughty from now on."

"Thank you. I don't want to lose you as a friend." I smile and kiss her on the forehead. I'm not entirely sure why I did that last gesture, but it seems to have appeased her.

"Perhaps I should go, before I drink too much and need to stay the night." She bends forward to put her boots back on then stands up.

We hug in the way soldiers probably hugged their wives or girlfriends before leaving to fight on the frontline. It feels like we will never meet again in that special way. Probably for the best, though.

Colette

I've had another bad night's sleep, and the medication isn't working. I know the nurse told me to give it a few more doses for it to kick in, but the fatigue has already taken a hold of my body, so the days and nights are harder to cope with.

It looks less grey outside my window, but by the look of people, with arms folded and collars turned-up, walking through the quadrant, it's clearly still cold. I long to join them, to remove myself from the cloying central-heated air of the hospital, but the effort's unsurmountable.

I'm dressed in case Finn comes in later. I daren't ask the nurse if she's heard anything in case it is bad news; I want to live with the sliver of hope afforded me by not knowing.

Although dressed, I can't face applying makeup to disguise my ghost-like state, and my hair is unruly without gel, which Finn keeps forgetting to bring me. Little curls now border the nape of my neck and my forehead.

I turn around at the sound of someone at my door and see Lois standing there. She's a vision of womanly perfection, the antithesis of me, and it hurts.

"I hope you don't mind me visiting. I asked Finn if I could come."

"It's okay, I suppose. A surprise, but okay."

"I thought you might think I'd abandoned you after only visiting you once."

"To be honest, all the days and nights merge; I've no idea where I am in the scheme of things. How's Finn?"

"Doing okay, I think. He has his hands full with Dylan, who's also doing well, by the way."

I'm touched by a ripple of annoyance. What does she know, she's not a mother? *Lucky her.*

I suggest we take a walk in the enclosed courtyard which passes for a garden thanks to the hanging baskets and pots containing winter pansies and heathers. Lois complains it's cold and I reply that she has a coat. We walk out of my room in silence.

"Do you see much of Finn and Dylan?" I ask, pulling my coat around me.

"Not daily, but I pop in from time to time just to see how they're doing and how you are, of course."

"Does Dylan like you?"

"How would I know, he's only tiny. What a strange question to ask."

"I *am* strange now, or hadn't you noticed?"

"You're not strange, you're ill. There's a vast difference."

"I can't help thinking Dylan would be better off with a different mummy. A mummy like you."

Lois stops walking and puts her hand on my arm. "Are you nuts? Oh God . . ." Her face is puce. "That's a poor choice of phrase. Sorry."

"It's all right; you used to call me nuts before I had Dylan. I seem to remember you calling me that when I told you I was pregnant. And who knew you were right."

"It was a turn of phrase. I was envious of your new-found life. You were married then pregnant, whereas I have nothing."

"You had, and have, so much more than me. You're a successful businesswoman who works from your gorgeous home. You date eligible men who adore you. And you're just so beautiful."

"Where's all this coming from?"

"Call it the madness, the medication, or being housed in here. I always thought you were more accomplished at everything than me. I imagined Finn would have fallen for you back then."

"Really? I think perhaps I scared him; I used to beat him at golf, cards, scrabble, you name it. A man doesn't like to lose to a woman."

Talking about the past tips me into a memory soup that swills around my mind, so when we arrive at a bench I need to sit down.

Huddling close together to keep warm, I'm enjoying the feel of another familiar person being so close to me. When Finn visits, he never sits close to me, always needing a barrier between us like a tamer and a lion.

"Tell me about your love life," I ask, desperately needing a distraction from the mental torture assaulting my mind.

"Not much to say, really. The business is keeping me busy, there's a growing demand for alpaca pashminas. Did I tell you Harrods are going to stock them now?"

"I'm impressed." I say the right thing but I don't mean it. I've no interest in her prowess as a businesswoman; I need to live a love life vicariously through her. Mine is now a mere corpse in the ground.

The cold, however, starts biting into my flesh and gnawing at my bones. I want to go inside, and I want her to leave. Somehow, a strain has developed between us, which saddens, but doesn't surprise me.

She walks a pace behind me as I trudge inside.

"I'm tired now. You don't mind leaving, do you?"

"Of course not." She leans in and gives me a hug and a peck on the cheek; her face and hands feel decidedly chilly.

I remain rigid in her embrace before watching her walk away, her slender hips rolling from side to side as she recedes into the distance.

Only my room offers me sanctuary from this world which now frightens and puzzles me. How on earth am I supposed to care for a child in this menacing world? I was wrong to even try; I can never protect him from all the harm that exists. Maybe he knows that, and that's why he's got rid of me?

Finn

"Colette's sister is flying over from Spain tomorrow. She's coming to stay here so she can visit Colette," I tell Diana as I finish changing Dylan's nappy.

"At least it'll give you a break from visiting that place."

"Lois is already doing that now. I can't keep avoiding her, she is my wife."

"You seem to be seeing quite a lot of Lois. She's such a wonderful girl. Beautiful and successful. I bought one of her pashminas; they're so soft. Did you know Harrods are now stocking them? She's amazing."

"Anyone would think you wished I'd married her and not Colette." I pick up Dylan and pop him over my shoulder, where he proceeds to gum my ear.

"I was always surprised you didn't date her. Colette seemed too wishy-washy for you."

I don't want to be having this conversation, so I suggest we join Dad who's reading the paper in the lounge. Not waiting for her to respond, I quickly descend the stairs to find him.

George glances over the top of the newspaper then returns to reading.

"Anything interesting in the news, Dad?"

"Just the same old guff about politics. The government is struggling to win the hearts of the country, so nothing new there."

Diana sits next to me, teasing Dylan away from my arms.

"I was just telling Finn we were surprised at him marrying Colette rather than Lois."

George remains hidden; his grip tightening on the paper.

"I know you're listening George, don't be obtuse. We're worried about Colette's future in this family, aren't we?"

I feel I'm in the audience, watching a play where my character doesn't exist. Folding my arms, I wait for George's words to reach me.

"That's all rather academic now; he married Colette and they have a child. We'll help them pull through this the best way we can."

"You're being unreasonable, George. We can't trust her to be alone with our grandson, and they certainly can't have any more children. The psychiatrist said this would happen again."

"He said there's a strong chance, Mum. But it may not happen again."

She looks at me as though I'd thrown a rotten tomato onto the stage. I half expect her to eject me from my seat.

"And we can take that risk, can we? Look at your handsome baby boy, doesn't he deserve the best?"

"His own mother is the best for him; she's just unwell at the moment. I can't believe you."

"Can't believe what? Believe that I have the courage to voice what everyone around us is thinking, that I have the conviction to do what's right for my grandson? You'd better believe it, Finn."

"Dad, can't you talk some sense into her. I can't take the emotional pressure right now."

"In the forty-two years we've been together, I've never once turned your mother around to my way of thinking. I'm a Labrador and your mother's a lion in this relationship; I learnt to live that way the day we married."

They're the most words I've heard my father string together in a long while, and I know exactly what he means. There's no point in arguing with her.

"Right, now I have you both on board, what are we going to do about this situation?"

My nerves tingle as I rub my sweaty palms on my jeans; I wait for my head to stop spinning. "I've got Gabriella coming tomorrow, and I don't want her hearing this type of conversation. I promise I won't do anything to put Dylan in danger. Now can we please drop this subject?"

I notice Diana's jaw muscles twitching, so I know she's far from happy, but Gabriella's arrival is just the diversion I need for now. But I know the battle has only just begun.

I recognize Gabriella straight away as she strides into the arrival's lounge. She sees me at the same time and waves enthusiastically. I can see men around me thinking I'm a lucky devil.

"Hola, Finn," she coos, flinging her slender arms around my neck. "How's the new papa doing?"

"Holding up, thanks."

"I can't wait to give him a cuddle. I bet he looks just like you."

"He's got Colette's nose, though."

I carry her large carpet bag as we weave our way through the excited throng to the car park. I pay for the parking ticket, refusing Gabriella's offer to pay, then put her bag in the back of the car.

"How's Colette doing?"

"I can't lie; her head's not in a good place right now. She's on Lithium which they hope will help balance her mental state."

"Do you know how long she'll be in there?"

I see her twiddling her hair in my peripheral vision.

"Could be up to eight weeks, depends on how quickly she gets better."

"Our mum could be quite depressed at times. I wonder if Colette's like this because of her."

I shrug as I pull off the motorway and head in the direction of home. I've never had difficulty conversing with Gabriella in the past, but it's different in the car right now. I wonder if she feels guilty about her infrequent visits.

"How's life in Spain, still hectic?"

"People still want to holiday in Spain, and the English love to have someone on hand to translate for them, or direct them to a restaurant where they can have double egg and chips."

"Sounds like my idea of a nightmare."

"Don't knock it; it keeps me in a job."

As I pull outside the house I sense Gabriella's excitement is palpable.

My parents greet Gabriella with a dignified distance. They've heard what holiday reps get up to, and I imagine Diana thinks Gabriella will talk about the ins and outs of the job, with precise, vulgar detail.

"Oh, let me hold my little nephew," she coos, walking towards Diana.

I wonder if I might have to intervene, but Diana places Dylan in his auntie's arms. Gabriella murmurs Spanish words, which sound exotic. Diana hovers around the pair so I suggest Gabriella takes a seat.

"He is so divine; you're so lucky."

"Everything would be easier if your sister wasn't ill," pipes up Diana.

"Well obviously, but Colette hardly meant for this to happen. I bet she loves him and misses him loads," Gabriella retorts.

I know my face has blanched and Diana has noticed. Whether she can deduce what the problem is, I'm not sure, but I'm eager to move the conversation on, and fast.

"Are you any closer to settling down yourself?" I know it's a risky topic, but I'm jammed into a corner

"There's no shortage of potential suitors, but I'm too young to settle down, Finn. I've more of my life to explore before I descend into the free-fall of marital boredom."

"I'll have you know that marriage is not boring, is it George?"

"No dear, it's a daily joyous experience."

Diana glares in his direction and purses her lips, clearly toying with the idea of shredding his cock-sure attitude, so I jump in yet again.

"What's it like holding your nephew?"

"He's the first baby I've held; he feels rather fragile. I feel I could hurt him accidently."

"You're doing just fine."

"It's time for Dylan to have a nap," Diana says, whisking him from Gabriella's arms.

When the baby monitor is switched on upstairs, music filters through and fills the lounge. Gabriella looks at me with wide eyes.

"Mum read that classical music helps a baby's brain develop."

"Really?"

"Who knows, but I indulge her. It can't do any harm."

"Can we go and see Colette now; I haven't come all this way to sit in your lounge," she says with a wink.

Colette

As Gabriella puts her arms around me, I'm transported back to our childhood, to times of carefree fun, safety, and teenage ideology.

"It's so wonderful to see you," she gushes.

"And you, although I wish I wasn't here."

"You won't be for long. Finn's told me all about your condition, it sucks."

She pulls a chair closer to my bed and holds my hand, giving it a squeeze whilst just staring at me.

"I'm not dying, you know."

"I'm sorry; I'm not good around ill people. You remember how I was around Mum?"

"Have you seen Dylan?"

"He's absolutely gorgeous, and he has your nose."

"Does he also have my madness?"

She lets go of my hand and leans into me so I can smell her minty breath.

"I don't know what you mean."

"It stands to reason. Mum was depressed, now I'm like this, so he's bound to have problems too."

She's stumped for what to say, so she stands up, opens the door, and calls Finn in. Why does everyone think he's my solution out of here?

"Hello darling, did you sleep well?"

"Not really. Where's Dylan?"

"Mum's looking after him, don't worry."

"That's all I do in here. Worry. I worry about him, you, me, the world. It never ends."

"Isn't the medication helping?" he says, sitting on the bed.

"Apparently it will, but then I'm worried I won't be able to think at all."

"Of course you will," my sister butts in. "You'll be the same old you in no time."

With one of them on either side of me I feel I have nowhere to turn, unless I lie on my stomach and shove my head under the pillow.

"I'll go and grab us some coffee. Love you, sis," she says, bending down to kiss me on my cheek. She smells of freesias.

"I've had a chat with the doctor and I'm bringing Dylan in tomorrow. Isn't that exciting?" says Finn.

"I don't know if I'm a good enough mother for him. What if I can't love him or he can't love me."

"Of course you'll love him. He's our baby, a baby we wanted. And he'll adore you."

I try to feel comforted by his words, but all I feel is a buzzing numbness which muffles my brain and heart. I want to reach out to him, from some elusive grey part of my mind, but I can't coordinate my synapses and sinews to make that movement.

Against my will I feel a tear run along the rim of my eye. It's too late to blink it back.

"Oh darling, don't cry. We'll get through this together."

"Will we? Will our marriage survive this?"

His eyes dart away from me for a brief second and I see his jaw clench in the way it does when he's stressed. They're the little signs only people with an intimate knowledge of someone would pick up.

He gets up, shoving his hands in the pockets of his jeans, and moves to the window to look out at the concrete quadrant. Something catches his attention.

"What are you looking at?"

"Just a couple sitting on the bench. They're having an argument. She's swinging her arms around like a juggler on speed."

"Don't we have enough worries of our own without getting involved in someone else's?"

"I'm just observing the amount of pain that comes with being in love. Love and pain co-exist everywhere, it seems impossible to love peacefully."

"Didn't we love peacefully before I gave birth? Or was that an illusion?"

He turns towards me, leaning against the windowsill. He clenches his hands in his pockets and puffs out his cheeks.

"We need time to rebuild our relationship, including with Dylan."

"I don't feel I have an attachment to him yet."

"I bet when you hold him tomorrow, love will flow between you both."

"What if it doesn't? What do we do then?"

He frowns, shaking his head slightly and clamping his lips together.

Gabriella returns with the coffees, placing my plastic cup on the bedside cabinet.

"I'm sorry, but I'm really tired now. I'll see you tomorrow."

Gabriella looks sad, but I know she'll understand. When Finn bends down to kiss me on the lips, I turn my head so he connects with my cheek.

Tomorrow I see my son.

The night devils are gnawing at my brain. I desperately want to sink into the silken clutches of sleep, to have my night thoughts quashed by the dense, rolling clouds of slumber.

Instead, I'm treated to a trembling hand and feelings of irritation. I want the daylight hours to pierce the darkness that's cloaking me, even though the thought of seeing my baby is terrifying.

The nurse suggests I sit in the comfy chair in my room in preparation for Dylan's arrival. It feels strange being in my room and not being in the bed.

When the knock at the door comes, I see Finn through the window and my heart explodes into tiny pulsating particles, taking my breath away.

I watch him walking towards me in slow motion, carrying Dylan bundled in a buttermilk coloured blanket.

"Would you like to hold him?" he asks, standing before me.

I flinch, without opening my arms. I sense the nurse and Gabriella standing by the door, observing my every move. I feel powerless and miserable, but incapable of expressing this.

Finn sits on the edge of the bed and tips Dylan so I can see his face. He has chubby cheeks like the Dough Boy, and a pouting mouth with a perfect Cupid's bow. He has the blackest hair thanks to the combination of our genes. He looks perfect.

"I'll try and hold him," I whisper.

Finn stands before gently placing Dylan in my arms.

His weight surprises me; for such a little boy he's heavy, like a dead-weight. He shifts around in my arms to get comfortable and I open the blanket so he doesn't get too warm; an instinctive move which surprises me.

Finn sits back on the bed, feigning being relaxed, but he can't hide his clenching jaw and watchful eyes.

The nurse and Gabriella remain close to the door, but are now smiling at my success.

"Am I like this because I'm an older mother?" I ask.

"Thirty isn't old. You're doing well, but we'll take things slowly," says the nurse, smiling so widely she looks like a toothpaste advert.

"Let me take a photo of you both," Gabriella suggests, moving forward with her camera in hand. "How about a photo of mother and baby, and then one of all three of you?"

I shift around uncomfortably, I know my hair looks a mess and I'm wearing no makeup. Gabriella positions Dylan's head gently so as not to wake him.

After several minutes of the flash permeating the room, Dylan stirs and begins whimpering. My body stiffens as he opens his eyes and mouth. He stretches out his arms and wails so loudly it reverberates around my skull and grates on my teeth. My breasts throb in response.

"Please take him off me," I urge Finn.

He's too slow to respond. I begin shaking and feel my grip on Dylan loosen. His cries become more forceful, and I've no notion to placate him, but rather to rid myself of the squirming creature.

Finn rushes towards me, whisking Dylan out of my arms. He starts bouncing and rocking him whilst making soothing sounds.

I don't look in the direction of the nurse or Gabriella. I'm not remotely interested in their platitudes or admonishment.

"I think he needs a nappy change," Finn says calmly. "I'll just pop him on the bed."

I watch Finn deftly remove the offending item, before cleaning the mess. He puts a fresh nappy on and Dylan is placated.

Even with the nappy wrapped in a scented bag, the unpleasant stench lingers in the air, and I really want everyone out of my room. They've conspired to make me unhappy, and now I want them gone.

With Dylan back in Finn's arms, the bed is vacant, so I climb on and turn my back to them. Gabriella tries to coax a farewell out of me, so I grunt and listen to them shuffling out of the room.

My mind drifts, rudderless, as fragmented thoughts of the baby and the family bombard me. They'd be better off without me, they'll soon see that.

Finn

"Well that was uncomfortable," Gabriella says as she slips into the passenger seat. "I was shocked to see how she responded to Dylan."

I smile weakly.

The low hum of the engine coupled with the movement sends Dylan to sleep. I'm relieved he's calm after the hospital fiasco.

"Let's play down the visit to Diana; she'll only be full of *I told you so* if we tell her the truth," I mutter.

"She might have a point, but I understand we mustn't let her know that. I remember her well."

The only sound filling the void is the swish of the windscreen wipers sweeping the sheet of rain away. The clicking sound of the indicator reminds me of the metronome on the piano when I was a child. It's comforting, regular beat soothes my frazzled mind, lulling me back to gentler times, where the intricacies of the world were far removed from my adolescent brain.

Once home, we stand in the hallway, dripping water onto the floor. Gabriella takes her coat off and shakes her hair, tossing crystal droplets into the air. In certain light I see her resemblance to Colette, the familial button nose and bohemian air. The sight plucks at my heart.

I move to the kitchen to warm a bottle for Dylan, when I hear Gabriella talking to someone.

"Is it too early to open a bottle of wine?" Lois asks.

My heart stops momentarily. "How did you get in?"

"Diana gave me the spare key. She insisted I be here for you on your return. She thought you might need someone to talk to."

"That's bizarre considering I'm here," Gabriella chips in, looking between us both.

I'm worried she can see what we've done, and I'm worried what Lois will divulge.

"Do you mind if I go up for a bath and leave you two in peace?" Gabriella asks. "I still feel I have Spanish sand between my toes."

As she leaves, I sit down to feed Dylan, just as I hear wine glugging into two glasses. Lois brings them over to the table and sits opposite me.

"Are you taking Dylan in tomorrow?" she asks.

"I'm not sure. I don't want to think about it right now." I watch her run her middle finger around the rim of the glass. "What are you thinking about?"

"I thought only women asked that question," she giggles. "I'm thinking about us, if you really want to know."

I prop the bottle on Dylan's stomach for a second whilst I take a large mouthful of wine. "Please keep your voice down. And could you clarify what 'us' implicates?"

Lois twines strands of hair around her fingers. "You must know that even when you married Colette, I was in the church willing you to turn around and declare your love for me."

I swallow hard. "But you're Colette's best friend."

"If I was to remain part of the splintering group, I had to accept her like a sister. It was hard at first, but grew easier over time. And at least I've remained close to you."

"You're concerning me. Perhaps sleeping together was a bigger mistake than I realised."

"It was no mistake, and it was even better than I'd imagined. It should've always been this way. Perhaps the gods are conspiring to push us together at last, by making Colette ill."

I look at her, praying she's joking, but her face is darkly solemn. Dylan finishes his bottle so I sit him up and rub his back rhythmically. The sound of his wind being expelled usually makes me laugh, but not today.

"But I did marry Colette, and now we have a baby together. She'll be home soon and things will get back to normal."

"But will they though? Or will a soupçon of madness linger in her, driving you insane? And what type of mother will she be?"

"I can't believe you're talking like this. You're supposed to be our friend. We want you to be Dylan's Godmother. Christ Almighty," I hiss, standing up and rocking Dylan vigorously. I need to think. Panic rises in me as Gabriella is upstairs and could be privy to this conversation if I don't take it in hand.

Dylan is disturbed by my actions, and Lois is quick to take him from me, placing him over her shoulder. I watch him nestle in the curve of her neck, just under her ear. I'm sapped of energy, and so confused.

"He's so adorable," she whispers, swaying from side to side. "I sense it didn't go well today with Colette. How can you take him back there, you could be damaging his emotional wellbeing."

She's sounding like Diana. Here I am hoping for Colette's triumphal return, yet these two women are fearing the worse and seemingly wanting to keep her locked away.

Panic is blinding me, so I don't notice Lois moving upstairs, until I hear the baby monitor activate. I listen to her sure-footed steps as she returns to the lounge and refills our glasses.

"So where do we go from here?" she asks, handing me one.

"Lois, I can't be the man you need." I put the glass down and push it away from me.

"And what kind of man would that be?"

"There for you exclusively."

"I know you come with Dylan in tow. That really doesn't worry me. Besides, I think he's already fond of me."

I don't know how to respond. And yet, how can I blame her for thinking this way after what we did?

"We need to talk, Lois. I feel there's been a gross misunderstanding."

"I'm not sure I like where this conversation's going."

"When we slept together, I was feeling selfish. I needed someone to make me feel like a man. I thought you understood that. Colette has been void of emotions since . . ." I feel a lump in my throat.

"So you don't find me attractive?"

"To be honest, you could have been anybody, and for that I'm truly sorry." I'm painfully aware of hearing the bathroom door open upstairs.

Lois sinks back into the chair, gazing at her hands resting in her lap. Her heavy fringe falls over her eyes, like a curtain at the interval of a play. I brace myself for her reaction.

"Well Finn, I can't say I'm not disappointed. Colette has always had a grasp on you. But I'm happy to wait. You'll return to me one day."

She looks up from under the blond canopy, with a buttery innocence that could fool any man, except me.

I will always be looking over my shoulder, watching for her in the shadows. What a fool I've been.

Colette

Doctor Gerry Holland peruses his notes of the past six weeks. I've returned to the bad habit of chewing the skin around my fingernails until they bleed. The soreness and blood makes me feel alive.

"You've made marvellous progress over the past few weeks. The nurses are satisfied with the advancement you've made with your son. So, we'll have a pre-discharge planning meeting before sending you home."

"When will that happen?"

"In a few days; I anticipate you leaving in about a week's time."

I feel my heart squeeze extra hard at the news. A squeeze of excitement and of fear. I just hope I'm ready.

I wander back to the dayroom and realize with an edge of melancholy that I'm going to miss the ward. Not the encounter of the first few days, but the place it has come to represent: a place of safety for my lack of confidence in myself and in being a mother. I'm cradled in the capable hands of the staff who urge me to develop and grow. I am also part of a little group of likeminded people who are also crushed under the array of emotional turmoil, and the blackmail our minds play with our sanity.

I'm soon to leave it all behind and return home to a husband and baby, who will both require me to organise every millisecond of their days. I'm not sure I'm up to it. Was I ever?

"That's great," enthuses Finn as I tell him the news. "Here, hold your son, he's missed you."

"I doubt that. As long as he's fed and changed, I imagine anyone will do for him."

"But you're his mummy and no one can replace you."

"Even though some may try."

He doesn't even try to hide his rolling eyes. "I thought you'd moved on from there. My mother is a doting grandmother, that's all, and Lois hasn't been coming 'round as often."

I shrug my shoulders and sit Dylan on my knee facing me so I can gaze at him. He looks cute in his blue-and-white-stripe Breton jumper.

"Are we going to cope?" I ask quietly.

"What with? Being a couple or being parents?"

"I think many people struggle with the latter generally. No, I mean as a couple."

I watch him search the ceiling for the right words to say, in fact, for any words to say. I want to put him out of his misery, to offer him a way out, but I'm not feeling magnanimous.

"We'll get there, no doubt."

His words hang in the air, like particles of sweat, suspended in the cloying heat. I can visualize each letter, the round shapes and straight lines, but not the sentiments behind them.

"I won't want your mother visiting daily. I need time with Dylan to build the bond that's missing between us."

"Not sure I can promise that. She's been used to seeing him daily."

"Well I need you to be strong for me. You'll need to stand up to her, otherwise this will never work."

Dylan senses my distress, arches his back and grizzles, turning his face crimson. He pushes his feet into my stomach, helping him to maintain rigidity.

"This is going to happen each time I get stressed out. This is what your mother does to me."

"Enough already. I'll have a word with her, that's all I can promise."

I can tell he's resisting the urge to take Dylan from me. During our sessions with the nurse, she'd told him not to be so overprotective of Dylan; to let me parent and make mistakes, safe mistakes. When he tried to protest, she said I wouldn't harm Dylan. It wasn't a competition of who cared for the child the best. Finn didn't like being spoken to like that. That's a trait from Diana.

An unpleasant smell emits from Dylan's nappy, but like Finn, I too have to realize that I can't hand him over every time a nappy needs changing, or his behaviour becomes intolerable.

I lay him down and reach into the changing bag for a nappy and wipes. I sense I'm being assessed by Finn as he watches every step of the process. Being assessed by a doctor or nurse was one thing, but being assessed by Finn is an altogether different experience. *Doesn't he trust me?*

Dylan is soothed once more and has morphed into the cuddly baby I long to hold; only now he's becoming a more fidgety and mobile, not quite the tranquil baby that nestles in the crook of my arm and falls asleep whilst I watch TV.

I relent and hand him over to Finn's awaiting arms, where he proceeds to coo and gurgle. His perceived happiness in his father's arms floods me with a sense of inadequacy.

I woke at five this morning, and was washed and dressed by six. The meeting isn't until nine, so I've plenty of time to pace my room and fret about what people might say about me. This constant focus on me is wearing.

The rain lashes ominously against the window, reminding me of the cell-like room I've been in for the past seven weeks. When someone knocks at my door, I jump, clutching my hand to my chest.

"Breakfast," chimes the catering lady, bringing in a tray.

Once she's left, I stare at the bowl of cereal and the slice of cardboard-like toast, with a tiny pot of honey on the side, and wonder how I'm going to swallow even a crumb. The overly-milky cup of tea doesn't look like it will offer much assistance.

Even the tiniest morsel of toast feels like it's lacerating my throat. A gulp of the tea washes it down, but not without it catching on my throat, causing me to heave.

I resort to chewing the skin around my nails with such vigour that each finger is dotted and streaked with blood. I look like I've self-harmed with the prongs of a fork.

The nurse takes me into the meeting room to await the arrival of the others. Within minutes of being seated I hear footsteps and voices reverberating down the corridor.

As Finn walks in I see dark shadows under his eyes, and the lines either side of his mouth have deepened. Then I see why. Diana.

My heart catapults out of my chest and hits the wall opposite, and I'm gasping for breath. Dark spots swim before my eyes as I grip the edge of the table to prevent myself from slipping off the chair.

Doctor Holland arrives swiftly behind her, giving me no time to voice my shock and objection. I try to catch Finn's eyes, but he resolutely fixes his gaze on the table.

"Where's Dylan?" I whisper to the nurse next to me.

"Your father-in-law and your sister are looking after him," she replies.

Her words flit around my head like butterflies unable to find nectar.

The meeting begins with a nurse mapping out my progress since my arrival, followed by a nurse from the community mental health team telling me what support I'll receive until I'm completely recovered.

"But is she safe, in your opinion, Doctor, to be left alone with Dylan?" demands Diana.

Everyone shifts their attention between Diana and Gerry Holland. Everyone except me; I am looking at Finn waiting for him to defend me.

"But of course, Mrs Forbes. Colette is left alone with Dylan for several hours on the ward."

"Is she?" she replies in her clipped manner, swinging her glance towards Finn. "But in here she has access to staff all the time, and she won't at home, will she?"

"Colette will have her community nurse, her support group, her husband, and you, which is more than lots of mothers have."

"But *most* mothers aren't mentally ill, are they, Doctor?"

Diana's remark slices through the atmosphere, cutting the gathered into two distinct camps. For me, and against me. Only, I can't tell which camp Finn is in.

I zone out of the rest of the meeting, only nodding occasionally to demonstrate my participation. Diana's voice is heard loudly and often, with her main fear being will I be a good enough wife and mother to her two darling boys.

My attention is drawn back to the room when I hear the scraping of chairs on the lino floor. Low mutterings pass between everyone as they shake hands and depart.

I sense Finn standing next to me; his musky aftershave creeping up my nostrils.

"I'll collect you tomorrow morning around nine. Are you excited or nervous?" he asks.

"A bit of both really. How about you?"

"Same here—"

He's interrupted by Diana requesting to leave as she has a luncheon. She gives me a curt nod before leaving the room, followed closely by Finn.

There goes my future.

Finn

A suffocating silence enrobes Diana and me in the car, so I crack open the window to allow a stream of cold air to seep in and help me breathe.

"You weren't very vocal in there," she chides.

"You were vocal enough for the pair of us," I mutter under my breath, but she's so busy huffing and puffing, she doesn't hear my remark.

My mind's so distracted I nearly run a red light, and Diana exclaims I'm out to kill her. *She's such a drama queen.*

"Hello you two. Shall I put the kettle on?" says Gabriella as we step through the front door.

"I'm in dire need of a strong cup of tea. I'll be in the lounge," replies Diana, without looking at her.

"What Mum meant to say is *that would be very nice, thank you*," I add as I follow her into the kitchen.

"How did it go?"

"She's coming home tomorrow; the doctor is pleased with her progress. She'll still get support from a community mental health team, as there is a risk she may become ill again. Returning home is a big step." I sit down at the table, letting the morning's information sink in.

"Your dad's been great with Dylan. In fact," she begins, lowering her voice, "I think he's enjoyed his time alone with his grandson without Diana being around."

"Doesn't surprise me."

Gabriella moves around the kitchen as though it's her own, preparing a tray of tea and cake to take in to my parents.

I hear murmurings in the lounge but I can't make out what's being said. I suspect Gabriella will divulge all on her return.

"Diana said she's no longer going to the luncheon, she's too chewed up about something."

"Did she say what about?"

"No, but it's obvious something's troubling her. Are you sure the meeting went okay?"

"I think Diana imagined somehow that Colette would remain in hospital longer so she could have more control over Dylan."

"And over you," she interjects.

I watch her pour the tea and push the cup towards me. I refuse the slice of cake. I stir sugar into the tea for so long, Gabriella puts her hand on mine to get me to stop.

"I'm not sure I like the idea of strangers coming into the house to check on Colette and Dylan. It feels like an invasion of privacy."

"They're not checking up on the housework, or how weed-free your lawn is. They want to see if Colette's settled back home and if her relationship with Dylan is strengthening."

"You always did talk a lot of sense."

Leaning back on the chair, balancing on the back legs, I peer at Gabriella through semi-closed eyes, and see her likeness to Colette. Only Gabriella has tanned skin, with a band of freckles across the bridge of the same button nose, and more refined features.

"You know Colette will pull through. She's a strong woman, and she truly loves you and Dylan."

"I don't doubt it."

"Well then what's troubling you? I can see something's pecking at your brain."

"I've done something foolish. It was silly and pathetic, but it could potentially ruin my life."

"What have you done?"

Mercifully, we're disturbed by the doorbell; I hadn't planned on confessing.

Lois is standing on the doorstep; raindrops glistening like a blanket of dew on her shoulders.

"Aren't you going to invite me in?"

I'm in a dreamlike state; every movement I make takes ten times longer than normal.

"Could you take my coat?" she asks, backing into me, pushing me into a corner.

I slip her coat from her shoulders, revealing her waist-length ponytail hidden beneath. She presses up against me with the guise of warming herself up. Out of the corner of my eye I catch Gabriella watching us from the kitchen door. She slinks back into the kitchen as I guide Lois to the safety of the lounge to sit with my parents.

The women are soon wrapped up in each other and cooing over Dylan, so I retreat quietly to the kitchen.

"Don't tell me your faux pas involves a woman, *that* woman to be precise," Gabriella hisses.

I'd never seen her eyes so black and frightening. "I made a mistake, a one-time mistake. God knows I regret it now. Please, *please* don't tell Colette, it would kill her."

"But all the while you and Colette remain friends with *her*. How's that supposed to pan out?"

"Look, we've all been friends for years, and we're adults now. Lois knows I love Colette and Dylan and that nothing's going to wrench me away from them."

"I'm not sure she does after watching that charade. I'm only sorry I live too far away to check up on you. I'm going to have to trust you for now."

"Will you tell Colette?"

"I think in this current climate she's better off not knowing. But if you hurt her, I'll fly straight back and heave you out of this house."

"I can believe that."

"Your son's woken up requesting lunch. And you shouldn't leave your guest for too long, she's been a rock for you, Finn," Diana says, entering the kitchen, looking down her nose at Gabriella.

"Are we talking about Lois?" Gabriella asks.

I stare at her, half begging and half in anger. I don't want Diana involved.

"Be a dear and get a bottle ready, would you?" she tells Gabriella. "Finn, I need to speak with you out here," she demands, cocking her head in the direction of the hallway.

"What?" I ask as we hover in the narrow space.

"Get in there and entertain Lois, your father is doing a terrible job. She's come to see you, not your father and I."

I'm transported back to being a terrorized altar boy, pushed into singing a solo. As she thrusts me into the lounge, I find Lois cradling a fractious Dylan in her arms.

"This baby lark's quite hard, I hope Colette's up to all this when she comes home tomorrow," she purrs.

Diana has obviously been talking to her. My father has his nose in a book in order to ostracize himself from the proceedings. *Wise man.*

"I'm sure she'll do just fine. Gabriella's still here for a few more days," I reply.

"Indeed I am," Gabriella snaps as she marches into the room with a warm bottle of milk in her hand. "I'll also be around to check up on everything and everyone." She takes Dylan from Lois and sits down in the armchair to feed him, pointedly ignoring me.

Lois looks at me with a smirk on her face. Nothing seems to phase her, which is a worrying trait. Perhaps she loves taking risks, and I was just one of those.

"Perhaps you should take Lois out tonight to thank her for all her help. You may not get another opportunity when Colette returns," Diana says on entering.

In my peripheral vision I see Gabriella glaring at me. I realize I can only please one person at a time. Who's that going to be?

Colette

Packing away my toothbrush triggers a rush of panic. The act signifies the greater realization that I'm finally going home. My room's now devoid of flowers and cards, and with my suitcase on the stripped bed, it looks like I've never been here at all.

I cast my mind back to my first day, and I don't recognize myself. The paranoid thoughts, the crushing lows, the periodic highs, and not caring for myself or anyone else. It doesn't seem real now.

The room seems bigger than on that first day, less cell-like. Perhaps my mind has expanded rather than the room? My therapist would be proud.

A nurse enters the room with a green plastic bag containing a week's worth of medication. There's a prescription inside to obtain more. She doesn't hang around. Perhaps I'm no longer interesting now that my mental state is stable?

Suddenly, Finn walks in.

"Are you ready?" he asks.

I nod, picking up my case, giving the room a once over.

Saying goodbye to the staff and other patients is more poignant than I imagined. I gulp back the tears and sobs that want to escape with each hug. I mustn't show too much raw emotion; everyone's still watching me.

It feels odd sitting in the passenger seat of our car, with an empty baby seat in the rear. I try not to look at it.

"Just so I'm prepared, who's at home right now?" I ask.

"Your sister and our son."

"Not your parents?"

"No, I've just told you. Sorry, I didn't mean to sound sharp."

"I just want to start as we mean to go on. I want to settle and get to know Dylan at home rather than on a hospital ward."

"I think I can make that happen," he replies softly.

Bare trees line the street where we live, and the uneven pavement harbours tiny coves of puddles, ready to catch out an unobservant pedestrian.

I float to the front door. Nothing seems real. The black door appears glossier, the brass knocker shinier, and winter pansies bloom brightly in the hanging basket. These are all touches of Diana; they are not signs of me. I am far too disorganized and laisser-faire for all of that.

Finn puts the key in the door, and as soon as it swings open Gabriella comes bouncing towards me, holding Dylan in her arms.

"So wonderful to see you back home," she squeals.

"It's great to be back . . . I think."

She falters briefly before ushering me into the lounge. A huge bouquet of flowers in a crystal vase sits on the table in the bay window. I know that's Gabriella's touch, Finn never bought flowers from one birthday to the next.

I perch gingerly on the edge of the sofa as though I am in a stranger's house. The air smells different and the light seems grainier.

"Are you all right?" Gabriella asks, her brow furrowed. "Go and make her a cup of tea, Finn." She speaks sternly, like a school teacher to a naughty pupil.

I tell her I am okay, but my voice sounds strained. She moves to sit next to me with Dylan still in her arms.

"Would you like to hold him?"

I nod cautiously as I still have an undercurrent of ennui in my mind. I open my arms and twist towards her before feeling the weight of his plump body in my arms.

Perhaps he senses my discomfort, as he wriggles excessively then begins to wail. My body freezes. I no longer feel resentment towards him; instead, a lump of sorrow hits the pit of my stomach.

"He doesn't like me," I whisper.

"Of course he does. Sit back and relax, he can probably feel you're tense."

I shuffle backwards and rest against the back of the sofa. I try making soothing noises, and soon he is calm and distracted by the ring on my finger.

"There, what did I tell you? You're doing great, you're a natural mummy," Gabriella says brightly.

I let out a tiny laugh and tell her that nothing's coming to me naturally. Dylan cranes to look up at me when I make the sound. I imagine it was because I've never done that in front of him before.

Finn enters with a cup of tea and a chocolate biscuit in the saucer, and puts it on the table before me. I can't work out how I'm supposed to drink it whilst holding the baby. And my mouth is so dry.

After a minute, Finn takes Dylan from me so I can drink my tea. For a brief second, I miss the weight of him sitting in my lap, but the tea moistening my mouth swiftly takes that notion away.

"When are you returning to Spain?" I ask Gabriella.

"In a couple of days. Sorry it's so short; it's the best I could do."

"Sometimes our best is not good enough," I whisper back.

"But sometimes that's all a person can give. Don't be so hard on everyone, or yourself," she retorts.

"Sorry, I didn't mean to offend you. I just feel stupid for what's happened lately. I've a healthy baby boy and a husband who loves me, so I don't understand."

"They told you it was hormonal, not your fault. Just stop berating yourself and start getting to know Dylan better."

I know she's making sense and that it's time I move on. I just wish I knew what she was hiding from me. I could always sense her doing that, even when we were children.

I watch Finn as he rocks Dylan until he's asleep in his arms, before taking him upstairs. He's in the hallway when the doorbell rings, and the next thing I hear is Diana's voice. I look towards Gabriella with panic in my eyes.

I recognize Diana's heeled footsteps as she approaches the lounge. Gabriella puts her hand on my arm and gives it a gentle squeeze.

"Hello Colette, how are you feeling?"

I want to say I was feeling better before she arrived, but instead I tell her I'm fine. She sits in the chair where Finn's been sitting, and surveys the room as though she owns the place.

"When are you returning to Spain?" she asks Gabriella.

"In a couple of days."

"I see. That will mean you'll need me here after then, I suppose." This time she directs her question towards me.

"I'll be fine. Finn will be here if I need anything."

"Finn has to go to work. He can't be here to watch over you."

I am parched once again, so my tongue sticks to the roof of my mouth. I hastily take another sip of tea.

"I'm sure I'll be fine Diana, I—"

"The psychiatrist said you were to have support to see you through the next few weeks," she interjects.

"She'll have her nurse and mother-and-baby group to support her. I'm sure my sister will cope, she's a strong person."

"I thought that too until she ended up in hospital."

I've been made immobile by fear and panic, and I'm thankful for Gabriella's support. *What will I do when she's gone?*

Finn's arrival defuses the tension that's strung across the room like bunting. However, it's not long before he's under her influence and is beginning to worry about leaving me alone with the baby.

"Perhaps you two could go out for a quiet meal tonight to discuss how to plan for moments of difficulty. I'm here to babysit. Get yourselves sorted before I fly back," Gabriella encourages.

Gabriella holds my hand as she speaks so I profit from her hope and strength that radiates into me.

"Eating out again, Finn?" chips in Diana, her haughty voice hanging in the air.

I turn to look at Finn, questioning him in my mind, because the words are nothing but dry lumps in my throat. I want to claw at my arm, allowing blood to seep out, in order to feel present in the room. The lack of clarity is screwing my mind to the inside of my skull, begging me to scream out loud.

"Where did you go?" I finally whisper.

"Just the local pub."

"Alone?"

"No, with Lois. She's been a rock for Finn over these past few weeks," replies Diana, checking her French manicure.

I notice Gabriella puff out her chest and her face is stippled with red blotches. It's my turn to pat her hand to reassure her I'm okay.

"I'm glad Finn had her for support and comfort, not to mention her help with Dylan," Diana continued.

"Yes, Lois has been an invaluable friend to me, but she didn't replace Colette. No one can replace my wife."

I see him exchange a heated glance with Gabriella. Diana shuffles around in her seat looking at the baby monitor, probably hoping to see the lights flicker to announce the waking of her grandson.

"Finn and I have known Lois for years. I'm not jealous they've been in each other's company, or had a few meals together. No one needs to be concerned on my behalf," I say.

Dylan chooses just this time to expand his lungs to maximum capacity. Grateful for the excuse, I leave the room, noticing Finn holding Diana back with his outstretched arm.

Finn's moved Dylan into the nursery from our bedroom. I wander over to the cot, where he lies reaching out with his dough-like arms, and his eyes screwed-up tightly with fat tears streaming down his pudgy cheeks.

I pick him up and realize he needs changing. It's the first time I've done it alone, which is unsettling, but I place him on the changing table and undo his sleep suit, revealing his rotund tummy.

As I reach for a clean nappy, something catches my eye and I turn to see Diana watching me from just outside the door.

"Did you want something?" I ask her, monitoring my tone.

"I was just going to the bathroom."

I feel my face reddening as she hovers in the doorway.

"Finn needs a strong, reliable wife. Someone who can be a competent mother, a homemaker, and an elegant hostess for his business soirees. Do you think you're up to all of that?"

"I managed before."

"Only now you have Dylan. How long will it take for him to realize you're not up to it? Six months? A year?"

Dylan is wriggling about as I try to put on a clean nappy. Before the nappy is fastened, he urinates all over my top. My initial reaction is annoyance, but I'm quick to find my peaceful place. I hear Diana tut behind me.

"I can't see this working, Colette, if you're not going to take your role seriously."

With Dylan finally changed and in my arms, I turn to face her head on. Her face projects a virulent dislike of me, more than I'd ever seen before.

"I will do my best, but if it's not good enough, Finn is free to find another woman. I wouldn't want to stand in his way of a successful life."

"I'll be watching you carefully; I'm not sure I can trust you and your madness around my son and grandson."

Diana steps closer to me so I can smell her expensive perfume and feel her breath on my cheek.

"I'll take Dylan back downstairs so you can get changed," she says, taking him from my arms and walking out of the nursery.

I head to my bedroom to select a clean top. Taking off my urine-soaked shirt, I feel the soft skin on my inner arms. When my fingers reach my forearm, I touch the thin, worm-like ridges under my fingertips, which still look red and angry as I'm now feeling.

The thought of slicing my flesh suddenly engulfs me; I know if I get the blood flowing, it will release the tension that's bubbling up in me. I look around for something to use, but it's useless. I have to let the mood pass, cold turkey.

I take a quick look in the mirror before re-joining everyone downstairs.

Returning to the lounge, I find Lois sitting next to Diana, who's gently bouncing Dylan on her knee. They don't notice me return.

Finn

I'm living in a nightmare; Colette and Lois are together in the same room. And as for my mother, could she be more obvious about preferring Lois to Colette?

My father's doing the crossword in the paper, thus separating himself from the awkward proceedings, whilst still observing from the periphery.

"It's brightening up outside. Why don't you and Lois take Dylan out for some fresh air, then Colette can have a nap," Diana says.

"What a good idea," Lois pipes up, taking her leather jacket from the arm of the sofa.

I'm disappointed Colette doesn't object, but then why should she; everyone's innocent in her mind. I avoid Gabriella's gaze.

I know it always aggravates Colette when I obey Diana's demands, and don't stand up for myself. Growing up, Diana always had the power in the household, so I know no other way to react.

"It's okay, Finn, a nap would probably do me good," Colette says, smiling.

Colette's comment spurs Lois into fetching the buggy from the hallway. Diana puts Dylan in and tucks a powder blue cashmere blanket around him. Colette leaves the room before I have the chance to speak to her. I'll talk to her later.

As Lois and I step outside, the crisp air smacks my cheeks. I pull my scarf tighter around my neck and glance into the buggy to check on Dylan. His little nose looks pink and his eyes are alert.

We stroll down the street, side by side in silence, listening to the magpies mocking racket from the bare branches. I'm aware of people smiling at us as the quintessential couple with their baby.

"It feels kind of special, doesn't it?" Lois smiles.

"What does?"

"Strangers wanting to see the baby and smiling at us as though we've produced the next Messiah."

"I suppose so, although I'm not pretending to be the father, I am his father."

"I could be his mother. That is, if you want me to be."

I feel my lungs instinctively stop inhaling air, as though I've just stuck my head in a plastic bag. I stop walking but Lois continues with the buggy, unaware of my receding proximity.

Suddenly she stops and looks 'round at me, her face crumpled like a deflated balloon. I momentarily think she's going to cry. *What is it with women and crying?*

I walk towards her. Drawing level, I see her eyes glistening with un-shed tears.

"Can we just talk about something else?"

"Okay, I understand," she sniffs.

Her hand on my arm feels strange, yet paradoxically familiar and comforting. Before I realize what I am doing, I put my hand on top of hers. Suddenly, I'm transported back to that night in bed, when her flesh felt like silk next to mine.

"I keep thinking about it too," she says, startling me with her tele-pathic understanding. "I haven't stopped thinking about that night."

"How did you guess?" I withdraw my hand rapidly.

"I see the longing in your eyes, and the way your breathing becomes shallow around me. We can't hide this forever, Finn."

"Well we have to. I'm a married man; I have more to lose than you."

"Not necessarily."

"What does that mean?"

"A judge may rule Colette an unfit mother due to her mental state. You could get sole custody and we could raise him together. He knows me more than her anyway."

"Stop talking this way, you don't know what you're saying."

"But I do. We're made for one another."

"If that were true, I'd have dated you, not Colette."

"You were afraid of me back then. I was too overtly sexual. Colette was demure and quiet. Now we know why, she was shielding us from her madness within."

I've the urge to take the buggy from her as I'm suddenly feeling exceedingly possessive of my son. She resists little and I pick up the pace so Dylan's face is buffeted by the chilled air. He protests with short spurts of coughing, so I stop. "We should return. He's getting fractious."

I turn the buggy around and feel Lois mould to my side.

"I'm willing to wait for you," she says, gazing up at me, her head tilting towards me.

"Please, Lois. Don't make this difficult. I've got to look after Colette and Dylan, they both depend on me."

She doesn't reply, but walks closer to me so our arms are pressed firmly together.

Diana looks disappointed when we return so soon, but Gabriella looks relieved.

"You weren't long," Gabriella says, picking up Dylan. "Oh, his poor face is frozen."

"That's why we turned back, it's bitter out there," I reply as casually as possible.

"Perhaps you should go and check on your wife," Gabriella says directly to me, rolling her eyes as though I don't know where the bedroom is.

I withdraw quietly, hearing Diana and Lois talking in hushed tones.

Colette

I'm sitting on the spare bed watching Gabriella pack her suitcase.

"I wish you weren't going; it's been so lovely spending time with you."

"I'm sorry; I wish I could stay longer, but I've got work commitments. Anyway, I think you need to be alone with Finn and Dylan, without outside interference."

"Fat chance of that with Diana."

Gabriella stops folding clothes and looks at me. "Don't let anyone bully you. Be the quietly strong woman you are."

"I'm no longer that person. Two months in that place has damaged me." I cross my legs as though sitting on a toadstool.

"Nonsense. Every day you spend at home will make you stronger and happier." She closes the lid, straining to fasten the locks.

"What happens if having a baby doesn't bring me the happiness it should?" My knees are bouncing in rapid successions.

She moves closer and sits on the bed next to me, wrapping her arm around my shoulders. "You're still recovering; things will still seem difficult currently. Be gentle on yourself and lean on Finn, he's your husband after all."

"Talking of Finn, has something happened between you both? You were rather sharp with him earlier."

Gabriella pulls away and stands up. "I suppose I blame him for all of this."

"That's not rational."

"I know, but I feel very protective of you and I don't feel he does enough."

I pull my knees up under my chin and hug them tightly. I can tell there's something else that she's reticent to tell me.

"Did Finn say he's stopped loving me?"

"Of course not, that's a ludicrous suggestion. I've just been worried; you know how that makes me cranky."

I smile at her and she smiles back before Finn calls up to say the taxi's here. We hug each other hard before she bumps her suitcase down the stairs and out the front door. *I miss her already.*

"What do you want to do now?" Finn asks me, in a voice that resonates with both pity and boredom.

"What are new parents supposed to do but wait and watch their young one in case they're needed? This is our role from now on."

"Our life doesn't stop because we have Dylan, why don't we have a cup of tea and plan all the things we wish to do, with or without him. You know my parents will babysit anytime."

I know he's right, but relying on Diana may bring more misery upon me; unhinge my fragile mental stability.

I follow him to the kitchen and watch him make a pot of tea. He looks more at home in the kitchen now than he ever did previously. Perhaps fatherhood suits him, and perhaps this will nudge him into finally cutting the umbilical cord with Diana.

He puts everything on the table then produces a pad and paper.

"I think we should go out for a meal soon, gives us both a break from cooking and washing up. There's a new Indian restaurant I'd like to try."

I nod as enthusiastically as I can, having nothing to add to his list. When the doorbell rings, he heads for the door with an air of relief.

"Hello," says Lois, stepping into the kitchen. "Nice to see you looking so well." She bends and kisses me on the cheek.

I smile, noticing her hair has acquired some butterscotch highlights, which accentuates her eyes. I always felt inferior to her appearance, but now I have some lingering baby fat around my waist and thighs, and my hair is parched and in dire need of a cut. I want to shrink away from her image of perfection.

"I'm going to book a hair appointment," I announce, getting up.

Neither of them answers me as though my words ride on a breeze, taking them beyond ear-shot. I make the call and have an appointment in an hour.

"I'm sorry to leave you both. I shouldn't be longer than a couple of hours." I head upstairs to get ready.

The salon is buzzing with the sound of music, hairdryers, and chatter. It's a little overwhelming, but my desire to return to my sharp elfin crop overrides all anxieties.

I can't help thinking about Finn's reaction to Lois's arrival. He seemed torn between being happy to see her and fearful. What does he have to fear?

As the hairdresser runs his fingers through my hair, the psychiatrist's words enter my thoughts. I'm reminded of the false beliefs that played havoc with my logical thinking during my time in hospital. And now, I'm left with depression, anxiety, and low social confidence. *How will I climb out of this chasm?*

I close my eyes to block my reflection in the mirror, as I'm finding fault with every feature of my face. My pale skin is more insipid than usual, highlighting the splash of freckles across the bridge of my nose and merging into the shadows under my eyes. I look like I've blown onto a hot cup of frothy coffee. My green eyes now have the poor luminosity of an energy-saving bulb that has just been switched on.

With my eyes closed, I'm aware of my increased heartbeat. It's thudding through my temples, and making the slices on my wrists throb, as though they could erupt.

I open my eyes and feel the room spinning, my hearing is impeded by the rushing blood. My breaths are shallow, and beads of perspiration are prickling my clammy flesh.

"Are you all right?" he asks, scissors poised.

"Are you nearly finished? I need to go." I'm aware of my pathetic-sounding voice, but I'm conserving all my energy to keep myself from running from the chair all the way home.

"Just need to feather your fringe and run some wax through, and you're done."

I valiantly try to slow things down by taking deep breaths and focusing on the image of a tranquil island in my mind. But nothing is working.

As soon as he finishes, I push myself out of my chair, and hurriedly pay the receptionist before scurrying along the pavement towards the bus stop, praying I don't bump into someone I know.

I hope Finn is ready to support me when I get home; I feel I'm spiralling out of control.

Finn

"It seems we keep getting thrown together," Lois purrs, as soon as Colette shuts the front door.

"It doesn't mean anything, it's just circumstance."

She's standing in front of me with her hands on my chest. I imagine she can feel my pounding heart.

"I know you think of me often, and I know this is hard because of our long-standing friendship, with Colette also, but our love's real and strong."

I'm intoxicated by her breath that brushes my lips like a butterfly in flight. Before I know what I am doing, I've pulled her towards me. The passion is unlike anything I've known; it tastes good, yet with a decidedly bitter aftertaste, so I pull away.

"I'm sorry. I don't want to hurt you or Colette. We have to stop this now; it's tearing me apart."

She looks up at me. "I will wait for as long as it takes. She will damage your life with her madness, but I'll be on the side-lines waiting to pick up the pieces and nurture you back to the sane world. You'll need me one day, Finn."

The sound of the front door opening makes me jump and push Lois away from me, more forcefully than I intend to. I call out and get a whimper back from Colette.

I rush to her, recognizing the torment in her voice. Her hair's returned to its former glory, but the rest of her demeanour is in tatters. She looks wide-eyed and terrified.

"What's happened?"

"I'm eaten up by anxiety. Oh God, Finn." She crumples against me.

"Sounds like a panic attack. They said you'd experience periods of anxiety and depression and low self-esteem. Come and have a cup of tea, sit with me for a bit."

She allows me to guide her to the kitchen where we find Lois buttoning up her blouse, her hair ruffled with a sheepish look on her face. My heart momentarily misses a beat.

"Colette, you're back sooner than anticipated. Your hair looks lovely," she says breathlessly.

I glare balefully at her over the top of Colette's head. *What the hell are you doing?*

Colette has retreated into a dense foggy silence, and I can't fathom what she's thinking. Has she seen something that should be hidden and forgotten?

"I'll make a pot of tea for us," Lois says, switching on the kettle.

"That's kind of you, but I thought you had to be going," I say flatly.

"I can't go without giving Colette my gift," she says as she pulls a beautifully wrapped parcel from her bag and hands it to Colette.

Colette stares at it, lightly touching the purple ribbon tied around it. In a painfully slow fashion she picks at the paper, gradually tearing it back one corner at a time. Lois looks at me, rolling her eyes before pouring boiling water into the teapot.

After a few restorative sips of tea, Colette resumes opening the gift until she finally reaches the pea green pashmina inside. She runs her tapered fingers over the cloth, seemingly appreciating it.

"I think the colour enhances your eyes, plus it's a great item to throw on in the chilly evenings," says Lois.

"It's beautiful, thank you. You're a good friend."

I knot inside hearing those words, but Lois seems insouciant. After a moment's reflection, I ask Colette if she wants to lie down.

"I don't want to rest, I want to get better," she replies tersely.

"And you will, with time and rest. Be patient."

"Easy for you to say, when getting out of bed doesn't present you with an insurmountable task every day."

I feel chagrined. "I can't pretend to know how you feel, but it's not easy for me either, I have Dylan to care for."

"It's always harder for the man, isn't it," she scolds. "Perhaps you'd be better off with me dead then you could replace me with a proper woman." She slams her palm on the table before dashing upstairs. I move to follow her, but Lois puts her hand on my arm.

"Give her time to calm down. I'll go and see her."

I wait until she's gone before tiptoeing after her, to eavesdrop at the top of the stairs.

"He doesn't mean to be thoughtless, Colette. I think he's just tired with all the worry about you."

"I'm sapped of energy continually, I need him to bolster me up, not put-upon me. God I sound so selfish."

"You've had a tough time, you both have. It will get easier."

Lois's compassion surprises me. Reassured she's not going to divulge our sordid secret, I descend quietly and return to the kitchen.

I am just about to pour myself a second cup of tea when Dylan stirs, but before I have time to mount the stairs, Lois descends with him in her arms.

"Colette's fallen asleep," she whispers as she brushes past me and heads for the kitchen. "Can you warm a bottle, please?"

We slip into an effortless routine, so natural it's frightening. I'm pleased Colette's not here to witness it.

Hearing the front door open startles me until I realise Diana still has a key. Her heels clatter on the wooden floorboards, and the inevitable smell of Chanel No5 edges its way into the kitchen before she does.

"Oh, my grandson's awake," she exclaims, approaching Lois. She smiles fondly at the pair before turning to me. "When are you returning to work?"

"Tomorrow, why?"

"Who's going to look after Dylan?"

"Colette of course. The nurse is calling in to see how she's doing."

"Popping in but not staying with her all day. I suppose it's down to me to fill that role," she says stoically.

"I'll help you too," pipes up Lois. "That's the joy of running one's own business; I can do it almost anywhere with Internet access."

A cold frisson trickles down my spine as I listen to them conspiring to monitor—or is it control—my wife. A soupçon of pity gravitates towards her sleeping body upstairs, but I have to return to work to cover the mortgage and bills. *Colette will cope, won't she?*

Colette

"Do you have to go back so soon?" I ask Finn as he straightens his tie.

"My boss has been very understanding, but I need to get back."

"What happens if something bad happens to you?"

"I've been a probation officer for eight years and nothing bad has happened to me so far."

"But you have me and Dylan to care for now."

"All the more reason for me to get back to work to earn the money; my paternity leave is over."

I know what he's saying makes sense, but I'm overwhelmed by anxiety, gnawing at my bones. I'm shaking inside; I need him to know I can't cope with Dylan on my own.

"What about Dylan? How will I manage?"

"My mum's coming 'round at nine, and the nurse will be here at ten thirty. You'll have plenty of—"

"Diana's coming here." My head's spinning. "I can't cope with her sanctimonious attitude towards me, and her smothering ways with Dylan. You promised you'd keep her away from me."

"The psychiatrist advised you not to be alone for too long in the early days. You need to be supported and I can't be here any longer. I'm sorry. I'll be home before you know it."

I don't want to sound callous, so how can I tell him I think his mother's a controlling cow, especially where he and Dylan, her boys, are concerned? I've never been good enough in her eyes.

"You'll be fine," he comments as though reading my thoughts.

"I've no choice really," I sigh.

We descend together and he kisses me on the cheek before closing the door behind him. I imagine he's relieved to be out of the house, in clothes void of the smell of baby sick.

The stillness of the house brings reality sharply into focus. I'm alone in charge of a tiny baby. The thought sends ripples of nausea washing over my stomach, and a bubble of the putrid taste bursting in the back of my throat.

Crying tells me Dylan's disturbed by the silence. I tentatively approach him and see his crumpled red face, screwed up like a festive paper napkin, with fat tears creeping down his dumpling-like cheeks, and pooling in his ears. He doesn't see me, but I get the feeling the sight of me would not calm him. I fear he'd be more comforted by the sight of Finn or Lois, or God forbid, Diana.

I reach down and lift him out of his cot. He is silenced briefly, until I get a whiff of his nappy and discover the cause of his *malheure*.

After ten minutes of discomfort for both of us, I descend the stairs only to be greeted by Diana entering the front door.

"How's my grandson?"

"How did you get in?"

"I have a key. Didn't Finn tell you?"

No he bloody didn't.

Diane trots to the kitchen and puts the kettle on before turning to me and holding out her arms.

"Come to your grandmother," she says in a ridiculous sing-song voice. Why do women do that?

I hand him over and begin making coffee. I sense her staring at me, raising the hairs on the back of my neck.

"You've got that nurse coming, haven't you?" she asks.

"I have. I haven't met her yet, but I'm sure she'll be nice."

"It's not nice you want, it's effective. She needs to ensure Dylan's safety at all cost."

A headache's brewing in my temples. Dylan's snuggled into her ample breast and they make a contented vision, making me feel inept and surplus to requirement.

I whimper into the lounge and flop on the sofa, hoping it will swallow me whole. I can't do this mother thing; I have no affinity with

Dylan. It's painful to admit, but I don't think I've bonded with him like Finn has. There's an empty cavern where my love should be.

Nurse Hannah Morley is sitting before me waiting for me to answer her question.

"I'm riddled with guilt. Guilt at being ill, at not being able to cope alone, and missing Dylan's early baby stages. I'm an inadequate mother." I don't feel any better after telling her this.

"What you're feeling is normal for any woman who's experienced postpartum psychosis. But all new mums feel anxious about coping and about being a good parent. Dylan looks a content baby."

"I've hardly had any input in his welfare. It's all been down to Finn, Lois, and Diana, and they know it."

"You're being too hard on yourself; he's sitting here happily with you now."

"Only because his grandmother fed and changed him before you arrived. As soon as you've gone he'll be in her arms again."

"Is that how you want it to be?"

"It's the best for Dylan. I have little patience and tolerance for him, and I don't know if that'll change."

"It will, give it time. Have you thought anymore about the mother-and-baby group?"

"I'm not ready to do something like that just yet." I feel like screaming, but, fortunately, Dylan does it for me.

The lounge door opens and in bustles Diana. She swoops on Dylan, whisking him out of my arms and onto her shoulder. My overriding emotion is relief.

"I'm Diana Forbes, Dylan's grandmother," she enunciates every word.

"Hannah Morley."

"May I have a word with you in private?"

"Only if Colette is happy with that," Hannah replies, turning to me.

Amazingly, I don't care. I suspect people talk about me behind my back all the time, so I'm used to it. I get up and leave the room, giving

Hannah her answer without actually speaking.

In the past, I'd have been curious in this situation and hovered by the doorway to eavesdrop. However, I find myself feeling neither curiosity nor concern. I must still be ill.

With the mug of tepid coffee in my hands, I stare at the desolate garden, with trees stripped of leaves, and borders devoid of colour and love. The dappled-grey sky hails rain in the distance, cloaking the day in Mother Nature's misery. A gentle breeze toys with the parched leaves scattered across the weed-infested lawn.

I see Hannah enter the kitchen in the reflection of the window.

"I'm going now, but you have my number if you need to speak to me. I'll see you next week at the same time."

Diana hijacks her space, holding Dylan in her arms, and staring at me with contempt in her eyes. I consider turning around but I feel catatonic. By the time I lift my eyes to see her again, I hear her footsteps slowly mount the stairs.

Before I know it, she's returned and is now standing by my side, invading my personal space.

"I wanted to talk to Hannah about something I'd read on the Internet. She confirmed that over half the women with postpartum psychosis go on to have a further episode of mental illness not related to childbirth."

I only hear every other word, so she's not making sense. Turning to face her, I hope to see a chink of support or compassion breaking through her armour, but I see nothing but resentment and disappointment. *Does Finn feel the same?*

Finn

It's such a relief to be sitting at my desk, wading through correspondence and e-mails accumulated during my paternity leave. The female co-workers have showered me with support and kindness, whereas my male counterparts have avoided the topic of Colette's illness and Dylan altogether, which suits me.

I've four home visits booked, but I've still time for a coffee; one I can drink hot rather than leave on the kitchen work surface whilst I tend to Dylan.

My mobile rings and I see the caller is Lois. Against my better judgement, I answer.

"How does it feel to be free?" she asks.

"It feels like being back at work."

"When's your lunch break?"

"In an hour, why?"

"I'd like to see you."

I burn my throat swallowing a mouthful of scorching liquid. "We can't do this, Colette needs our support not our deception," I hiss.

"Only for a chat, nothing more. I got used to seeing you regularly whilst she was in hospital, and I miss you."

I can't help feeling flattered, but I know it's wrong. Mind you, I challenge any man not to feel the same where Lois is concerned.

What am I thinking? I'm a father now; I need to focus on my son. I tell her I am having lunch at my desk and hang up.

I have to focus on nurturing Colette back to normality. But Lois will always be around us. She's always been different; sexy in a way that Colette never was; Colette was the safest option back then.

Strolling to my car at the end of a very busy day, I find Lois leaning against the bonnet, donned in an astrakhan coat and faux fur hat. She's clutching her leather bag closely to her chest.

"Hello stranger," she says hoarsely, thanks to the cold air. "I was hoping you weren't working late; I'm freezing out here."

"What do you want?" I ask, unlocking the car before we both climb in.

"God that's better. I told you, I just wanted a chat."

"You could come 'round to the house rather than parade yourself in front of my work colleagues."

"I can't really tell you, in front of Colette, that I'm offering you unencumbered sex. I'm capable of remaining good friends, but with the bonus of sleeping together from time to time."

I can't believe I'm not only listening to her, I'm actually considering her offer. She was the unobtainable of the group, surrounded by eager men. And now here she is, offering me her body like a stamen to a bee.

"Your silence says so much," she purrs provocatively.

I turn the key in the ignition to warm the car and to stop the trail of condensation filtering from her mouth and making her look like an old-time movie star.

"It's too dangerous. What if Colette found out?"

"If only you and I know, how could she?"

"Feminine intuition."

"I think her medication may have dampened that talent."

I offer her a wry smile.

"Why don't you take me back with you now, and I'll prove that not only can I be discreet, but that Colette won't suspect a thing."

Against my better judgement, I agree to her suggestion. She rests her hand on my thigh as I drive home.

Colette's sitting in the lounge staring out the window when we arrive. The air is void of cooking smells, and Dylan is not with her. The baby monitor is on the coffee table.

"Where's Diana?" I ask.

"You've just missed her. She and George have a table booked for dinner before going to the theatre."

"Where's Dylan?"

"In the nursery, asleep."

"And dinner?"

"If you've got nothing planned, why don't I make a pasta dish?" Lois butts in.

It's only now Colette notices Lois in the room, and she doesn't appear to mind.

I leave to go and check on Dylan as Lois heads to the kitchen, giving me a rub on my shoulder as we part in the hallway.

Satisfied with Dylan's wellbeing I return downstairs to find both women in the kitchen, the air infused with basil and garlic.

"Dinner's nearly ready, why don't you get us all a drink," commands Lois.

"Not quite what I had in mind," she comments on seeing me with a carton of orange juice.

"Colette can't drink with her meds and I'm driving you home after this, so no point in opening a bottle of wine for one person." I throw her an infuriated glance

She shrugs as she serves the food into three bowls, and places them on the table.

Colette picks at her food, as do I; but Lois is savouring every mouthful. After ten minutes Colette pushes her bowl away, before leaving the table and heading for the garden.

"I'll go and check on her. Eat your dinner, you need to keep your strength up," smiles Lois.

I have to trust her; I can't be around all the time.

Colette

The rain's ceased, but the cold air is damp and foreboding, as I stand in the naked garden.

"Are you all right?" Lois asks, arriving at my side.

"Not really."

"Talking is supposed to be healing, and I'm a good listener."

She's right; she was always a good person to talk to; she had the ability to reframe my thoughts and situations.

"I fear Finn may leave me now I'm mentally ill."

"What makes you say that?"

"I'm no longer a complete woman or wife. I daren't . . . you know . . . in bed in case I get pregnant. All this can happen again."

"You can guard against that. Your first priority is getting better."

Panic is still fluttering over my heart. "Do you think he's capable of having an affair?"

"You're worrying unnecessarily; he loves you, regardless of all this," she concludes, waving her arms around.

I wish I could believe her. I sense my rising paranoia taking hold of my mind and showing me false images, or are they premonitions?

She puts her arm around my shoulders and pulls me towards her. It feels good to connect. She will see I am okay; I know she will.

The temperature dips further so I suggest we move back inside. She gives me one last squeeze before linking her arm through mine and leading me back.

Finn is nowhere to be seen. I imagine he's upstairs with Dylan, so I flop onto the sofa and nestle amongst the cushions, pulling one over my still disgustingly squishy stomach.

"I'll go and check on the boys, let you rest awhile."

She sounds like Diana. I hug the cushion tighter and close my eyes, in the hope that sleep will welcome me in. Sadly, it eludes me.

I hear them talking through the ceiling. Their words invisible, but I sense some irritation in Finn's voice. Dylan is quiet, which is a blessing.

A tear rolls down my cheek as I contemplate whether I like being a parent or not. The tear dribbles into the corner of my mouth, and my tongue reaches out to saviour the salty taste. I'm not sure why I'm crying, but it feels the right thing to do at this moment in time.

Hearing footsteps coming down the stairs, I wipe my eyes with the heel of my hand, then hug the cushion hard.

"Look who I've brought to see Mummy," Finn says in a light voice.

I turn to see as if I don't know the answer, but of course I know its Dylan. *Why can't I dredge up some joy at seeing him?*

Finn bends down to place Dylan in my arms but I keep the cushion clamped in place. I can't look either of them in the eye, fearing they can see my indifference and parental inadequacy.

"Try and hold him," Finn encourages.

I want to tell him that forcing the baby upon me is not the way to go. Dylan senses my apathy and begins to whimper.

Lois moves into my eyeline, gently removing Dylan from Finn. She cradles him and sways from side to side until his sobs are intermittent hiccups. Finn backs away from me, and Lois conveys *it doesn't matter* to me via a wink, before sidling up to him.

Their hushed tones float on the air but I can't be bothered to work out what they're saying. Whatever it is, I know they're probably right.

The sound of the front door opening pre-empts the sound of Diana's voice echoing in the hallway.

"So, how's the invalid?" she asks, viewing me from the lounge doorway.

I feel all three of them waiting for my response to validate their presence. I search for something pertinent to say, but all I can find is, "Not bad."

Diana moves swiftly on. "Pleased to see you're here, Lois. How's business?"

"Harrods have increased their order to include the baby pashminas too."

"Oh you are a clever girl, isn't she Finn?"

"Indeed she is. Cup of tea?" he offers the room.

Diana and Lois accept and I nod, knowing that it's sufficient for Finn; he knows me well enough.

The two women enter into a complicit conversation about mutual acquaintances and finally about Dylan's progress, for which Diana credits the three of them. I would like to say her comment hurts me, but that requires a certain amount of effort.

Without them noticing, I peer at them from under my eyelashes. They look comfortable together, and Dylan's sucking his thumb whilst gazing up at his grandmother. If a stranger came upon the scene they would cast Lois in the role of leading lady, and I wouldn't blame them.

Finn returns with a tray of tea. He looks uncomfortable and agitated for which I blame myself. It can't be pleasant parading your mentally ill wife in front of family and friends. Perhaps I should take myself out of the equation, permanently.

I excuse myself with a whisper and disappear to the kitchen, where I quietly source a sharp knife from the drawer. Fearful of being discovered, I slip upstairs and lock myself in the bathroom before perching on the side of the bath.

I roll up my sleeve and run the side of the blade along my alabaster skin. The coldness alerts my mind to the task in hand. I so want to feel better, I decide not to wait.

Positioning the blade on the upper inside part of my arm, I push the tip into my skin. There's a popping noise as it breaches the flesh, and the first trickle of blood slips out. I slide the blade in a sideways motion, leaving a trail of blood appearing behind it.

I watch a teardrop of blood slowly creep towards the pit of my elbow. All the negative thoughts are carried away on the red stream and I instantly feel better. This is what I needed to do. The doctor said counselling and a mother-and-baby group would be the answer, but why did he not mention this? Because it's so wrong, which is probably why it feels so good.

I wash the blood away then bandage my arm crudely before floating downstairs and returning the clean knife to the drawer.

"He's not settling, so Finn and I are taking him for a stroll in his buggy, if that's all right with you?" Lois says, as I return to the lounge.

"Of course it's all right," replies Diana, barely glancing at me.

I give her the faintest smile. Perhaps next time I will cut myself deeper.

Finn

I'm alone again with Lois and Dylan, which I fear is becoming a regular habit, even with Colette home. The fresh air and walking motion has soothed Dylan, which in turn has calmed me. At least I think it's that and not the fact I'm with Lois, who seems to be getting sexier every time I see her.

"What are you thinking about?" she asks me, knowing it's a dangerous question to ask.

"I'm thinking about you," I reply without thinking of the consequences. Maybe subconsciously I want her to react favourably.

"I see. Good things, I hope."

"Nothing is good about the way I feel about you. This is possibly the worst situation I've ever been in."

"Explain?"

"I'm in love with two very different women who offer me diverse things."

"In love? You're in love with me?" She pauses. "What do we both offer?"

"Colette's given me a child, and a stable relationship and home life. And you . . . well you offer me the most amazing sex and you make me feel wanted, as a man."

She lets go of the buggy with one hand and grabs my hand with the other.

I pull it away quickly. "We can't be affectionate in public; that would complicate things."

"Sorry, it was a natural reaction."

Before I know where I am, we're standing outside her terraced house and she's pushing the buggy up to her front door. I look at her questioningly as she turns the key and lets us in.

She pushes the buggy into the kitchen-diner then takes me by the hand and leads me to the lounge. She pushes me onto the black leather sofa and straddles my lap. I am uncontrollably aroused, and not even the thought of Dylan in the next room dampens my spirits.

I close my eyes and let her take control of me, knowing this is what she'll always give me for as long as we both want. *Oh, and I do so want it.*

We scurry back, both dishevelled and flushed, but happy. That is until I'm crushed by guilt. But what do I expect, loving two women, the way I do?

Colette is still upstairs when we return, and Diana is sitting in the lounge reading a gardening magazine. She looks up at us and smiles, a smile she rarely bestows on Colette.

"How's my gorgeous grandson?"

"Still sleeping. How's Colette?" I whisper.

"Probably doing the same, although how much sleep does she really need?"

"I should be getting off," says Lois as she gives my elbow a surreptitious squeeze. "Call me if you need me. Bye, Diana."

"Goodbye dear, and thanks for all your support."

The house feels strangely empty with her gone, and I have to stop myself from running after her. *Grow up, Finn.*

Feeling too embarrassed to stay in Diana's company lest she sense my infidelity, I move to the kitchen to see what I can cook for dinner.

"You were gone a fair while," Diana says from the kitchen doorway. "Anything you care to share with me?"

"I don't know what you're getting at. We got talking and lost track of time."

"You spend more time talking to her than you do your wife. That's got to mean something."

"Mum, Colette isn't well, and can barely hold a conversation. It's not her fault."

"I imagine if Lois had a baby, she'd be at her computer selling pashminas in no time."

I don't want this conversation with her, not with all the guilt raining down on me. She'd never understand my ability to love two women for two very different reasons, and I'm not going to even try to explain to her. I know which woman she'd want me to keep.

"Has Diana gone?" Colette asks as I peer around the bedroom door.

"Yes, she and George are going out for dinner with friends. Talking of which, I've made a shepherd's pie. Do you fancy some?"

"I'm not hungry."

I sigh inwardly. Dealing with someone who's depressed is much harder than I thought.

As though tuning in to the situation, Dylan wakes and begins gurgling in his cot. I'm surprised how buoyant he makes me feel as I lift him up, his warm body snuggling into mine. This is how Colette should be feeling; it would do her good to hold him and let his innocent strength lift her spirits.

I return to Colette and place Dylan on the bed next to her. It's on doing this that I notice deep red stains on her sleeve. My throat constricts. Is it what I think it is? *How could you?*

She glances at Dylan then rolls over, turning her back on him. This time I don't sigh inwardly, but let it out with one rasping noise before whisking him up and taking him downstairs.

Perhaps Diana and Lois are right. Perhaps Dylan and I would be better off without her?

Colette

I think by the look on Finn's face, he's noticed the blood that's leaked through the bandage. I want the cutting to belong to me, I want to own and control it. I'm fed up of belonging to the psychiatrist, the mental health nurse, Diana, Finn, and even Dylan. I've lost *me* somewhere along the way, and cutting allows me to feel again, to release the pain in my mind, which if left untreated would explode my brain so it seeped through every orifice in my skull.

I know I'm being wholly ungracious. Some women can't conceive, or have suffered numerous miscarriages. Perhaps I was born to be barren but cheated my way into motherhood, only to discover cheats never win.

Dylan's crying again; I suspect he's suffering with colic. Or did I hear that via Diana? Whatever, his wailing is gnawing at my bones like a blunt chainsaw.

Footsteps bring his noise encroaching on my silent sanctuary, and I brace myself for his entrance.

"I know you're in recovery, Colette, but quite frankly, I'm back at work and struggling to cope with this." His face is puce, but not as violently vivid as the colour plastered across Dylan's cheeks.

I slink further down the bed and pull the pillow around my head with both hands. I falsely believe I am safe until Finn rips the quilt off the bed.

"Colette, you've got to try," he yells, causing Dylan's screams to intensify.

"I can't do this." I clutch the pillow over my ears. "Do it with someone else."

"Maybe I should have." He slams the door behind him.

As the noise retreats, a calming aura embraces me and my breathing slows down. I hear Finn talking to someone; I hope to God he's not asking Diana to come over; she could tip me over the edge.

I sleep for a few hours and the house is mercifully quiet. The smell of shepherd's pie lingers in the air, folding over my stomach as bile rises in my throat.

Dimness resides outside the window, with only pin pricks of stars daubed on the velvet-like sky. The window rattles gently in the breeze and I subconsciously pull my cardigan around me.

I ease myself off the bed and tiptoe to the top of the stairs to listen to the whispers of the house. Beneath the dark rumblings, I hear low voices and I recognise them both.

Creeping down the stairs, I strain to hear what's being said. I hear Diana's words first.

"You should bypass the nurse and speak to the psychiatrist; you can't go on like this."

"And say what?"

"That you want her committed until she's completely better, that's if she ever gets better. I mean, thousands of women have babies and don't go mad afterwards."

There's venom in her voice, but I can't blame her.

"I still love her though."

"Love makes you weak and gullible."

"You're hardly either, and you're in love with Dad."

"That's a matter of opinion. Anyway, this isn't about me it's about you and Colette, and *you* have to do what's best for my grandson."

"I think I know what's best for Dylan."

"I don't think you do and I'm not going to stand by and let you jeopardise his future. Having a mad mother won't go down well with the playground mothers, or future public schools."

"He can't even crawl yet, and you're already worrying about school."

"Don't be flippant, Finn. I'll give you a few days then I'm taking over."

Diana's voice sounds closer, so I press my back against the wall and melt into the shadow cast by the hall light. The front door closes and her car is set in motion.

Before I have time to retreat, Finn begins mounting the stairs.

"God you startled me," he snaps.

"I was coming down to find you."

"You've just missed Diana, but perhaps that's no bad thing."

"What do you mean?"

"Your relationship's always been . . . fragile, but now—"

"It's thorny," I interject.

He says nothing and just nods. *Coward.*

I descend, brushing past him on my way to the kitchen to find solace in some chocolate.

"When are you seeing the nurse again?" he asks from the doorway.

"Next week, why?"

"Do you talk about your lack of attachment with Dylan?"

I shrug my shoulders, not knowing what to say, but knowing he wants to find a way to jettison me into the loony bin.

He brushes his hand over the top of his head, another sign he's stressed. His eyes are dark hollows within which I can see both heaven and hell; two places he can send me to.

"I want to pop out and meet the guys in the pub. Do you think you'll be all right with Dylan for an hour? He's been fed and changed."

"Of course." I really want to tell him I've no interest in the baby that made me ill. Why is Dylan more important than me?

Finn leaves and I wonder where he's really going. Is he leaving me alone with Dylan in the hope that I'll harm him? Surely not.

The chocolate hasn't given me the comfort I crave, so I pour a gin and tonic and throw some ice into the glass. Fatigue crushes every muscle and joint, and I plod around as though trudging through a bog; I have no desire to survive, death presents a favourable option to me right now. But I mustn't vocalise these thoughts, I'd made them believe such ideas had evaporated.

Dylan makes a snuffling sound which ripples through the monitor. Instead of checking on him, I sip my drink and stare through the window, trying to imagine my life without a baby in tow. My dreams fade as Dylan wakes and murmurs loudly, demanding attention. My well-honed morality kicks in, so I shuffle upstairs.

It saddens me I'm not moved by peering into his cot; perhaps he's sapped all my energy and *joie de vie* so I can't possibly feel any sense of happiness or achievement. Who invented the image of perfect motherhood for me to compare myself with?

He catches my eye and I swear a brief smile graces his lips, as though letting me know he knows my love is tenuous. Can a baby's smile mean so much?

He starts grizzling, so I pick him up and smell the powdery scent of his little head. It's surprisingly comforting. He holds his head up for less than a second, gazes around before falling forward and colliding with my clavicle.

Stepping gingerly down the stairs, I make my way to the kitchen and take a bottle from the fridge to warm, whilst he gums my neck.

Hearing the key in the door, I brace myself for company.

Finn

A group of young men stand outside the pub smoking rollups, encasing them in a thick toxic smog. I hesitate near the entrance before moving on and picking up the pace.

It doesn't take long for Lois to answer her door, before dragging me inside.

"What brings you here?"

"Do you need it spelling out?"

Her finger slips between the buttons of my shirt as she looks up and smiles. "How long can you stay?"

"Colette's alone with Dylan, so not that long."

"Is that wise?"

I pull away, cross she's even mentioned it. "I came for a quick hug with sanity, not for a debate."

"My, you're tetchy." She backs away, her face melting into a sulk.

I apologise and return to tasting her lips, but she's not reciprocating.

"Although I cherish these moments with you, are you sure you can trust her with your baby? Diana would go mad if she knew you'd left them alone."

"Then we had better not tell her."

She moves to the lounge and drapes herself over the sofa, waving me over with a flick of her wrist.

I arrive home to find Colette in the lounge giving Dylan his bottle. She has a thunderous look on her face which I'm half expecting, but when I round the door I find Diana sitting on the sofa, her arms firmly crossed and eyes glued on me.

"And where have you been?" she snaps.

I glance at Colette who's staring intently at Dylan.

"I had a drink with some guys. I was only down the road, and Colette isn't going to harm him."

"How can you be so sure?"

"The psychiatrist said so. Besides, I wouldn't leave Dylan if I was worried."

"Well I worry, and that counts for a lot."

I sit down and look across at Colette who's rubbing Dylan's back to wind him. Even though she appears disconnected from the conversation, I feel uncomfortable having it in front of her.

"Why don't we go in the kitchen," I suggest.

"I'm not staying now you're back," she replies. "I'll return in the morning so you can go to work."

I accompany her to the front door. "Perhaps we should monitor what we say in front of Colette. I don't want to upset her."

"Well she's upset all of us without caring. I dread to think what she'll do next, which is why she needs monitoring around Dylan."

I'm about to protest when she raises her hand in the same stop motion she used when I was a child; I know better than to disobey. As she walks away I feel my ears burning as they did when I was a boy.

Turning around, I see Colette mounting the stairs slowly.

"Are you taking him to bed?"

"Yes, do you want to come and check I don't smother him with a pillow?"

"No. I'm sorry for my mother's insensitivity."

"I'm not sure that's true; you never stand up for me and that's because basically you only see me as mad too."

I can't answer her. Instead, I watch her troop upstairs and into the nursery where she only stays long enough to put him in his cot before going into our bedroom and closing the door.

And here I am again, alone. The house is darker, my wife is distant, my mother over-bearing; only Lois brings me light relief from this terminal cancer ravaging my life. And Dylan offers me respite in this melee, although I can't help blaming him from time to time for my current situation. Poor mite.

Rummaging around in the drawer to find a matching pair of socks, I manage to disturb Colette who's still in bed.

"Dylan will need feeding soon; I've got to leave in fifteen minutes."

"When's your mother coming 'round?"

"I don't know."

"She doesn't trust me. Do you?"

"I haven't time for this now," I reply, grabbing my wallet from the dressing table. "I'll see you tonight." I know I'm being unfair.

My shoulders relax as I leave the house, closing the door just as Dylan starts crying. I'm surprised I haven't bumped into Diana on my way out, but no doubt her distressed grandson radar will be on alert and she'll be here in a flash.

"Sorry to call you at work, but I want to know if I'll be seeing you later?" I find Lois's voice tremendously evocative on the phone.

"I'll try, but I'm in court this afternoon so I don't know when I'll be finished."

"That's okay, just as long as I get a hug."

I find I'm now distracted but I need to focus on work. I have to hold one part of my life together.

Court goes on longer than expected, but Lois doesn't give me a hard time when she opens her front door. She leads me inside and takes me through to the kitchen where the table is set for two, adorned with a lit candle.

"I can't eat here; I'll be expected to eat at home when I get in."

"Colette won't have cooked for you."

"No, but my mother probably will have."

"Tell her the truth, she won't mind."

"That may be, but I don't want her reading too much into it."

"What you mean is she might be pleased."

"I'm not sure what I mean, I just want you to be here for me."

She hugs me and apologises for her impatience. It feels good to be held by a strong-minded woman, but it niggles me that I may be starting to need her too much.

She's made a delicious light meal of lambs' livers, baby potatoes, and peas, and I've got the time to taste it without anticipating Dylan needing attention at any moment. The candlelight catches her prominent cheekbones and the butterscotch highlights in her hair. Her oriental perfume cuts through the smell of the meal and envelops me in a comforting blanket.

The peace and relaxed atmosphere is a welcome backdrop for my troubled mind. I feel more me with her.

After finishing the meal, we move to the lounge where Lois sits next to me on the sofa and pulls my arm around her shoulder.

"I wish you could stay the night," she whispers.

"You know that's impossible—"

My mobile interrupts me, saving me.

"Where the devil are you?" Diana blasts down the phone.

"Just finishing work. I've had a long afternoon in court. I'm just packing up now. Why, where are you?"

"Looking after Dylan, of course."

"What's Colette doing?"

"Oh, I don't know; in her room, I think. She has no interest in your son whatsoever."

"Please, not now. I'm just heading to my car." I hang up before she can goad me further about what a useless wife and mother I've married.

"Sorry, Lois, I've got to go." I kiss her on the forehead before dashing out and heading off without a last look in her direction.

I hear Dylan crying as I walk up the path to my front door and my heart sinks in anticipation of the night ahead. Diana is pacing up and down the hallway with Dylan thrown over her shoulder, frantically rubbing his back in circular motions.

"Thank God you're home. You need to buy some more gripe water, or whatever it's called these days," she says, handing Dylan over to me.

She unhooks her coat from the rack and leaves without saying another word. Dylan is fractious and the house has an underlying menace about it. I wish I could let it all out as Dylan is now doing.

Colette

The sound of the front door closing enters my mind, and I know I'm free of Diana until tomorrow. Her ascorbic words clatter around my brain like dodgem cars, colliding periodically and hurting my head.

"If you love my boys the way you proclaim you do, you'd leave them and let them find happiness elsewhere," she had said when we were sitting in the lounge, shortly after Finn left for work.

"This illness will pass," I uttered.

"Not in all cases. Sometimes it can be the catalyst for future mental health issues," she replied. "I always thought you were unhinged. I never understood why he chose you out of all the female friends he had. Lois was far more in-keeping with him, and still is, come to that."

Her gaze sliced across at me, but I was too lethargic to retaliate. So I decided to keep out of her way and retreat to my bedroom, leaving her to dote on her grandson.

I wait for Finn to come up and see me, so when he remains downstairs I decide to go and find him.

The radio's playing in the kitchen where I find him listening to the news and sitting at the table nursing a beer.

"Mum said you were asleep," he says, excusing his absence.

"No, just keeping out of her way."

"Please don't be mean. You know she needs to be here so you can recover; it's what the psychiatrist advised."

"I know, but I'd like a break from her. Perhaps Lois could come tomorrow for a change; she said she can work anywhere. Will you phone her?"

"Why can't you?"

"It feels like too much effort. You promised you'd support me." I can't understand his reticence to speak with her; she's his friend too.

He gulps down his beer then pulls his mobile from his jacket pocket. It doesn't take Lois long to answer.

"Colette asked me to call you to see whether you could stay with her tomorrow to give her a rest from Diana, but we understand if you're too busy." She's quick to respond and he nods at me.

By the time Finn comes to bed it's almost midnight; something he would never have normally done on a work night. But what's normal these days?

The mattress sags as he climbs in so I roll slightly towards him. His breathing is heavy and loud, no longer the restful sound I used to hear. He doesn't lean in to kiss me; yet another change that's emerged since Dylan's birth.

I wake to find Finn's already up. Lifting myself up on my elbows I hear Lois's sweet laugh rising from downstairs. *No Diana, thank God.*

I ease myself out of bed, slide my feet into my slippers, and creep downstairs. I hear their voices but I can't decipher what they're saying, and as I step into the kitchen, they cease their chatter.

"I'm here as you requested," Lois says as she shimmies towards me, pecking me on the cheek. "You and I are going to have a girly day; the pashminas will sell themselves today."

We hug and it feels both a relief and alien to have human contact.

"I'm off to work. Have a good day," Finn says before disappearing.

I feel shabby in contrast to Lois's ethereal image. The dressing gown does me no favours, so I depart for a shower whilst Lois plays with Dylan.

Lois is feeding Dylan when I return; she looks the picture of idyllic mother-dom. A twinge of jealousy snags my heart. But this is Lois I'm talking about; I've known her for fourteen years and we've always been such good friends. So why am I feeling uncomfortable?

"How's Finn coping with my illness?" I ask her.

"How would I know?"

"You've seen him more than me lately."

"He doesn't discuss his feelings. He's a man, remember."

I pour myself a coffee from the pot and sit opposite her at the table. Dylan is now wriggling in her arms and we both ignore the fact I haven't asked to hold him.

"Do you think Finn still loves me?"

"Of course he does. You worry too much." She pauses to wind Dylan. "Why don't we go out, visit an art gallery or something?"

"With a baby?"

"Of course, I've seen plenty of mums in galleries and cafés with little ones in tow. You can wrap the pashmina around him for extra warmth."

"I'm not sure. What about feeding and changing him? What if he cries non-stop and annoys people?" A barrage of negative thoughts bluster through my mind, and panic rises within me.

"I'm with you; we'll sort it out between us. Come on." And with that, she hurries upstairs to prepare Dylan for his first outing with me.

My knees are locked in paralysing numbness. I'm rooted to the chair listening to Lois singing to Dylan. She has a sweet voice.

An hour later, we're ready to head into London. Lois bustles around competently with me struggling to keep pace. I'm mortified when we step outside and she hands the buggy over to me. I'm not ready for this.

I try to speak but my mouth is too dry. Lois opens the gate and waits for me to go through, like a patient mother waiting for her child to take their first steps.

My hands slip on the buggy handle and Dylan looks at me as though I am a stranger, which of course I am. Lois walks next to me trying to take my mind off my anxieties by talking non-stop. Her words pass before my eyes like wisps of cloud on a summer's day, and I can't make sense of anything.

On arriving at the Tate Gallery, Lois helps me carry the buggy up the inordinate amount of stone steps. I notice people staring at our madness, but Lois appears immune to such acts. I envy her ability to rebuff others when necessary.

I love the hushed reverence inside galleries, and I pray Dylan doesn't shatter the mood. We wander to the Pre-Raphaelites rooms. Millais, Rossetti, and Hunt overshadow all the other artists for me. Their scientific precision and imaginative grandeur makes me breathless whenever I see their works.

But my enjoyment is short-lived as Dylan wakes and protests at being . . . what exactly? Hungry? Thirsty? A dirty nappy? I'm flummoxed and rooted to the spot with crippling embarrassment, as a guided group turn to face the offending noise. Lois raises a hand in an apologetic gesture before removing him from the buggy and smelling his bottom.

"Not the problem," she says. "He must be hungry. Let's go to the café."

I'm relieved she's taken command of the situation. The café didn't even occur to me.

There's a buzz in here, so Dylan's protestations seem less audible. Lois points to a chair at an empty table then hands me Dylan whilst she goes in search of refreshments and a jug of hot water to warm his bottle.

Across from me is a mother breastfeeding her baby. She gives me a knowing smile which fades as I retrieve a bottle from the nappy bag. Her NCT preaching's have obviously impacted on her view of bottle-fed babies. How quick people are to judge.

"Here we go," announces Lois on her return. "A jug for the young master and two cappuccinos and carrot cakes for us."

The drink I can handle, but not food. Whenever I'm stressed or anxious, my stomach shrinks and rejects the idea of eating. Dylan is causing me both emotions right now.

"How are you and Finn doing, as a couple I mean?" she asks.

"Being a couple is not a priority at the moment. Being parents has overtaken that."

"But surely you are both deeper in love now you've created another human being together." I notice she has a dainty cappuccino froth moustache.

"You'd imagine, but in reality, the sleepless nights create a tension all of their own."

I can't tell whether she's satisfied by my answer as she masks her reaction by eating some cake. I pick at mine before feeding Dylan the warmed milk.

Time passes slowly and I'm keen to get home to retreat to my bedroom, seeking solace under the quilt, leaving Lois with Dylan to await Finn.

Finn

I smell Lois's perfume as soon as I step through the front door, and the scent makes my heart lurch.

"Hello, Finn, how was your day?"

I scan the room looking for Colette, but only see Lois holding Dylan whilst pouring two glasses of red wine. She brandishes one at me, and as I take it the tips of our fingers touch, sending a spark ricocheting up my arm.

"Where's Colette?"

"In bed. We went to the Tate, which tired her out somewhat. So, how was your day?"

"The usual, interviewing young offenders, trying to find ways of keeping them out of trouble."

"Does it work?"

"Sometimes, depends on the willingness of the individual and the support they have around them; like family and friends."

"Did you think about me today?"

She's speaking louder than I'd like, and I instinctively look towards the hallway.

"She won't hear us."

"I was wondering whether I could trust you around her, if you really want to know."

"I'm offended," she turns her nose up mockingly. "I'm not a marriage wrecker. I'm a good friend who doesn't mind sharing her man."

"I'm *your* man am I? I'm not sure Colette would see it that way."

"She doesn't need to know, makes our liaison more passionate in my view."

She walks over and puts her hand over my heart. Her close proximity is torture so I put my glass down and take Dylan from her, holding him closely like a shield.

"I must go and see her." I walk away quickly, preventing her from stopping me.

I knock quietly and peer around the door to find her lying on the bed staring at the ceiling.

"I hear you went out today, that's great progress."

"I didn't enjoy it," she sighs.

"Early days, give yourself time." I move closer with Dylan, but neither he nor Colette seems bothered about each other's company.

"I need to speak to a mother in my situation. None of you understand how I'm feeling which is making me feel isolated."

I'm pleased she is actually holding a conversation with me, albeit a grim one. "Perhaps you should go to the mother-and-baby group the nurse mentioned."

"Too much pressure. I thought I might find a group online; I like the idea of talking to faceless people."

Keen to encourage her I suggest I bring her laptop up. She pushes herself into a sitting position and awaits me to bring it up. With Dylan now clasped tightly onto my hair, I rush down to fetch the item and bring it up to her. She thanks me quietly then asks to be alone. I'm saddened that I feel relieved.

I put Dylan to bed and descend to find Lois cooking a rice dish.

"I've made enough for Colette; you can take it up to her when it's ready."

"She wants to be left alone. I'll reheat it later if she wants it."

"Another romantic dinner for two then," she says coquettishly.

I smile but inside I am twisted and torn. The fine line between right and wrong is blurred and all I can see is Dylan straddling the three of us before falling down a crevice.

The steam from the dish placed before me acts as a flimsy screen behind which I find sanctuary for a brief moment. The aroma of salmon and parsley mixed with the rice is pleasing. Lois is a good cook.

"What happens if Colette never recovers to her old self? Will you remain by her side, or will you give Dylan a happier environment to grow up in?"

"I can't allow myself to think like that. She has to get better."

"Dylan's okay now, but eventually he'll notice that his mummy is different from other mummies."

"Lois please, let's talk about something else."

"How about us?"

I stare at her and let my eyes respond. I'm too tired for this now, and I know I probably have another night of interrupted sleep ahead of me. I finish my meal then take the bowl to the sink. I see her watching me adoringly in the refection in the window. *How did it get to this?*

I tell her I'm tired and she takes the hint to leave, but not without tasting my lips before she goes.

After my shower I check Dylan and find him asleep sucking his thumb. He looks carefree. *Enjoy it whilst you can little man.*

Colette's still awake, intently looking at her laptop and barely noticing my arrival. She certainly doesn't look at me adoringly.

"Found anything interesting?" I ask.

"A group for other sufferers of postpartum psychosis. I am chatting with a woman about her experience, we totally understand one another."

"That must be helpful."

"More than you know."

I climb into bed and lean into her tentatively to kiss her on her cheek, but she leans way from me, her eyes never leaving the screen.

The morning comes too soon and I'm surprised to find Colette's not in bed. Bleary eyed, I pad into the nursery hoping to find her there, but Dylan's on his own playing with the blanket as though it has magical properties. He sees me and I swear he smiles, so I lift him out and head for the kitchen.

Colette's sitting at the table with half a mug of coffee in front of her. At least she's made a pot, so I help myself then warm Dylan's bottle.

"How are you?" I ask, fearful of knowing.

"Fine."

I notice her pulling on the sleeve of her dressing gown, the fabric trapped between her thumb and forefinger. She looks guilty, and before I can stop to think, I speak. "Have you been cutting yourself again?"

She ignores my question and evades eye contact.

"If you have, we need to let the nurse know. Self-harming is a serious matter." I'm fluctuating between anger and concern.

"You can't control every aspect of my life, Finn." Her voice sounds stronger and sharper.

"I'll wait for Diana to arrive before leaving for work."

"Why, worried I'll slit Dylan's wrists?"

"That's a horrible thing to say, that never occurred to me."

"So why the worry?"

"I care about you and I don't want you hurting yourself."

The discussion is futile as Diana enters the house with her key and brings a dark molasses-like cloyingness with her. Colette sinks down in the chair, putting her arm under the table.

"Where are my darling boys," she says, entering the room.

I need to go to work but I feel bad about leaving Colette with my mother, her overbearing and interfering traits can be testing. But I have no choice. *Sorry Colette.*

Colette

This is all I need, being left alone with Diana and Dylan. All the stress released by cutting has amounted to very little now that she's here. Life feels so hopeless in moments like this.

"Are you going to get dressed? You look a mess," she says snidely.

Without replying, I get up and head upstairs, wondering how long I can remain away from her without looking rude or mental. Hell, I am mental; I might as well use it.

I squeeze into my jeans, although a rubber ring of flesh bulges over the top. Faint coffee-coloured lines are spread over the offending flesh; I'm disgusted by the sight of myself, and I can't imagine anyone loving me now.

I flop onto the bed and check my laptop for a message from Chloe. I so need to hear her words; she understands me. Her words embody the pain I feel. She understands exactly how I feel about Dylan as she feels the same about her baby, Rachel.

I send her a message telling her I've the mother-in-law from hell here, and that I may need to chat with her quite a lot during the day.

Then I hesitantly tread down the stairs and find Diana in the lounge with Dylan in her arms.

"About time. For the amount of time you spent up there you don't look that special." She looks at me with the same eyes as Finn, which breaks my heart.

"I might take Dylan out for a walk," I venture.

"Not without me you won't. Besides, it's raining. Good God, girl, you really need to pull yourself together."

I've no answer to bat back to her, so I sit down and pick up the news-paper and pretend to read. I hear her cooing to Dylan and repeating the word *nanna* to him. She's determined he say that before he says mummy. And strangely I don't care.

The paper yields nothing of interest, but I hold it in front of me for protection.

"You really should prepare an evening meal for Finn. See what you've got in. My Finn needs looking after. Lois has been doing a good job in your absence."

She hasn't got a mental illness, I want to say, but I remain mute and go to the kitchen just to get out of her way.

The cupboards are full of nothing inspiring, but I resolve to make a three-bean curry with borlotti, kidney, and butter beans. A vegetarian meal will not be seen as wholesome by Diana, but I haven't got around to ordering more food online; another chore I need to build up enthusiasm for.

"How long do you think Finn will put up with you like this?" Diana says from behind me.

"As long as it takes, I imagine."

"You're more a fool than I thought. Men don't hang around weak women. They are the main earners and need a wife to support them. Finn can't hold down his stressful job and care for you and Dylan. Something has to give."

I chop an onion, keeping my back to her. Each slice is cut with precision.

"Lois has been a darling; I don't know where Finn would have been without her. She's so clever with her business too."

I can't contradict anything she says, after all, Lois is successful in everything she does apart from her love life, which puzzles me. Plenty of men are attracted to her when we go out, but she tells me she is waiting for Mr Right. She's rather picky though; no man meets her standards.

"Did you hear what I said?" Diana questions.

"No, sorry, I was miles away."

"If only that were the case," she mutters. "I said, have you and Finn talked about the christening yet?"

"Not as yet."

"Well I suggest you do. The church is always booked up in advance."

I make a non-committal sound before dropping the onion slices in sizzling oil, releasing their potent scent into the air, and sending Diana scurrying away.

The idea of a big gathering for the christening shreds my nerves and brings up old feelings about the wedding. My parents live in Spain, so Diana took it upon herself to meddle with every aspect of the ceremony and day itself. Not only did she decide the church and reception venue, but she also interfered with my choice of dress and bridesmaid outfits. I had wanted a small affair in a registry office, but that was not the Forbes way, she informed me at regular intervals.

I can see the christening being no different and it makes my heart hang heavily. With the bean curry finished and ready to heat up later, I tell Diana I am going for a lie down before climbing the stairs and returning to my laptop.

I decide to write an e-mail to Chloe, explaining all my difficulties with life. It will feel good to write it down to hopefully distance myself from it, as my nurse suggested.

Dear Chloe,

I'm so glad we found each other. It's wonderful having someone who understands what I'm going through. Diana wants to organise the christening and I know I haven't the strength to fight her wishes. How do you cope with forceful characters in your life?

I've started self-harming again. It feels so good at the time, but the shame and guilt that follows negates any benefits. I feel trapped in a vicious cycle as sometimes my only reason for getting out of bed is to cut myself. You mentioned you also self-harm. What do you do?

Not only is my connection with Dylan tenuous, but my feelings towards Finn are almost as numb. I say almost as I know I want him to nurture me, but he's so busy with Dylan and his mum that he has no energy or patience left for me. I feel isolated and the only person who has true time and understanding for me is you. Don't get me wrong, the nurse is as understanding as a medical person can be.

Perhaps one day we could meet? I know we're in a regional group, so you can't be far from me. I live in North London.

Best wishes, Colette.

I press send and hope she replies soon; I long for human contact that doesn't involve me feeling inferior or belittled. I like the absence of pretence between us.

I don't have to wait long for Chloe to respond.

Hi Colette,

I am a seasoned self-harmer. I started after having my first baby when I first got postpartum psychosis. I slice my thighs, as my arms are quite badly scarred. My nurse thinks I've stopped as she doesn't know about my new site. Always trick your nurse into thinking you're getting better, that way they visit less often.

I don't know why you think Finn will be there for you, both my children's dads fucked off when my behaviour became erratic. As a single mum, I only have me and the kids to worry about. You can have that one day, if you want it.

It'd be fab to meet up. I live in East London.

Cheers, Chloe.

I feel as alive as I can be, as I swiftly reply.

Dear Chloe,

I hope you don't feel I'm pushing you into meeting, but I really want to be in the company of someone who gets me, as you say.

Diana would be more than happy to babysit while I come and see you, if that's better for you. Your eldest is at nursery so you've more time constraints than I do. I'll tell Diana I have a hospital appointment to stop her interfering.

I know I am eight years older than you, but I hope this doesn't mean you'll

find me boring. I'm very low at the moment and barely talking to anyone,
but I know I'll be able to talk to you.
In anticipation, Colette.

My hands are trembling. Reaching out to a stranger is alien to me, but I feel Chloe knows me better than anyone currently. I'm staring at the screen, willing her to reply. But again, I don't have to wait long.

Meeting up sounds good. It would be easier here as Kerry has nursery in the morning. Could you come at ten? I live at 11, Burnham Road, East Ham E6.
Chloe.

I send a speedy reply then search on the web how best to get to her. The tube is my best bet, even though the thought of being in close proximity with a plethora of people is making my skin crawl.

Excited and invigorated by my accomplishment, I decide to brave downstairs to see what Diana's doing, out of curiosity rather than companionship.

I find her sitting in the lounge watching a gardening programme with Dylan asleep in her arms. How I wish I had that connection with him.

Tomorrow can't come fast enough for me.

Finn

I've had a stressful day at work and the last thing I need is Diana hassling me about Dylan's christening.

"But it's the Forbes' way, he needs to be christened, and a celebratory soiree."

"I hear what you're saying, but we've enough going without the stress of organising that."

"By that you mean Colette's illness, I suppose. Well I can organise everything, you won't have to worry about a thing."

"I'm not sure Colette will be happy with that."

"I don't think she's in a position to complain. She doesn't even have to attend if she's too ill."

"We can't christen Dylan without her present; that's outrageous."

"Dylan doesn't deserve a mad mother."

"Colette's ill after having him, this is not a life-long illness. The doctor said that giving her time and support will help her, and you don't seem to be giving her either."

"I'm here almost every day; if that's not time and support then I don't know what is. Anyway, I don't see you lavishing her with love and support. Lois seems to be your focus lately."

My face flushes, no doubt signalling my guilt to her. I swallow hard. "I don't see what you're getting at. Lois and I have been friends for years."

"A mother knows things. I've observed you together and there's more to you both than meets the eye. Why you didn't date her, I will never know."

"Obviously because I was more attracted to Colette. I'm not going to dredge-up the past, I'm more concerned with the here and now."

"And I'm concerned about yours and Dylan's future."

"Colette, how have you been today?" I ask as I spot her standing in the doorway. I wonder how long she has been standing there.

"Fine, thank you."

I know *fine* is code for *not that good, actually*. But I resist challenging her in front of Diana.

"I've an appointment at ten tomorrow, so could you come at nine to give me time to travel please, Diana?"

"What's the appointment for? Should I go with you?" I ask, knowing that work won't like short notice for absence.

"No, I'm just visiting a group the nurse mentioned."

I'm stunned and Diana is also speechless, but somehow looks like she's relishing the prospect of having Dylan to herself.

Unsurprisingly, Colette doesn't hang around and evaporates from our presence like dissipating cigarette smoke. I wish I could do the same, but Diana's determined to trap me into agreeing to a date for the damn christening. Where is Lois when I need her?

"I suspect you think the topic of the christening has been forgotten after that interlude," she says smugly. "Well, I've brought my diary so we can pencil in a few dates, then I'll phone the church and see what's available."

I know it is futile so I agree to some dates and hope that's the end of the conversation.

"I have your christening gown we can use; I think a family heirloom is important on these occasions. For the meal I suggest we book a room in the Noble Hotel in Greenwich; they do a fabulous roast pheasant."

She's really thought of everything; but why am I so surprised?

"I've worked out there will be around sixty people for a sit-down meal, and I've found a lovely string quartet to play."

"It's sounding more like a wedding than a christening. I'm not sure it warrants so much." Big mistake.

"Dylan is our first and possibly our last grandchild, and he deserves a Forbes welcome to the world. I've been dreaming of this day; you can't deny me."

"Why would he be your last grandchild?"

"We can't go through all of this again with Colette, but if you marry again we may be lucky and have a grandchild without all the drama."

I can't believe what I'm hearing, this is a complete turnaround. I mean, the word *divorce* is blasphemous to Diana, and here she is suggesting I marry again so she can have more grandchildren without the shame of my wife becoming mentally ill.

But what can I say to her? That perhaps she should have had more children; a daughter who would have provided multiple children sanely.

If I'm to keep her happy, I must let her organise the christening, and to hell with how Colette and I feel about it. I'm positive it's the last thing Colette will want to attend; she'll feel like a freak show, with people staring and whispering behind their hands. Perhaps I won't tell her just yet? Hell, I could do with talking things through with Lois; she always reframes things for me.

I remember when my parents were disappointed I wanted to be a probation officer and not a barrister, Lois reframed it for them so they viewed me as a profound philanthropist. I don't know how she did it, I wasn't there, but she did and I was and am eternally grateful, although I could do with a barrister's wage to pay for this blasted christening.

"You look troubled," she tells me. "If you're worried about paying for this function, don't be. Your father and I will pay. What are grandparents for?"

"Don't go overboard, though. The cost will soon mount up."

"It's vulgar to talk about money; Dylan's worth every penny. And as I've mentioned before, Colette doesn't have to attend if it's too much, we can always say she has influenza."

My smile is as weak as my strength of character where Diana's concerned. But at work, I'm rigid and tough, keeping the offenders in line; if only I had an ounce of that strength now.

I retrieve my mobile from my jacket and move into the garden to make a call.

"Hello, I was wondering if we could meet up tomorrow after work."

"You know I always have time for you, Finn."

Tomorrow can't come soon enough.

Colette

Leaving Diana and Dylan is liberating, although the prospect of travelling to East Ham on my own is daunting.

The bus is packed and I have to stand in the aisle, holding on to a cold metal pole. As the bus lurches away, I am thrown into the back of the person next to me. Apologising, I receive an ill-tempered grunt in return. I feel like crying.

At each stop more people flood onto the bus until I truly believe I won't be able to breathe. Just as I think I am going to enter the realms of a panic attack, my stop arrives.

The tube is far worse than the bus, but fortunately I only have four stops until I arrive at Upton Park station. We judder along the track until I arrive at my stop. I weave my way through the mass until I arrive outside to be greeted by torrential rain.

I search for road names whilst manoeuvring around umbrellas and buggies, until I find Burnham Road. I arrive at number eleven and I'm surprised to discover that Chloe omitted to mention she lives above a fish and chip shop.

I ring the buzzer and hear her voice for the first time; she has an east-end accent that makes me think of a market trader, but with a softer lilt. She buzzes me in and I'm immediately faced with a steep flight of narrow stairs. How does she manage with the buggy?

At the top of the stairs a shaft of light appears from an open door, where a figure waits for me. On reaching the top, Chloe greets me like a long-lost friend, and I must say I feel much the same about her.

"This is unreal," she says. "It's so strange meeting you in person. You look younger than I imagined."

I think that's a compliment so I blush as we move inside.

The first thing that strikes me is the faint odour of cooking fat clinging to the curtains, dusty carpet, and furniture. We're standing in a fairly spacious room which is cluttered with toys and a mound of ironing.

There's a tiny kitchen, with grubby white cupboards and tiles, and a worktop littered with cartons of formula and baby bottles. She catches me snooping.

"I know I should have tidied before your visit, it's just . . . I don't have the energy . . ."

"You don't have to explain yourself; I know how it feels. My house would be a disaster-zone if Diana didn't tidy every day."

"How does she know where things go?"

"She doesn't, she puts them where *she* thinks they should go."

"Nightmare."

Chloe indicates for me to sit down as she fetches baby Rachel, who's started crying. I brush fragments of crisps from the seat before sitting down on the saggy sofa, feeling a tad overdressed for the occasion.

"It's relentless, this parenting lark," Chloe says loudly as she returns with Rachel in her arms.

"Do their fathers ever help out or give you money?" I ask, trying to ignore the now screaming baby.

"Not bloody likely. The first one saw Kerry until she was a one-year-old, then nothing. This one's dad has never seen her. I live off benefits, what else can I do?"

What indeed? The baby's ceased her infernal racket thanks to the bottle in her mouth. She's smaller than Dylan, with fragile fingers which paw at the bottle.

"Do you ever, like, think of ending it all?" she asks, perching on the arm of the chair.

"I attempted once, but it was more of a cry for help. I'm not really that brave. Have you thought how you'd do it?"

"I'd kill the kids first; drown them in the bath."

"You'd kill your babies?" I'm incredulous.

"There'd be no one to look after them, and I don't want them going into care."

"I couldn't do that, besides there's always Finn and Diana. Would you take an overdose?"

"Too slow and risky; could vomit them up or get found before I'm dead. I'm going to jump from the multi-storey car park."

"Going to?"

"This is my second bout of post-thingy illness and I never get better. I'm a single mum who hates being a mother. I've no money, no social life, and no friends."

"You have me."

"No offence, Col, but we don't have much in common except this illness. If we didn't have that, we'd never have met."

"That may be, but we have connected and I want to help you."

"You're sweet, but you can barely help yourself."

I know she's right. I admit putting an end to this relentless misery is mighty tempting, but that takes courage; something I haven't got.

"Are you seriously thinking about ending it? 'Cause if you are, we could do it together." Chloe's looking at me wide-eyed.

"How?"

"We could jump together, holding hands in our last moments."

I think about what she's saying as she winds Rachel. It would teach Finn a lesson, but I imagine he and his mother would forget me very quickly. It would be hard on my parents and Gabriella; I would have to leave her a note.

"You've gone quiet. Have I said something wrong?" she checks.

"Not at all. I was thinking who would actually miss me when I'm gone, and it wouldn't be Finn. I suspect even Dylan wouldn't miss me as he'd still have Diana and Lois as female roles."

"No one will miss me. Society will be better off without me."

"But jumping?"

"What would you prefer? Hanging, drowning, bleeding to death—"

"Stop. None of those sound easy."

"Suicide isn't supposed to be easy; it's a life-changing event."

I look at her and she laughs dryly. She puts Rachel in the playpen before throwing herself into the chair and lighting a cigarette. *So that's what that other smell is.*

She blows the noxious fumes into the air so an ash cloud hangs over the baby's head. I'd feel bad for her, but she may not live long enough to get cancer, if Chloe has her way.

"What happens if you kill your babies and then can't kill yourself?"

"I'd have to; I don't want to go to prison."

"You'd go to a psychiatric hospital, get treatment."

"Even worse than my life now. Only death will do for me; but I'm not forcing you into it."

The atmosphere stings my eyes and burns my nostrils, but I'm transfixed by Chloe and her resolve to leave this world. I'm not sure I'm as loyal to the concept, but how would I feel in a world without Chloe? At this moment in time, I'd rather go with her than remain friendless.

Chloe stubs her cigarette out in a saucer then picks up a glass of flat coke. She offers me a drink but I decline.

Her dull blond hair is pulled back in a very tight ponytail, so her forehead's rigid. Chipped blue nail polish on her fingernails looks like a throwback to the Eighties, and her tracksuit looks in dire need of a wash.

We're dissimilar in every way apart from our mental health, which is a great leveller. Perhaps fate has drawn us together, uniting us in our grief and mental torture, and enabling us to finally be free.

"When are you doing all of this?" I ask, trying to sound nonchalant.

"Anytime soon. I can wait until you're ready, but don't take too long."

I cough. She's serious and I believe I may be too.

Diana is playing with Dylan in the lounge and he's making babbling sounds. They both look very happy until I walk in the room, turning the atmosphere glacial.

"So you're back. How was your meeting?"

"Informative."

"Hope they informed you how to be a good wife and mother."

I feel the blade of her verbal knife splice me between the shoulder blades, but I don't want to give her the satisfaction of crumbling in front of her, so I take a deep breath and move towards Dylan. Holding my arms out I await a reaction but he remains transfixed on Diana, and she in turn looks self-satisfied.

"Perhaps I'll see what I can cook for tea," I suggest lamely.

"Remember my Finn's a carnivore, not a vegetarian," she calls out as I disappear.

Chloe's words remind me there's a way to get away from all of this, and by the looks of it, Dylan would be better off without me. But Chloe's children?

Finn

"I think you should have this," Lois tells me, handing over a door key.

"I'm flattered but don't you think it's a little risky?"

"How is anyone ever going to know what it's for?"

I smile. "I might feel a tad guilty every time I see it."

"I rather hope you'll feel something other than guilt."

I encase her in my arms, and brace myself for the wave of self-reproaching emotions to hit me like a Tsunami.

"How's Colette?" Her voice is muffled by my chest.

"I don't want to talk about her; I want to concentrate on feeling relaxed."

"We can't ignore her, she's my friend."

I'm aghast. "And she's *my* wife. Lois this isn't a game."

"There are no rules for having an affair except for making sure another party doesn't find out. A game is what you make of it; how would you categorise an affair, then?"

"I don't see in slotting into any category, unless it falls in the *I am a total git* category. You don't have as much guilt as I do."

"If you're feeling so guilty, then why are we doing this?"

"You know the answer."

"But I want to hear you say it." Her blue eyes dance with coquettish mischief, taking my breath away.

She grabs my hand and leads me upstairs before pushing me onto the bed.

"You still haven't said it properly, only once in a sentence."

"I love you . . ."

On opening the front door, the smell of burning greets me, followed by the voice of my mother.

"I'm so sorry, Finn dear, *I* should have cooked your dinner."

Colette is standing in the kitchen doorway with her arms folded across her chest, and a piercing look in her eye which appears to see right through me. *Damn Lois's oriental perfume.*

"I'm sorry I'm late and I'm sorry I've caused you to burn dinner."

"You're too kind, Finn. She could have turned the oven down," Diana quips.

"Where's Dylan?" I ask, trying to move on.

"Asleep in his cot. Would you like a drink?" Diana asks.

"Actually, shouldn't you be getting home to Dad, you've been away from him all day."

"It does him good to fend for himself once in a while. But if you think you can manage."

"Of course we'll manage, I'm home with my wife and baby. Thanks for everything," I reply, pecking her on the cheek.

She gives a cursory wave to Colette before grabbing her handbag from the console table and leaving.

"So what's for dinner?" I ask lightly.

"Cremated chicken pie. We might be able to salvage the filling, but the crust took the heat."

She has a strange look in her eyes, and when I move to kiss her on her forehead, she turns away.

I sit at the kitchen table and assess the plate of food before me, wondering whether suggesting a takeaway would be rude. I notice Colette sits down without a plate in front of her.

"You're not eating?"

"I'm not really hungry; being with Diana takes its toll on me."

"How was your meeting?"

"Interesting."

"I didn't really get what it was about."

"It's a self-help group. I think I'll return."

"That's great. Hopefully this is the start of your journey to being you again."

"That's corny, but I appreciate the sentiment."

I pour the wine and take a large gulp; I can feel my face prickling with heat. "Will you need Diana to babysit each time you go?"

"To start with, but eventually I hope to take Dylan. I just need to gain in confidence first."

"She loves caring for him."

"But she's not his mother, I am. She seems to forget that."

"I know, it's just we need her so I daren't tackle her about it. You know how she can get. Soon you'll be okay to be on your own and all this will be a bad memory."

"Do you think? I'm not sure I'll ever forget and I bet Diana doesn't."

"We'll manage that when the time comes."

"It's made me think about having another baby, and I think it's best I don't. Diana gave me a rundown of statistics of having this illness after another one."

"Good grief, we're not planning a baby just yet. We don't know what the future holds."

"What would you like the future to hold?"

"I can't think past tomorrow let alone the future. Let's take it one day at a time, eh?" I can see she's crying.

Dylan's snuffling sounds are projected through the baby monitor offering me the distraction I so desperately require. I bound out of the room before she has time to say anything else.

Holding Dylan against my chest fills me with warmth. Yet my heart is shredded as I reflect on our family unit and whether it will survive all that is happening to us.

The power is with me; I just don't know what to do with it.

Colette

I hardly slept last night; ruminating over Chloe's plans, and trying to decide when I would be ready to join her. She said she couldn't wait too long, and once she'd killed her babies there'd be no turning back.

As I lay in the dark with Finn's low rumbling snore at my side, I tried to imagine what falling from a great height would feel like. Would my life flash before me as was commonly reported? Would we be able to hold hands until we hit the ground? Would it hurt? And lastly, would I regret my decision halfway down? That last thought troubles me still.

Needless to say, I'm now shattered, so I remain in bed as Finn gets ready for work.

"Thank God it's Friday; this has been a gruelling week," he says, donning a tie. "I'm in court for two offenders today, so I may be home late. Don't bother cooking I'll get a takeaway on the way home."

I would have once been excited about a takeaway and relieved about not cooking, but the prospect of a day with Diana without the respite at Chloe's weighs heavily on my mind. I pull the quilt over my head in the vain attempt to shield me from the impending day.

"You need to give Dylan his bottle," Finn instructs me. "Diana will be here soon."

"Oh joy," I mutter quietly before emerging from the quilt like a snake shedding its skin.

Finn kisses me on top of my head before heading downstairs. I hear him talking before the front door closes.

I screw my eyes shut and massage my temples as footsteps approach. The knock at the door is lighter than usual.

"Are you decent?" Lois calls out.

My eyes shoot open as a smile inches across my face. "What are you doing here?"

"I phoned Diana and said I wanted to spend the day with you. I thought I'd give you a rest from her."

Dylan's forming noises that travel through the monitor, and before I have chance to get to my feet, Lois has left the room and I hear her talking to him in a singsong voice. I wish I could emulate that.

After I'm dressed, I descend to find Lois swirling gently around the lounge with Dylan in her arms. I think he's looking happy.

Lois smiles at me and ceases being so energetic, swaying gently from side to side instead. Dylan has entwined his fingers in her hair which is flowing freely over her shoulders like a cornfield on a hill.

"I was wondering if I could go to the self-help group if it's on today," I ask her.

"Sure, Dylan and I will be just fine."

I slip upstairs and phone Chloe hoping that today's good for her. The incessant ringing worries me as I hold my breath with anxiety, imagining her dead babies and her crumpled body on the pavement. I feel like passing out when suddenly I hear her whisper-like voice.

"Chloe, it's me, Colette. Would I be able to come and see you today?"

"Have you decided that today's the day then?"

It takes me a few seconds to comprehend her. "Oh no . . . sorry. I just want to talk some more if that's all right."

Her pause is painful as though she's concentrating on murdering a baby as we speak. I feel sick.

"Yeah, why not. Bring a bottle."

"A bottle of what?"

"Whatever you've got; whisky, gin, wine . . ."

My mind's racing. Does she just intend to get drunk, or is it Dutch courage to perform the task without me? I tell her I'll bring something. *I don't suppose orange squash will do?*

By the time I'm washed and dressed, Dylan's asleep in his recliner and Lois is arranging an ostentatious bouquet of flowers in my grandmother's old crystal vase on the table in the bay window. She doesn't notice me, so I tread quietly to the drinks cabinet and stealthily remove a bottle of sloe gin and slip it into my handbag.

"I'll be off then, if that's okay with you," I say in a flat voice.

It takes her a couple of seconds to register. "Of course, Dylan and I will be fine. Take as long as you need."

I don't feel guilty as I leave, as my desire to explore dark avenues with Chloe is stronger than anything else. In fact, her plans for death are paradoxically making me feel alive.

The fish and chip shop is open for business as I arrive, and the smell of fat coats the air with rancid grease. Another reason for Chloe to want to die, no doubt.

"This is the best I can do," I say, handing over the bottle of sloe gin.

"Perfect," she replies, grabbing it off me and closing the front door behind me.

"What's this all about?" I ask.

"You tell me, it's you who called to say you wanted to visit."

"No, I mean drinking alcohol so early in the day."

"Haven't you ever had a day when you want to obliterate all thoughts and sounds from your mind?"

"I suppose I have, I just thought that's what the medication's for."

"If they work for you that's great, but living here with two kids I need more of a hit."

I see what she means. I'm lucky compared to her; I live in a nice home with a husband to support me. Guilt swamps me as I watch her unscrew the bottle cap. I wish I hadn't made her spell out her misery to me.

"How are Kerry and Rachel?"

"Kerry's brought a cold home from nursery and I think Rachel's getting it." She pours a large amount of gin in a tumbler and adds a dash of lemonade. "Do you want one?"

"I can't drink during the day; it makes me sleepy."

Chloe shrugs then downs half the glass. Soft crying comes from the room next door but Chloe remains immune to the sound. The louder the crying gets, the more Chloe drinks.

"I hope you're not going to take too long deciding if you want to jump with me, I'm not sure I can wait much longer."

"Can't someone help you for a bit whilst I build up to it?"

"Like who?"

"The nurse, a friend . . ."

"You know the nurse will talk to the social worker who's waiting for any excuse to take them away from me. And you're the only friend I have. Do you want to look after them?"

I smile apologetically. She knows the answer.

Rachel's obviously given up on expecting comfort, love, or milk, as her crying has ceased. *Poor mite.*

Chloe pours herself another drink, this time not bothering with lemonade. I swear her eyes are glistening. She catches me watching her.

"If you think I'm being a shit mum, then say so."

"I'm not judging you, Chloe. We're both crushed by our inability to cope with our children. We're both ousted by society for not being the norm."

"But at least you have a husband. I know his mum's a bloody nightmare, but you're not alone."

Now I'm hit with more guilt.

"Would you like to come to my house next time?"

"And see how you live so I feel even more shit, no thanks."

What's happened to the Chloe I met online? I know we can all be affected by mood swings, but this is throwing me off balance. I can see she feels wretched but I'm powerless to help.

"Is . . . there some other way . . . I can help you?" I clumsily trip over my words as tears spill down my cheeks.

She slumps back into the chair, expelling a lungful of air. "I just can't wait to end it all."

I want to ask why she's waiting for me if things are that bad, but I resist, and say something else. "I find cutting helps release my stress, have you thought of doing that again?" I pull my sleeves down over my hands to hide the tiny threads of dull red and angry scarlet worms.

Chloe stands up and unbuttons her jeans before pulling them down over her flaccid thighs to display her cuts. The raised lines look like the thick edges of bacon rind, forming intricate patterns on her mottled skin.

"I've returned to this old site so no one knows but you. I may be younger than you, but I have been doing this a lot longer." She takes another swig. "Now tell me what's stopping you from ending it all today."

I knew she'd ask sooner or later, and now I need to give her an answer. "Diana's arranging a christening for Dylan. I'd like to be here for that, then I'm happy to go."

"When's that?"

"Later this month, I don't know exactly when."

"You want Dylan christened?"

"Not really, I'm agnostic."

"Does agnostic mean you don't believe in God?"

"It means I know there's something, but I'm not sure it's the God everyone talks about."

"I wish I were like you. I was raised a Catholic and so I know I'm going to hell after killing myself. But I'm already there now."

"There's no such thing as hell; religion concocted it to control society, making people fearful. Religion is only a theory."

"So we're not going to hell after our suicides?"

"No, just a long peaceful sleep."

"And our babies?"

"I assume the same." I take a deep breath. "You know I'm not taking Dylan with me."

"He's got family, my two have no one." She pours another glass of gin. "I know what you're thinking, but I have no choice, I'm all they have."

I can't form a coherent sentence to express my concern over her plans for them. It will have to wait for another day. I want to stay longer, but I know I should get back home before too many questions are asked.

"If you need to talk later, contact me online or text me. The darkness of the evening can be crushing."

She nods, but doesn't get up. I make my way to the door just as Rachel protests again at being alone. Chloe pours herself another drink. I want to help, but I know I can't. No one understands our pain, and it saddens me to watch a young woman so screwed up by dark, intrusive thoughts. I wish our babies brought us joy like they do to other mothers. *Who's to blame?*

Finn

Dylan's crying wakes me but not Colette. I think her antidepressants make her sleep more deeply.

I pad softly to his room and pick him up, knowing he needs his early morning feed. I realise weekend lie-ins are now a thing of the past, something I hadn't considered when Colette first became pregnant; in fact, I hadn't considered fatherhood at all up until then. Even when I did consider it, I saw it as an idyllic union between two people who both played a role in raising their child.

As it is, I'm in the kitchen at six in the morning, warming a bottle for my son, as his mother lies sleeping upstairs. I can't help but feel disappointed and badly done to.

Now satiated, Dylan is calm but his nappy is full, so I return to the nursery to sort him out.

"Your son's awake," I say when I enter our bedroom.

She stirs slightly as I place him next to her on the bed. He stretches out his arm and grabs her nose, by hooking his thumb up her nostril.

"What's Dylan doing?"

"Trying to get your attention, I think."

"I'm not a morning person."

"You used to be."

"That was before he made me ill."

"I've told you before, this isn't Dylan's fault."

She removes Dylan's fingers from around her nose and sits up on her elbows. "I don't understand what I'm supposed to do with him all day."

"Bond with him through play and hugs. Take him to the mother-and-baby groups the health visitor mentioned. I don't know, what do they suggest at the support group?"

She looks at me puzzled for a few seconds. "Oh, the group . . . no, we don't really talk about things like that."

"What do you talk about, then?"

"Our feelings mostly. We understand one another and how it feels to be like this."

"Is everyone like you?"

"More or less."

"Is there anyone there who's getting better yet?"

"We're all at the same stage, you know, depressed, anxious, low social confidence."

I smile and nod to hide my disappointment. I fear compassion fatigue is already setting in and I'm going to be the impatient, distant husband the medical team hoped I wouldn't be. Would I feel this way if I wasn't involved with Lois?

Halfway through the day, I'm beginning to think like Colette, wondering what the hell we do with a tiny baby at the weekend. Once upon a time we'd have gone shopping, had lunch out before seeing friends in the evening, or a trip to the cinema or theatre. That life seems a distant memory now and I'm beginning to wonder whether having Dylan was the best idea for us. *What am I saying? It's not his fault.*

The doorbell pierces the air, blowing the whistle at halftime. Seeing as Colette isn't stirring from the sofa, I leave her to keep an eye on Dylan lying on the floor playing with his fingers.

"Lois, what are you doing here?" I ask in a low voice.

"Nothing to worry about," she smiles. "I've come to see how my good friends are doing."

The weak midday sun forms a halo around her flaxen hair; it's mesmerising.

"Aren't you going to invite me in?"

I step back, breathing in her heady perfume as she breezes through. Colette's voice sounds pleased to see her, weighing heavily on my conscious.

"I'm glad you're here, I've something to ask you," Colette says.

I look as surprised as Lois; I've no idea what she's going to say.

"Even though I am against Dylan being christened, I might as well have some choice in the proceedings. So, I was wondering whether you'd be his godmother?"

Lois squeals, rushing over to Colette, encasing her in a hug. She looks at me over Colette's shoulder and I shrug. For a fleeting moment, I wish I'd not sullied this scene by sleeping with Lois. What's been done cannot be erased like condensation on a windowpane.

I extrapolate myself from the saccharine scene and switch the kettle on, reverting to my role of invisible caregiver. Laughter comes from the other room, and I wonder whether I am the source of a malevolent joke.

By the time I return to the lounge, Colette's still in her seat and Lois is now on the floor tickling Dylan's gently rounded tummy. I place the tray unnoticed on the coffee table before sitting on the sofa, feeling excruciatingly out of place.

"Say, how about I go shopping and buy stuff to cook us a fabulous meal for this evening?" Lois suggests, sitting up and contorting her legs into the lotus position.

I daren't answer, lest my shrill voice reveal my emotions, sullying the atmosphere.

"That sounds very nice," Colette says as she stands up. "Do you mind if I go upstairs and lie down?"

Lois shakes her head coquettishly and I half rise out of the chair but Colette waves me back down saying she's fine.

"Well, Mr Forbes, I'd better buy some delicious ingredients to tantalise your tongue," Lois whispers as she presses her palm into my chest.

I'm rendered speechless by how the day is unfolding. I'm not in control, and I'm not sure if I like where I'm heading. I think an early whisky may help my quivering nerves.

Colette's been asleep for over an hour and I'm contemplating waking her, when Lois returns with three bags of shopping and a large bouquet of red tulips.

"Be a sweetie and help," she says as she sashays down the hallway.

Colette's suddenly been brushed from my mind, and like a well-trained puppy, I scamper after her, hoping she gives me some treats in the kitchen.

Colette

My ragged sleep doesn't refresh my mind, or elevate my spirit. My soul is nailed to the floor and dripping through the ceiling below, only no one can see it but me. My face is streaked with dried tears.

My thoughts shift to the knife concealed in my jewellery box; it calls to me loudly, ripping through the air. The stainless-steel blade glints fiercely in my mind, reverberating with echoes of previous cuts.

Tiptoeing from the bed so as not to alert those below, I open the pearl in-laid walnut lid and remove the upper layer to retrieve the knife wrapped in a monogrammed handkerchief. I listen hard to check no one is about to interrupt me, before slipping to the bathroom and locking the door.

Trepidation flutters in my heart as I run the flat of the blade along my inner arm. The healing scars scream self-hatred. Suddenly I remember Chloe's advice and raise my brown skirt and roll down my woollen tights before running the side of the blade along my gently dimpled flesh. My thighs are much larger than Chloe's, tempting me to carve off thick portions of flesh so they look more like hers.

I'm numb to the first cut, before the neuropathic pain releases the endorphins. Rivulets of blood dribble down my legs, and the relief is akin to the high of cocaine. The head rush is phenomenal.

A tear escapes and runs a jagged journey down my cheek. I'm a fool to think I'm relieved, I'm but distracted from my anguish for only a brief period.

I clean up the mess and dress my wounds before creeping back to the bedroom to sort out my tear-streaked face. Although every fibre of my being begs for me to remain upstairs, I feel I should join the others and form part of the family, albeit a dysfunctional one.

The smell of grilling peppers pervades the air, and the sound of chatter offers a balanced backdrop for Dylan to begin practicing his babbling noises.

"Feeling refreshed?" Lois asks as I enter the kitchen.

Her words show she doesn't truly comprehend my situation. Everyone accepted the postpartum psychosis when I was in hospital, but this depression that's followed seems too difficult for people to grasp now that I'm home. Depression is almost seen as a copout by everyone, except for Chloe who's my soul sister in all of this.

I decide to ignore her question and risk appearing rude in the process.

Dylan is bouncing gently in his rocker, whilst attempting to play with a towelling baby elephant. The scene before me is like a fairy tale, and the only thing spoiling it is me. I am beginning to truly believe Dylan, and Finn come to that, will be better off without me. *I'm almost ready, Chloe.*

I sit at the head of the pine table, tracing all the grooves and dents with my forefinger, whilst Lois stuffs the red and green peppers with pancetta and couscous, and Finn flicks through the newspaper.

I notice another vase of flowers on the windowsill. This time my green and yellow ceramic vase is full of tulips. The house is looking like a show home, with touches of Lois appearing subtly around the place. Not that I mind; she was always more stylish than me.

"I hope you're both hungry, it'll be ready soon," she says. "How about a glass of red to be going on with?" which she directs towards Finn, who folds his newspaper obediently.

Dylan is making louder noises synonymous with wanting his feed. Finn appears to prepare the bottle on automatic pilot, waltzing around Lois as though they have spent many an hour together in this very room. Perhaps they have. After all, I've been out of contact with my former life for a while now.

Lois is positively glowing with her borrowed life. I think she suits motherhood better than I do. Another reason to go, perhaps?

"Do you want to feed Dylan?" Finn asks me, holding our child expectantly.

Pretending to think about it by looking at the ceiling, I shake my head. I've no energy to hold him.

The meal is an explosion of flavours, and I can see Finn is blown away by her cooking. The dark cloud enveloping me is squeezing me harder so my lungs are unable to expand to garner more air. Pin pricks of black and red dots flash before my eyes, and my ears are irritated by a high-pitch buzz. I've lost sight of the room, and my feeble legs are trying to run. I hate how I feel, and I hate that no one can help me. The darkness is suffocating, without actually finishing the task altogether to free me.

Lois insists on clearing the table and making a pot of coffee, while Finn, Dylan, and I head to the lounge. I flop into an armchair and Finn gives me Dylan before returning to the kitchen. I hear their whispers then silence before I lay Dylan on the sheepskin rug.

On bending down, I notice patches of blood seeping through my skirt. I lift it up slightly to see the blood-soaked bandages, barely containing the flow. If Finn sees this, he'll send me back to the hospital for sure.

I quietly rush upstairs to change the bandages before my dark deeds are discovered.

As I peel away the sodden fabric, the sight of the blood overwhelms me and I only just manage to lift the toilet seat before vomiting the entire meal into the white bowl.

The acrid taste in my mouth is disgusting, and suddenly I'm considering taking that journey without Chloe. I could take Dylan for company instead.

Finn

"You're enjoying yourself a little too much," I whisper in Lois's ear, as we both lean against the worktop.

"I always enjoy myself in your company, no matter what we're doing," she replies dulcetly, slipping her hand underneath my jumper and massaging my chest.

I grab hold of her forearm. "This is too dangerous."

"Exactly."

"You have nothing to lose."

"I could lose you, and you mean everything to me."

"Why didn't you make a play for me when we were younger?"

"I did try but you were hopelessly in love with her. Whereas now, your love has dwindled."

"That's not true."

"Oh, it bloody is. Don't tell me you'd have slept with me if you still felt like you did back then."

She has me.

Dylan's distressed cry reaches my ear and rescues me from Lois's eager clutch.

I move to the lounge to find Colette absent, and Dylan lying red-faced on the floor. Scooping him up, I dash upstairs to find Colette, mainly out of anger.

Our bedroom door is shut, so I enter abruptly and wish I hadn't.

"What the hell have you been doing?" I ask, even though the bloody patches on her thighs tell me all I need to know.

"You shouldn't burst in like that," she snaps.

"This is our bedroom. Please don't tell me you're doing this again."

"I can't explain anything to you; you can't comprehend how I feel. I feel isolated."

"But this," I say, pointing to her legs. "This can't possibly help."

"You wouldn't understand."

I want her to try and explain, but I know it is hopeless.

Dylan is now quietly gumming my shirt, and I step forward to attempt to put him next to Colette.

"No," she shrieks. "Don't force him on me." She runs from the room and locks herself in the bathroom.

Hurried footsteps clamber up the stairs, and a tap on the open door announces Lois's arrival.

"Everything all right?"

"I don't think Colette's well. She's been self-harming again."

"Should we call a doctor or her nurse?"

"I don't know," I shrug.

She walks up to me and wraps her arm around my waist, hugging me into her. I close my eyes and smell Dylan's powdery head mixed with Lois's perfume, and imagine us as a unit. My eyes snap open, I'm a despicable man.

"I'm going to call the mental health team, see what they say I should do. Do you mind?" I say, handing over Dylan to her.

Lois follows me downstairs to the lounge where I rifle around in the address book for the number. Lois sits with Dylan as I recount my concerns to the team who agree to send someone 'round within the hour.

"There, now you can relax," she tells me, patting the seat next to her.

"I don't know if relax is the correct term, but at least I feel less powerless."

She snuggles into me with Dylan on her knee, but it feels wrong and I pull away.

"Have I done something wrong?"

"Everything's been wrong since Dylan was born. My joy at his birth was short lived, and the torment gets darker and deeper."

"Never mind, it will sort itself out sooner or later, you'll see."

The wind's picking up outside, and the light's fading, so Lois switches on the table lamp which casts a sinister shadow thanks to the red shade.

"We've been waiting well over an hour. Where the devil are they?" I mutter.

"I'll make a pot of tea, and I bet they're here before the kettle boils."

Her clattering around the kitchen is finally interrupted by the door-bell.

Lois reaches the door before me and lets the nurse in. I hear them talking as they walk towards the lounge where I stand with Dylan sleeping in my arms.

I hand him to Lois to put to bed whilst I take the nurse upstairs to see Colette.

"How long has she been in there?" the nurse asks, after my second attempt knocking on the door.

"About an hour." It sounds bad saying it aloud. And the look in her eye confirms my suspicion.

"Colette, it's Margery. Let me come in please."

The silence is ominous, dripping with menace. Voices in my head tell me how callous I've been leaving her alone for so long, just because I was intoxicated with Lois's effervescing company.

"Can you unlock the door from the outside?" Margery asks me.

I shake my head as beads of sweat trickle down my forehead.

"You'll have to break the door down, then," she concludes, moving away from me.

I've seen it done in films but I have never attempted it myself. My first contact with the door as I slam my shoulder against it causes a surge of pain to zigzag down my arm and into my fingers. I swear Margery rolls her eyes. Lois has now joined the scene, so I now have to display my inadequacies in front of her too.

My second attempt is a mockery to my manhood, as I nearly knock myself out as my head makes contact with the door before my shoulder does.

"I'm calling the police and ambulance," says Margery.

Oh God, what will the neighbours say? I holler her name and bang on the door with my fists, but to no avail.

Lois moves closer to me and begins talking to Colette, asking her if she could come in without the other two. I've been relegated to "the other two" by her of all people.

When even she cannot get a response, she looks at me with pity in her eyes.

It isn't long before thudding footsteps approach us as a policeman arrives with a battering ram in his hands.

Rubbing my shoulder, I watch the policeman smash the door open with one strike of the ram, only to discover the room's empty, and the window's wide open. He hurries in and looks out the window.

"Where would your wife go, sir?"

I can't think. The only person she could run to is in the house with me right now. He asks me for a photograph of her as Margery is very concerned for her emotional wellbeing.

I'm paralysed by fear and confusion. I find it hard to believe she's managed to escape, and yet she has.

"I hope she's not done anything stupid," Lois says. Do I detect a smidgen of hope in her voice?

"She wouldn't abandon me and Dylan," I say mainly to Margery.

"If she's been missing for an hour, she could have done quite a lot of damage by now."

"I suggest you start calling people she may have gone to. Make sure someone's always here in case she returns. Keep us informed." And with that, he disappears with her photograph.

I flick through the address book, seeking friends I hadn't thought of.

"Where can she be?" I question, as though the ethers in the room will answer me back.

"Why don't you stay here with Dylan and I'll go looking for her. You're too shaken up," says Lois, placing her hand on my arm earnestly.

Margery announces she's going too, and will check for Colette along her route. I somehow sense her hopelessness.

I watch both women leave and go their separate ways before returning to Dylan to look at his angelic, carefree face. I check my mobile in my pocket in case I have message.

Jagged thoughts rip through my mind, causing a vortex of black images to bore into my heart.

Where the bloody hell is she?

Colette

I'm still trembling from climbing out of the window. Sheer desperation overcame my fear, but I'm now suffering with an overdose of adrenaline coursing through my veins.

"Do you want a drink?" Chloe asks me. "I got my money today so you can have vodka or wine."

"Either." I don't rightly care; I just want something to soften the raw edges of fear.

She brings me a glass of orange squash with a hefty dose of vodka in it, which I knock back. I'm now spluttering over my still uncomfortably tight jeans.

"So now you're here, what do you plan to do?" she asks, taking my glass to refill.

"I want us to go ahead with ending it together, if the time's right for you?"

Chloe looks at Rachel who's playing with her feet as she lies on a blanket on the floor.

"You don't have to kill them, you know," I say.

"I don't want them going into care as I did. Look how I turned out."

"How old were you when you went into care?"

"Fourteen. My alcoholic mum couldn't care for me anymore."

"It'll be different for your daughters. They're both so young and pretty, I bet they get adopted in no time."

"They are pretty, aren't they? Kerry's doing well at nursery, everybody loves her."

"Shows what a good job you've done."

The grim silence speaks loudly to me, whispering the question I fear to ask, but feel I must.

"How will you kill them? You mentioned drowning, but that seems extremely scary and violent for them."

"I've decided to dose them up with cough syrup to make them sleepy, then put a pillow over their faces."

I am shuddering. "Would cough medicine do that?"

"I don't really know, but I can hardly type 'how to kill children' into the computer, can I?"

I feel bad for asking. I don't want to push her into this, but I need to escape, with or without her.

"I have to fetch Kerry from nursery soon. Do you want to come or stay here with Rachel?"

"I think I'd better stay here." I catch her glancing quickly at her baby. "I won't harm her."

She smiles weakly. "I was wondering about leaving her at the nursery and walking away from them both."

"That's so much kinder, but then they'd come looking for you and prevent us from killing ourselves."

"I hadn't thought of that," she sighs heavily. "You see how hard it is. I change from day to day. Some days I'm ready to do it then the next I feel like I do today. Could you do it?"

"Absolutely not. Sorry." I stare at her wide-eyed. "You could leave them outside a church. By the time they work out who they are, we'll be gone."

So here I am, desperate to leave this cloying, twisted world, and my partner of the deed is now backing out. I can't jump alone. I know that when she brings her eldest home, she'll find it even harder to do.

Outside, clouds are merging together, wreathing the day in early gloom. I watch Chloe through the window as she crosses the busy road, her head down as though she's constantly bowing to God.

Rachel gurgles behind me. I turn and feel saddened by her situation, but incapable of finding a way out from the intrusive thoughts that overpower my moral compass. Right from wrong hangs in the balance here, but one false move and it's all over.

It's not long before I hear the sound of footsteps and inane chatter coming up the stairs. I brace myself for the invasion of Kerry who is still demanding, yet more independent than a baby.

Kerry is clutching a poorly scribbled-in picture which she thrusts towards the fridge demanding Chloe stick it on the door with the others. She then points to the cupboard and Chloe takes out a packet of biscuits before giving her one. She offers me a biscuit but I am not hungry. How can people on death row eat prior to execution?

Kerry totters over to the TV and switches it on before dropping onto her nappy-padded bottom. Chloe is showing a legendary lack of interest despite her wavering over killing them or not.

"Drink?" Chloe asks, brandishing a bottle of cheap wine.

"Why not?" Perhaps it will give us both the impetus we need.

The wine has a sharp edge, puckering my mouth with its arid backnote. I feel I've licked the inside of a barrel, leaving splinters in my tongue.

Kerry starts complaining she's hungry, and her whiny pitch rallies Rachel into moaning mode. I find the combined noise unbearable so I force another mouthful of wine down my straining throat.

"You've come for a reason," Chloe begins as she hands Kerry a jam sandwich and heats a bottle for Rachel. "We both know what we want to do, so let's start making plans."

I'm pleased with her more positive attitude. "When will you be ready?"

"I need to get a couple of bottles of cough syrup for the girls and more alcohol for us, first."

"I've got money on me for that," I offer. "I need to write a suicide note for Finn and Dylan."

"Whatever for?"

"To say goodbye and to explain why, I suppose. Aren't you leaving one?"

"Who to?"

I dip my head, chagrined by my tactlessness. "I've thought of a way to put your girls to sleep forever." The word death is not sitting well in the same sentence as Kerry and Rachel.

"How?" Chloe says eagerly.

"You still give them cough syrup then we leave the gas oven and fire on, and try and seal the flat as much as possible. What do you think?"

I can see her reflecting as she feeds Rachel. "Sounds a good idea. Less gruesome than smothering them, I suppose."

"We could always stay in the flat with them and die the same way," I suggest, feeling this could answer everything.

"I worry it may be enough for their little lungs but not ours."

"We could take an overdose. Or what about throwing ourselves in front of a tube?"

"What's wrong with jumping?" She sounds irritated, and I suppose I would be in her situation.

"I'm worried that I'll get to the top of the car park and lose courage. I've never had a great head for heights."

"I don't know how we'd time the jump in front of a train? Besides, there'll be people there who might stop us. An empty top floor of a car park is more private."

I guess she's right. After all, she's been thinking about this longer than me. My pathetic attempts at slashing my wrists were clearly just a cry for help; I see that now.

Diana's words keep streaming through my mind, with the odd word screaming louder than others. If I love them, I would let them have a happier life by leaving. I think about Lois's reassuring smiles and hugs as she cares for me and the boys. She cares for us all; I see that now.

With both girls fed, the flat is quieter, enabling me to think. I ask Chloe for a pen and paper before sitting at the table to compose my suicide note.

Finn

I'm going out of my mind. Lois has been gone for over two hours, the phone has remained silent, and Colette hasn't returned home. Dylan has provided periodic relief from my insanity, but when he's quiet, the tumultuous thoughts return to ravage my mind.

"Colette?" I call out on hearing the front door open.

"No, just me," Lois replies. "I've searched all her favourite haunts, but no one's seen her. I even popped in to the beauty salon to see if she was being pampered."

"You think of everything."

"We've been friends for years, I know her well."

I make us both a coffee, anticipating a long night ahead.

"I hesitate to say this," she starts, "but I wonder whether she believes she's spoiling yours and Dylan's life with her illness."

"What do you mean? Why would she think that?"

"Perhaps she wants to disappear."

"You don't mean . . . suicide . . ." My lungs empty of air.

"Oh, I'm sorry; I didn't mean to upset you." She moves closer and wraps her arms around me. "I thought you might have wondered that yourself, what with her being so depressed."

"She wouldn't do that."

"Perhaps you've done the typical male thing of denying anything's wrong; or that you could fix it just by being here."

"You must think I'm a fool."

"No," she says, putting her hands either side of my face. "You've been admirable and stoic in the light of the adversity you've had since the birth of Dylan. I admire you."

"Sleeping with you hasn't been that admirable, though."

"I'm impossible to resist." She's smiling, but I sense she means it.

I jump when the phone rings. Rushing to answer it, I say Colette's name with panting breath.

"It's your mother. Why are you asking after Colette?"

"This isn't a good time, Mum."

"What's she done now?"

I explain as much as I know and she has nothing but harsh words about the mother of my child. *Do I expect a different reaction?*

She's regimental in dictating what I should do to protect myself and Dylan. She wants to come around and lead me into battle.

"It's okay, Lois is here taking care of us."

"She's such a rock for you. I hope you remember how good she's been when Colette returns; if she returns."

"Not you as well," I exclaim. "Colette is just going through a rough patch."

"I said she should have stayed in hospital longer."

I'm sorely tempted to slam the phone down on her, but the wrath I'd incur would be too great, so I meekly say something innocuous before saying I want to keep the phone line free in case Colette tries to call.

"Diana wanting to take control?" Lois asks.

"You know how she is. I wish Colette would contact me to say she's okay. I'm now thinking the worst thanks to you both."

She pouts, and I want to tell her off for being selfish, but what good would that do?

The sun's turned the sky orange behind the arching mantle of broken cloud, and the trees are casting ominous shadows on the tatty lawn. I want to call the police again to see if they have any news, but Lois says they'll call me if they have.

"Drink this," Lois says as she hands me a whisky on the rocks.

"I can't, I need to stay clear headed."

"One drink isn't going to harm. It'll help settle your nerves. I'm here to drive if need be."

I take a sip and appreciate the warm trail that descends to my stomach. I realise I've not eaten for hours.

"I'm going to stay the night so someone's here for Dylan if you need to go."

"I'm not sure that's wise. She could turn up at any time."

"I'll be in the spare room, silly."

I smile ruefully just as Dylan starts crying, seeking company.

I walk into the nursery and pick him up to dab his wet face. His eyes crease like Colette's when he cries. I pace and rock him to soothe his fractious mood before changing his nappy then taking him downstairs for a feed.

Lois is already heating his bottle when I arrive in the kitchen. She's barefoot and looking very Mother Earth, something I always thought Colette would blossom into.

She hands me the bottle before moving to the lounge and putting on the table lamps.

"Now it looks cosy. Do you fancy a sandwich? You really should eat."

"Still not hungry. Where is she? It's driving me crazy."

"Maybe she's with a friend."

"I know all her friends, remember?"

"I meant from the mother-and-baby group. My sister met her best friend through one of those groups. None of our group have babies, so we're not on the same wavelength."

"You're a genius; why didn't I think of that?" I get up and hand Dylan over to her.

"Where are you going?"

"To phone the health visitor."

I discover it's after working hours and a recorded message tells me to go to A&E if I have concerns about mother or baby, or call out-of-hours doctor. He is not going to be able to give me the names of the group. This is hopeless.

"Never mind, come and sit with me and have another drink. You've done all you can today."

"I've hardly done anything."

She kicks her legs up and over my lap. They look like fragile porcelain legs on an antique doll. But my reverie is broken by Dylan grizzling before bursting into full-lung-capacity screaming.

"What the hell's wrong with him?" I say, half-worried by the different tone in his cry, and half-irritated by the din which is grating on my raw nerves.

"Probably just wants his nappy changing," she says, getting up.

"Again? Look, you've done enough. I'll do it," I offer.

But she waves me to stay seated saying it's no trouble. I watch her sashay out the room before closing my eyes for a brief second.

My mobile sits on the table; its silence reminding me Colette is either in trouble or doesn't want to see me. Does that mean she doesn't want to see Dylan either? I'm not used to feeling such degrees of pain and despair. Is this how Colette feels all the time?

A key turns in the front door, and I'm racing to welcome her home.

Colette

I've never been one for writing letters or e-mails. Staring at this blank piece of paper is bringing me out in a prickly sweat, but I want my suicide note to explain things fully, so when Dylan's older he understands why I did it. I don't want to lay blame at anyone's door, especially his, but I need people to know that my suffering was so intense, it caused my demise.

Dear Finn,

By the time you read this, my body will have already been discovered. I hope identifying my body wasn't too traumatic for you. I want to explain to you and Dylan why I've done this.

I never expected having a baby would damage me and irrevocably change my mental health. Who knew this could happen? At the ante-natal classes they talked about the pain of giving birth and the sleepless nights, but no one ever mentioned this debilitating illness, only the baby blues for three days—huh.

I feel I've let you and Dylan down by not being a normal mother. My heart is sore with pain. I never felt like harming Dylan, only myself, and I thought cutting my flesh would deal with the misery, but it only went so far in helping. I've been lost for a while and you haven't been able to reach me, and I'm sorry for that. I haven't been able to bond with Dylan either and that's made me feel inadequate. I think he has a better bond with Lois and Diana, which doesn't make me feel good.

I wanted to talk to you about this, but I knew you'd dissuade me from killing myself, yet that's the only answer to the problem of being me. I hate and despise myself; I'm beyond repair. You and Dylan will be better off with someone like Lois; she'd be a wonderful substitute for me. Perhaps you already know that?

I'd like to say I'll watch over you both from above, but I don't believe in that, as you know. So, all I can say is I hope you both have a happy life. Diana said if I loved you both I'd leave you so you could pursue a happier future. I hope she at least approves of this action.

Goodbye Finn and Dylan. I did love you both very much in my own way.

Colette xx

Reading them back, the words seem trite; I don't feel I've got my message across. I swear the anti-depressants have dulled my mental agility. I can't live this miserable existence any longer.

"Have you finished?" Chloe asks.

"Kind of. The finality of it all is closing in around me, and it's scary."

"You know it makes sense. What have we got to live for?"

"I'd like to say our children?"

"I can't give mine a bright future; in fact, I can give them fuck all."

"And I believe Dylan will be happier without me, so I suppose you're right, it's time to go."

"You've got to help me get the flat air-tight. I need to start dosing them up."

A pang of sadness pinches my heart; if only she had someone to leave them to like I do.

I wonder if Dylan will have any memory of me; my scent or the sound of my voice. Maybe I will not have existed at all for him, which is perhaps for the best; after all I've been a fairly unloving and impatient mother.

And what about wife? I've not been attentive or loving of late. I've had no energy to love Finn either. He'll have no trouble replacing me; he's still young and handsome.

An image of him making love to another woman briefly flits into my mind, and my heart plummets to my stomach. Imagining him entwined with another woman, his breath on her neck and his soft moans filling the room is making me feel sick. I'm glad there's no heaven for me to watch him from. That would be the ultimate torture for my sin of suicide; if I believed in sin as a concept.

Chloe is spooning cough medicine into her eldest. The medicine is obviously sweet as Kerry willingly opens her mouth for another spoonful. A bottle of milk with a large dose awaits Rachel.

"What are you staring at?" Chloe snipes as she removes the spoon from Kerry's mouth.

"Nothing, I'm just daydreaming."

"Well that's not helping. How about sealing the windows with towels or sheets, or whatever needs doing?"

I walk over to the cupboard she's pointing at and remove a bale of towels. I roll each towel into a sausage shape before pressing them along the bottom of the window. I find some tape then tape a towel to the bottom of the front door so when we close it, it's sealed.

Chloe's now feeding Rachel the warm milky mixture and telling Kerry to lie on the sofa. She swings Rachel in her arm as she moves to the TV and switches it on. Children's programmes blare out as Kerry settles down under a blanket, her thumb firmly in her mouth.

Chloe places Rachel next to the sofa in her bouncy chair, also wrapped up tightly in a blanket.

"I'm ready," she declares.

"Are you sure you don't want to write a note?"

"Course I'm sure. My children will be dead. There's no one to read it."

"How about the policeman who finds their bodies."

"Why the fuck should I care about him?"

I shrug my shoulders, wishing I had never started this conversation.

We put our coats on, and I place my letter in my pocket ready to post along the way. Tears stream down my face as I watch her tenderly kiss each child and cocoon them once more before silently slipping to the kitchen to turn on the hobs and oven, leaving the door wide open. She surveys the room once more before beckoning me out then locking the door behind us.

We walk down the stairs in heavy silence, smelling the warming fat in the chip shop vats for the very last time. I don't want the nauseating smell to be my last memory.

"I've no choice, you know," she says finally.

"In what?"

"In doing away with my little ones. I can't bear to think of them in care."

"I understand why you feel the way you do, even if I don't agree. I'm not here to judge you."

"Everyone judges me, especially people like you. But whatever."

I don't know how to respond because she's right, and I feel ashamed of my perceived superiority.

As we pass people on the pavement, I'm aware they don't know we're walking to our deaths, as they jab us with their shopping bags and elbows. Seeing a dozing toddler in a pushchair makes me want to run back to the flat and rouse the children from their life-sucking slumber. Have I just witnessed two murders?

Chloe points to the multi-storey car park in the distance. I wonder if a person heading for the gallows felt as I do now, seeing the implement of their execution for the first time.

I stop and hover in front of a red post box on the pavement before retrieving the suicide note from my pocket. I turn it over and over before slipping it through the slot and hearing it land on the pile below. I wonder how Finn will respond on reading it; perhaps he'll be overcome with relief.

Chloe hasn't noticed I'm lagging behind, so I semi-trot to catch up with her, arriving at the car park entrance just as she does.

"It's emptying nicely as I said it would at this hour. Normally by now the top floor should be clear."

I nod and follow her inside and up the stairs.

"Can't risk getting into the lift and it breaking down on us; don't want to be trapped in it all bloody night," Chloe whispers.

"That would be ironic."

She looks at me blankly before continuing up the steep flight of concrete stairs. Her youth has her bounding up faster than me, making me breathless and slightly dizzy.

Finally, we arrive on the sixth floor, and as Chloe predicted, the space is clear of vehicles and people. The perfect place to leave a life behind. Only I'm experiencing a fear like I've never known before; not even when on the psychiatric ward. This fear is grabbing me by the throat and torso, and squeezing the air from my lungs, as a breeze abrades my cheeks.

Through the black dots floating before my eyes, I watch Chloe move closer to the edge and hold on to the metal railing. She turns to search for me, and for the first time since knowing her, her facial features have softened. She almost glows with serenity, and a peaceful aura encases her. I wonder whether I look the same to her.

"What are you waiting for?" she asks, holding out her hand.

"I was just thinking how relaxed you look."

"That's because I already feel free. Do you feel it too?"

"I'm more overwhelmed with trepidation, actually."

She thrusts her hand towards me again and I tentatively take hold of the tips of her fingers before she grabs my wrist with her free hand and pulls me closer.

"I've dreamt of this moment and now it's finally here. Thanks for sharing it with me."

My tongue is stuck to the roof of my mouth, preventing me from answering. A shadow travels across her eyes.

"You don't want to jump, do you?"

"I'm scared, and wonder whether this really is the right solution."

"It is for me."

"I wish I had your conviction."

"You're going to make me jump alone, aren't you?"

"I'm not making you do anything. I'm torn between supporting you and returning to my miserable life."

She releases my hand and grips the railing so hard her knuckles turn white. Panic rises within me, wondering whether I will have the physical strength to prevent her going over. But is that the right thing to do?

"I have to jump," she whispers. "My babies are dead and I'm not going to prison for killing them. I wouldn't cope. I've no choice."

I understand her reasoning in my warped perception of the situation, and I am also aware that if I wish to die, I can either do it with her now or alone in the future.

I ask her for one last hug then squeeze her hand tightly.

Finn

I can't help showing my disappointment as Diana strides into the house.

"I expect a warmer welcome than that," she says tersely.

"I hoped you were Colette."

"Still not back then? I hope you chastise her thoroughly for the worry she's put you through."

I roll my eyes as she marches past me, into the kitchen, where she offers an over-enthusiastic greeting to Lois.

"I'm just making a pot of tea, Diana."

"Oh you are wonderful, isn't she, Finn?"

"Yes Mum," I reply with minimal enthusiasm. *Why is no one as worried about Colette as I am?*

I try Colette's mobile again but it's still turned off. I'm now worrying she's found out about me and Lois, and I'm overwhelmed with remorse, but I've no one to discuss this with. My male friends and I never discuss personal or relationship issues—it's an un-said rule—and Lois and Diana would be biased in their views. I must stew in my own guilty conscious and be damned.

"Have you two eaten?" Diana asks.

"I'm not hungry," I reply as my stomach growls.

"I'll rustle up an omelette and salad. You need to keep your strength up for Dylan's sake," Lois says, looking at me briefly.

"She's right. Are you staying the night to look after him?"

"I am, Diana. I don't think he should be alone. Besides, when Colette turns up they'll need time to talk, so I'll be here to look after Dylan."

"How considerate of you, dear. I wouldn't have dropped by had I known." She smiles at us both. "I'll just finish my tea and be off."

I dislike the way she speaks to Lois and me, as though we're a couple in the early stage of forging a partnership. I wonder whether Lois has confided in Diana. *Now that is a scary thought.*

Diana replaces the cup in the saucer with a delicate chinking sound before announcing she's leaving.

"Thank you for looking after my boys," she gushes to Lois, hugging her tightly.

They exchange a conspiratorial look before Diana hugs me and tells me things will be sorted soon. I want to ask her what she means, but I'm too weak, or too scared of the answer.

Lois is busy preparing the food whilst I look absentmindedly at the lights on the baby monitor. When he shuffles around in his cot, the lights flicker as if showing how watchfully they are looking over him.

"Here you are," she says, sliding a plate in front of me.

I thank her feebly, feeling my stomach turn at the smell of the cheese. Once she sits down opposite me, I prod the omelette, cutting off small sections, forcing them between my lips and into my dry mouth.

"Are you hoping for Colette's return, or are you starting to move on in your heart?" she asks.

"That's a strange and hurtful question. I'm pretty angry with her at the moment, but I wish her no harm. I'm worried about her. As for my heart, I'm struggling."

"Tell me more."

"My thoughts about you and Colette are still the same. If I could mould you together, I'd have my perfect woman."

"Seeing as that won't happen, what are your intentions?"

"When she returns, I'll have a serious conversation with her about getting back on track."

"What about me?"

"I have to consider what's right for Dylan. I should be with his mother."

"Again, what about me? Seriously, Finn."

She's sounding vexed, yet anxious, and I don't know what to say to make her better. "I do have strong feelings for you. I still want you in my life."

"In a special way?"

I hear wistfulness in her voice.

"It depends on how things go with Colette. I'm sorry."

"Am I your consolation prize if everything fails with her?"

"I don't see you like that. You deserve someone to be with you exclusively. I'm not good enough."

"You *are* good enough for me. I only want you, and I'm happy to wait for you. You'll come back, I know you will."

I sigh and reach for her hand across the table. Her soft hand is so small in mine. I want to protect her from the complicated life I now possess. I'm a father, and that comes first.

"Let's move to the lounge," she suggests, scraping her chair back.

I follow her like a starling chick following his mum, nagging for food; only I'm actually begging for attention.

She sits on the sofa and pats the seat next to her. I sit and wrap my arm around her shoulders, pulling her into me tightly. Her hair smells of spring blossom; it comforts me like the scent of Dylan's tiny head. My heart's pumping wildly.

"I'm sure Dylan will be asleep for a while longer," she utters, smiling seductively.

A small voice in my head urges me to concentrate on Colette, but a much louder voice screams for me to envelope Lois in a passionate kiss. The latter voice wins.

Twenty minutes later, we're both breathless and glistening with shimmering beads of sweat. Just watching her button up her blouse stirs emotions in me, until Dylan chooses this moment to reawaken the father in me.

"I'll pour some wine," Lois says as I trundle upstairs.

The nursery reeks of dirty nappy, and on changing him I notice the watery, foul smelling mess he presents me with. His little stomach is slightly distended.

On returning to the lounge, I express my concern to Lois.

"Perhaps it's colic, or he senses the anxiety in the atmosphere," she replies.

"Surely not. I think colic sounds most likely."

Satisfied, as she's not overly concerned, I sit in the generous armchair and place him on my lap.

"I wonder about calling the police again," I say.

"And say what? Have you found my wife yet? If they haven't called you it's because they've nothing to say. No news is good news."

Again, I'm pacified, like antacid on a fiery stomach. However, that same quiet voice nudges me gently to worry about Colette. I wonder in the silent moments where she is and what she's doing. I've never considered her a person to have an affair, unlike Lois. Not sure she'd be a trustworthy wife.

But her absence is uncharacteristic, and I'm fretting she's hurt herself more than just cutting her arms or thighs. Has she managed to slice so deeply the blood's flowing freely, emptying her body of its life-force?

Dylan's now fast asleep on my lap, and I feel ready to shut out the troubled day. I stand slowly and Lois follows me with her china blue eyes. Her angular cheekbones look like plinths on which her eyes sit like trophies.

Without words, we clasp each other's hands and mount the stairs towards the bedroom. I tuck Dylan under his blanket and watch him snuggle down with his thumb firmly planted in his tiny mouth. He looks angelic, unlike me. I'm clearly turning into the devil as each hour passes.

I know I should feel shame as I watch Lois undress in my matrimonial bedroom. I should but I don't. What does that say about me?

As she slides under the quilt, I close my eyes and wonder briefly if it would not be easier for all concern if Colette returned and found us in bed. Yes, it would damage her, but it would also free her, she deserves someone better than me.

As I try and let the darkness drown my thoughts, I imagine Colette standing in the doorway; her eyes finally open to my betrayal.

Colette

Finn just stares at me as I walk into the kitchen. It's taken me all night to walk home, encountering men who thought I was a prostitute and drunkards offering me a swig from their battered cans and half-empty bottles of cider along the way.

"God, what's happened to you?" he asks me, standing up with Dylan in his arms. "You look like hell."

I don't know where to begin, nothing that's gone before feels real; and yet I know it's happened, but I can't speak. I daren't share my most profoundly dark experience lest I get blamed; no one would understand.

I'm unaware at first of Finn guiding me to a chair with his free arm. Once seated, fatigue hits me and tears dribble slowly down my dusty cheeks.

"Where have you been? I've been so worried about you."

I detect a hint of annoyance in his voice, but still I can't speak. I want to tell him about the horror of watching Chloe prepare her daughters for death, before watching her plummet to her own demise without a shriek or any utterance at all.

I want to share my last moments with a depressed young woman who'd been given very little chance in life by either her family or society. Her own short life had been a noose around her neck, which gradually tightened as each damning year passed.

And in the end I too let her down. That guilt will remain with me for the rest of my life; no amount of anti-depressants will remove the blackened scar on my mind.

I'm drawn to the noise of creaking floorboards above my head. I look at him and frown.

"Lois stayed the night to look after Dylan in case I was called away to tend to you."

I'm numb to what he's saying as everything seems so insipid compared to the vivid emotions I experienced with Chloe. She flits in and out of my thoughts constantly. And as for Kerry and Rachel, I just hope their souls were swept away by the angels, as it would be preferable to living and knowing your own mother tried to kill you before killing herself. *Poor mites.*

Lois arrives in the kitchen wearing my powder-blue dressing gown.

"Colette, wow, I didn't hear you come in," she says, clearly surprised by how florid her face is.

"She hasn't said a word since coming in. She's catatonic," Finn says.

"Let me make us all a coffee," offers Lois before filling the kettle then sitting at the head of the table. "We've been so worried about you. Did you spend the night with someone from the mum-and-baby group?"

I don't want to engage with them, in case they see too much of me. And once I starting talking I may never be able to stop.

"I suggest you phone her nurse seeing as we can't get through to her," says Lois, getting up to finish making the drinks. "We're not equipped to deal with this."

I want to protest, to tell them I'm fine, but of course I'm not, and I fear the nurse will wheedle the truth out of me. Then where will I be?

I hear Finn on the phone but I can't hear what he's saying. Lois is standing in the kitchen rocking Dylan gently in her arms.

"You can't keep messing Finn and Dylan around," she whispers. "They deserve a happy and stable life."

I know she's right, and I suddenly regret not jumping with Chloe. I'll never be brave enough to do it alone, unless I manage to store enough tablets, but the nurse told me I'd vomit before they took hold of me.

Finn returns and whispers in Lois's ear before taking Dylan from her.

"Do you want to hold your son?" he asks, holding Dylan just above my lap.

I believe Dylan senses my discomfort as he begins to whine before revving-up into a full-blown wail. Finn lifts him over his shoulder and pats his back gently whilst making soothing shushing sounds.

Lois places a mug of coffee in front of me, which I cup my hands around for warmth. She's looking concerned and I want to open up and let her reframe my experience; she was always good at doing that over a bottle of wine.

"The nurse is coming to see you within the hour. Perhaps you should get washed and changed; you look like you've slept in those clothes."

"I haven't slept at all," I reply in a voice I don't recognize.

"Hell, where have you been?" he asks sternly.

"Nowhere in particular."

"You must have been somewhere, or were you just wandering the streets all night? Do you realise how dangerous that was?"

He's snapping at me, so I close down; it's my only source of protection. I hope that by closing my eyes everyone in the room will disappear and I'll be transported back to Chloe's flat before it all happened.

Finn moves swiftly to the front door as the bell rings. I hear him talking rapidly to the nurse as they make their way to the kitchen. Nurse Hannah Morley arrives at my side and kneels.

"Hello, Colette. Everyone's been worried about you. Would you like to talk to me in private?"

I would like privacy from everyone, but I know that's not going to happen. I whisper in her ear that I'll speak to her alone. The others leave and Hannah closes the door.

"How have things been?" she asks, sitting in the chair next to me.

"Dark and confusing."

"In what way?"

"I don't know how I should be feeling. I feel one way but my head tells me I should feel another way." Talking to her is exhausting. All I want now is to sleep.

"Is that why you stayed out all night? Were you trying to sort out the confusion?"

Should I tell her I was trying to kill myself, or would that lead me straight back to hospital? I decide to hide the truth.

"I can't decide whether Finn and Dylan would be better off if I left them. Perhaps they'd be happier?"

"What do you mean by 'left them'?"

"Moved out and moved to a different part of the country," I lie.

"What makes you think that? Has Finn mentioned that?"

"No, it's just something I think about."

"Have you mentioned this to him? You may find it makes him sad that you think this way. It's been a difficult time for you both, but you're pulling through. Things will improve as each day passes; this time will eventually be a distant nightmare."

She means well, but she doesn't realise what I'm hiding. I'll never get over watching Chloe fall, wide-eyed and in silence, as though watching a film in slow-motion without sound. I failed Chloe and I failed her children.

"Are you still taking your medication?"

For a minute I'd forgotten she was here and her voice startles me. I reassure her that I am fighting to get well and I apologise for worrying everyone with my absence.

Hannah asks me about my times with Dylan, and whether I feel I am developing a bond with him. I lie and say I think so. I sense she knows I am lying.

After fifteen minutes of checking for any side effects to the medication and cross-examining me about self-harming, she decides to go. Relieved, I relax and return to the self-loathing I've come to accept as the norm.

Finn and Lois return to the kitchen and mollycoddle me until I feel close to suffocation.

"Why don't you two take a stroll around the garden and I'll prepare Dylan's bottle." Lois suggests.

Finn wraps his arm around my shoulder and guides me into the garden which is beginning to return to life. I pull the chunky-knit cardigan around me as I notice tiny signs of green shoots on the bare tree branches, and miniscule tips forming in clumps around the trunk and in the borders. Spring is burgeoning and I've not noticed until now. Have I become that self-absorbed?

"Are you going to tell me where you were last night?" he finally asks.

"Does it matter?"

"It might help me find you the next time . . . if there is a next time."

"Perhaps I don't want to be found. Are you worried I was with another man?"

"The thought never crossed my mind."

"Am I that unlovable?"

"It's not that, you've just always been a faithful and loyal girlfriend and wife . . ."

"What's wrong?" I ask, as his protracted pause prickles the hairs on the back of my neck.

"Nothing," he smiles, before remarking I look cold and ushers me back inside.

Lois is in the lounge feeding Dylan on the sofa whilst watching a house makeover programme. I've never noticed before how at-home she looks; I find it a touch unnerving but put it down to the remnants of paranoia still lurking in my brain.

She offers me Dylan to take over the feed but I decline, purporting to being tired after the bout of fresh air. I take myself off to lie down, leaving the three of them looking like a reconstituted family in a magazine photo shoot.

I hear them whispering together as I absentmindedly mount the stairs slowly. I try to block the nagging voice in my mind telling me they're talking about me. *Damn paranoia.*

I switch on the TV to block out the negative thoughts, and settle in bed with the duvet pulled up to my chin. Like a slap in the face, the newsreader announces the suspected suicide of a young mother after killing her two young daughters in East Ham. Chloe's photo is flashed up on the screen. *It wasn't a nightmare.*

I fling the quilt back and dash to the bathroom in time to vomit. I wonder whether someone recalls seeing me with her? Questions will be asked by the police and by Finn. The next few days of the inquiry into her death are going to be torturous; waiting for the knock on the door.

Then I remember. My suicide note.

Finn

I can't help feeling relief when Colette takes herself off to bed; which must make me the worst husband in the world. I'm chagrined at my attitude, yet Lois and Diana seem to believe I'm doing nothing wrong.

"I'm surprised the nurse did nothing more than talk to her," Lois says.

"Clearly she's not sick enough to be taken into hospital."

"But you have to go to work, and me or your mother have to care for her."

"You don't have to," I snap more than I intend to.

"But I want to. What I meant to say is having Colette at home is a lot of worry for *you*. I wish to unburden you of that, hence I'm here."

"I thought you were here because we're sleeping together." I know I am spoiling for a fight.

"That too, but Colette is also a dear friend."

As she puts her hand lightly on my arm, I feel my burgeoning anger dissipate and I apologise for my behaviour. She reaches up and puts the plump tip of her finger on my lips. My natural reaction is to kiss it which then progresses to kissing her on her lips. This all feels too normal, as though it's Lois who's the mother of my child and the keeper of my heart.

Instead, I'm married to a distant, uncommunicative, and undemonstrative woman, who prefers solitude to my company. There's little wonder I act as I do. *It's not my fault.*

The key in the front door announces Diana's arrival, and I sense her bristling nature enter before her.

"Was that the nurse I saw pulling away?" she asks in her clipped and proficient tone.

"She's just seen Colette."

"She's back? Are they sectioning her again?"

"No, just monitoring her. She's fine."

"Where is she now?"

"In bed."

"Then she's clearly not fine, is she?"

I clamp my lips shut. This isn't the time to argue.

"Did you find out where she went?" Diana continues.

"She wouldn't say."

"I hope she isn't being sexually promiscuous and touting for sex."

"What are you talking about?" My face is burning as I clench my fists in my pockets.

"I read it on a mental health site. It does happen, which is why she isn't telling you where she's been."

"You've never liked her, have you?" I finally have the argument I've been seeking, and I can't stop goading her for a deeper intensity.

"She's all right for a friend, but when you chose to marry her I knew it was wrong. Your father wouldn't let me persuade you otherwise, and now I blame you both for foisting this mentally incapacitated daughter-in-law on me."

"Maybe I should divorce her and marry Lois?"

"That would be the sensible thing to do, if I thought you were being serious. But you're not. This is an embarrassing mess."

"Oh that's right, you can't show off about your grandson as that would entail talking about Colette. She's ruined your boasting time, hasn't she?" I'm on a roll.

"Not only has she been in a psychiatric hospital, but you now have the mental health team invading your privacy. Is this what you want?"

"Of course it isn't what I bloody want, but Colette doesn't want it either. This isn't making her happy. God you're so blinkered. If you included Colette in the bigger picture, you'd take into consideration what all this is doing to her."

Diana's face is glowing with tiny droplets of sweat as she puffs out her chest to blast me again, only Lois enters the room with a groggy Dylan in her arms.

"I think I'll put him down, then make a pot of tea."

Her presence is like a breath of fresh air, mingled with her intoxicating perfume.

"You're an angel, Lois," Diana says, gazing adoringly at Dylan. "Where would my boys be without you?"

I'd be a faithful husband.

"Now you're here, Diana, I'd like to nip home and get changed," Lois says in her sing-song voice.

"Changed?" Diana says looking between us both. "Did you stay the night?"

"For moral support, and in case I was called out, someone needed to be here for Dylan. I couldn't trouble you in the middle of the night." My mind's racing, and unnecessary words are spewing out of my mouth. I always did over-explain as a child when I was flustered and guilty, and here I am, doing it again. She'll know; mothers always do.

"As I keep reiterating, thank goodness for Lois. So what are you going to do now?"

I look at her, confused.

"What are you going to do about Colette's behaviour? We can't babysit her forever."

"I've been running my business from here, Diana. In fact, I'm bringing some pashminas over to wrap and send off tomorrow. You see, it's all sorted."

Lois looks slightly smug as she declares her actions, and although I am indebted to her, I can't help wondering whether this is more about her needs rather than Colette's. But I suspect Colette would rather have her here than Diana, so I say nothing.

"Well I believe it won't be long until she requires sectioning again, mark my words." Diana moves on to showing the new outfits she's bought for Dylan, and whilst the pair coo over the cuteness, I take the opportunity to go upstairs and see Colette.

I push the door open slightly and peer in to see her lying on the bed, her eyes wide open, staring at the ceiling.

"Can I come in?"

"It's your bedroom too, why the need to ask?"

"I don't know really, everything's different and I'm not sure how to be at times."

"You're still my husband, and Dylan's father."

I nod, moving closer to her to perch on the edge of the bed. I see she's lost weight, hollowing her cheeks, and making her look older.

"Lois is taking over staying with you whilst I'm at work. You won't see much of Diana, which I'm sure will make you happy."

"I've forgotten what happy feels like."

"Doesn't holding your baby and smelling his head make you feel happy? It does me."

She shrugs, gazing past me, seemingly lost in her darkened world. I sense an element of compassion fatigue setting in my mind again, making work seem preferable compared to here.

"Would a trip to the hairdressers or café lift you?"

"I care for neither of those . . . I've seen things . . ."

She's making no sense to me as she trails off, and I wonder whether she's experiencing visual hallucinations. Perhaps Diana's right; we need to keep a close eye on her mental state.

I'm also riddled with anxiety about the regular close proximity of Lois. I'm not sure how it's going to affect me, and I'm not sure how she's going to behave. *Can I trust her?*

Colette

Lois puts a cup of coffee and the local newspaper in front of me, before wrapping a cornflower-blue pashmina on the kitchen table. It's pleasant sitting with her, and even nicer not having to talk.

I turn the newspaper over to find a picture of Chloe staring up at me. The article confirms the link between her death and the death of her two daughters, professing that the murder-suicide was the action of a depressed single mother.

It went on to talk about the state of her shabby flat, and toyed with the idea of her being involved with drugs, alcohol, or even prostitution. They belittle her attempt at motherhood, although the nursery declared Kerry was well cared for.

Remorse wells-up inside me; I shouldn't have let her jump alone, even though we're all alone in reality, and when death finally comes, we face the darkness unaccompanied. But I had that rare opportunity not to be alone and not to abandon Chloe. I hate myself on so many levels.

I wonder about Kerry and Rachel. Did they look just as angelic asleep as they did awake? Did they sense the closeness of their sibling when they drifted into the black soup that eventually engulfs us all, or were they painfully aware of abandonment?

I feel to blame for their demise; I helped seal the flat, and now I'm being punished by memories and sordid images. I almost told Finn about it last night, but I thought he'd freak out and call the police.

"What's that you're reading?" Lois asks.

I briefly tell the story and she listens gravely.

"At least she had the decency to kill herself, pity she took the children though."

"Why do you say that?"

"Because she was making life a misery for those around her, so suicide was the only answer. You have to admire her bravery at jumping."

Tears prickle my eyes as I think of those last seconds with Chloe. I wish I'd done the same so my photo was also on the front page.

"She could have survived had she had more help and money."

"How do you know that?" Lois replies incredulously.

"I don't know for sure, I'm just guessing. It can't be easy being a single mum to two under-fives."

"Then she shouldn't have got pregnant. Contraception's free."

"Maybe she wanted someone to love her or stick around. Life's never that straightforward."

I'm finding this conversation exhausting. I don't like the way she's judgemental about someone she's never met.

"You're very touchy. Are you feeling tired?" she asks.

"I'm shattered, but I can't sleep, so don't ask me to go to bed."

"I wasn't going to, but I wondered whether you'd like to make Dylan's bottle up or just feed him?"

I want to say neither, but choose to say the latter so as not to raise alarm.

"Has the post arrived?" I ask nonchalantly.

Lois stands with her back to me, making the feed. She shakes her head, so her waist-length ponytail brushes gently from side to side; I'm transfixed like watching a metronome.

"How come you've stayed single for so long?" I ask.

"The right man hasn't come along. Let's face it, Ian was a bloody bore. We couldn't open a bottle of wine without him giving me a fifteen-minute lecture on its origin and grape variety."

"He was attentive though."

"There wasn't that unfathomable physical attraction; I need that gravitational pull on a daily basis."

"You ask for too much. Sex always dwindles in long-term relationships."

"Not if you're with the right person."

"How would you know? The longest relationship you've had is about four years."

"I just know. So, you and Finn have been together about ten years, has the sex dwindled?"

I feel embarrassed. I'm used to dissecting a relationship over a few glasses of wine; it's harder and more intrusive sober.

I put the cool back of my hands against my fiery cheeks whilst considering what to say. "Well obviously, since Dylan's birth things haven't been the same."

"Is that more to do with you or Finn, would you say?"

I hadn't thought about it in depth, but on reflection I would say me. "This illness has taken its toll on me. I just don't feel the same."

"It must be hard on Finn too."

I shrug; I care not to answer as she hands me Dylan's warm bottle. She then passes over Dylan and watches me as I settle him in the crook of my arm, placing the teat in his mouth.

"There, you see, you've settled into the mummy-role nicely."

I smile weakly before staring into Dylan's eyes which are fixated on me. Perhaps he's wondering who I am. I wish him no harm, but I'm longing to slice my own flesh to relieve my internal pain and confusion.

I miss Chloe. Who can I talk to now? Do I risk meeting someone else on the site lest they also pull me into their suicidal intent?

Dylan starts spluttering on the milk and begins crying and wriggling around. He pushes his feet into my thigh and arches his back, causing a panicky sensation to rise up my throat. Lois swoops in and whisks him out of my arms. I feel relieved.

"He's such a colicky baby," Lois declares, slinging him over her shoulder and patting his back firmly, so his cries now sound like hiccups.

"I feel you know him more than I do," I tell her.

"Perhaps I do, but you're still his mother. Has this put you off having another baby?"

"Oh yes. The thought of being shut on a hospital ward with a bunch of mad people again is enough to put anyone off having a baby. I'd rather kill myself than go through that again." *I've said too much.*

"Would you jump off a high building if you had to?"

"I'm not good with heights, so no. I'd use tablets and alcohol."

"You've thought about it then."

"Only in passing." I don't want to be having this conversation, I feel she's tricking me.

Dylan's quietened down and has reverted to sucking his thumb. I ache to want to hold him, but I've no strong bond pulling me towards him. Lois takes him up to the nursery, leaving me stewing in my dark thoughts, and wondering whether I'll have enough privacy to cut myself soon.

"I thought I'd pop out and get some ingredients to make a meal for this evening; save you cooking," she says on returning, switching on the baby monitor. "It'll be a nice welcome home for Finn."

"You don't have to. Finn's been managing."

"That's my point, he needs caring for, life's been hard of late. I won't be long." She picks up her bag before grabbing her coat from the banister.

So here I am, alone at last. I walk over to the wooden knife block and study the stainless-steel handles; touching each one to decide which one to use for a change. I'm not sure my usual knife is working for me. I make my decision and slide it out of the slot before wrapping it in a tea towel.

Upstairs, I peer into the nursery to check he's asleep before creeping to the bathroom and locking the door.

I hardly recognise myself in the mirror. My angular cheekbones look like they could pierce through my skin at any given moment. My cheeks are hollow, and my mouth's in a permanent pinched position. I'm not surprised Finn's turned-off me.

I feel so angry about events, I want to slit my wrists and be done with life altogether, but I'm a coward.

Angrily, I push the point of the knife into my skin until it pops, then draw the blade along the inside of my arm until a thin line of blood bubbles through the sliver. I'm mesmerised by the sight of the red gloop, and imagine my illness and stress dripping out of my soul as the blood runs down my arm and splats into the white sink. It looks like art that would sell for thousands, making me smile briefly.

I start another slice; it makes me feel alive. In fact, it's the only thing to make me feel at all. Not one person around me can do this, although Chloe came close.

I'm lost in the vision of red when hearing the sound of the front door closing jolts me. Lois calls out and I call back, monitoring the tone of my voice.

Her premature arrival curtails my special time so my anxiety level rises uncontrollably. I reach for the plasters in the cabinet and quickly mask the two cuts, hoping they don't bleed through. I rinse out the sink then attempt to trot downstairs, pulling my sleeves down as far as they will go.

"I thought I'd cook lamb shanks with rosemary and roast Mediterranean vegetables," Lois informs me as she carries the shopping into the kitchen.

"That's Finn's favourite meal."

"Really? How fortuitous."

I watch her deftly move around the area and feel a dull pang of jealousy as she seems to own my kitchen.

Suddenly it dawns on me; I'm beginning to experience a variety of emotions rather than just the dull black gloom that's swaddled me for the past few months. Maybe the cutting's working? I decide not to divulge the shift in my wellbeing; I don't want to be abandoned until I'm truly ready.

"Would you like help with the veg?" I offer quietly.

"No, I'm fine thanks. You could prepare Dylan's next feed, though."

Everything comes back to Dylan, but I suppose I should take a more active role in his upbringing. I shuffle to the area of the kitchen, which is cluttered with his feeding paraphernalia, and begin to measure out the formula. I remember from antenatal class that breast milk is better for a baby but between my illness and medication regime, Dylan was not to be blessed with the natural feed. Another area I've failed in as a mother.

"Are you struggling?" Lois asks.

"No, I'm fine."

Dylan wakes with a thunderous cry, demanding attention from the very moment he opens his eyes. With leaden legs, I climb the stairs to fetch him, anxious to get everything right in front of an audience.

He sees me as I peek over the top of his cot, but the tone of his cry doesn't change. I lean in and hoist him out, waiting for his wail to abate, but it persists.

I place him over my shoulder, patting his back gently. But clearly milk is going to be the only pacifier, so I walk gingerly downstairs and pick up his warmed bottle. I choose to sit in the lounge away from Lois, whom I feel is watching me just that little bit too closely, but I don't blame her; I'd do the same in her position.

Dylan sucks hungrily on the teat, his eyes drawn to my face. His podgy fingers attempt to grasp and hold the bottle which is clearly too large for his little hand.

Once again, Dylan starts to squirm and writhe around on my lap, making it difficult to keep the teat in his mouth, forcing him to gulp down mouthfuls of air.

"That won't help his colic," tuts Lois, entering the room.

"What won't help his colic? What are you doing to my grandson?" snaps Diana, following behind.

I smile weakly with a helpless look in my eyes. Diana approaches and whisks Dylan from my arms before slinging him over her shoulder to try and extract the trapped wind in his stomach.

All I can think about is intercepting the letter. *Where the bloody hell is it?*

Finn

"You're a wicked, mad excuse for a wife and mother. You're not to be trusted with Dylan, and I'll make sure Finn sees things clearly."

I hear this on stepping inside. Rushing to where the commotion's coming from, I find the three women in my life and my son all gathered together. My heart plummets to my guts.

"About time, Finn. We need to deal with Colette before she kills your son," Diana implores.

"What's going on?" I dare ask, not really wanting this after my hard day at work.

"She can't even feed him properly with a bottle. The poor dear's swallowing air; no wonder he has tummy troubles."

"Lois?" I want her opinion.

"I was preparing dinner, but I'm sure Dylan was just being fidgety. I'm sure Colette wouldn't mean to harm him. It's still early days, Diana." Lois smiles weakly.

Diana's face softens momentarily until she glances in Colette's direction. Colette's eyes drift across mine before she rushes upstairs and slams the bedroom door.

"You didn't have to be so cruel," I comment.

"You should've heard your son. His distressed cry was so loud I swear the neighbours thought she was trying to kill him."

"I don't need this; I've only just got home."

"I'll make you a cup of tea or pour you a beer," offers Lois, placing her hand on my arm.

"Beer, please. Don't look at me like that, Mum. I'm an adult now."

"It's not the beer, it's your wife. I can't stand by and watch her destroy your life and that of Dylan's. She'll never be a Forbes in the true sense of the name, and I blame you."

"I don't know what you expect me to do? Are you suggesting I divorce her?"

"I'm suggesting you have her committed; not to be released until she's mentally sound."

I realise I'm grinding my teeth to prevent acrid words spewing out of my mouth. I know things are difficult with Colette, I really comprehend that deeply, but she *is* Dylan's mother.

"Here," Lois says, handing me a beer.

I savour the cool liquid as it descends my throat. Gazing at the scene from over the rim of the glass, I'm wondering what impact I'm having on it. Am I the glue to keep us all together, or am I the corrosion that will inevitability split us and leave us all damaged?

Diana's rubbing Dylan's back in slow, rhythmic movements, but nothing eases him. His crying is sawing through my temples like a jagged blade.

"Dylan needs to see a doctor," Diana declares over the din. "You never cried like this as a baby. My poor Dylan."

"I'll check the diary and see when the health visitor's next due," I reply, desperately trying to keep the situation under control, and away from the mental health aspect.

"I doubt he needs a doctor," Lois pipes up. "He's probably just stressed with the commotion in the house."

Diana seems pacified when Lois speaks, even though she has no children. I feel indignant, but relieved she's taken charge, and Dylan is now silently sucking his thumb. Praise to Lois indeed.

"Colette doesn't need watching by all of us at once," I say quietly.

"Am I not allowed to visit my grandson if Lois is here?"

"I didn't mean . . . you know what I mean. Don't be so facetious."

She rolls her eyes and pouts with a down-turned mouth; she always got 'round Dad with that look. And perhaps it works on me too as I now feel guilty. "You know you're welcome any time."

"I'm not sure Colette feels the same."

"She's still unwell. I'm sure she'll be back to normal soon." I cringe at my choice of word.

"Only time will tell," she sniffs.

Lois moves closer and places her hand on my shoulder. Her sly wink tells me she's on my side. I feel some kind of relief.

"Let's eat. I'll see if Colette wants to come down. You can sit with us with Dylan if you fancy," she says turning to Diana.

She bounds upstairs with the vitality of a fourteen-year-old. Diana and I sit at the table, enveloped in the mouth-watering aroma of lamb and rosemary.

Lois returns, informing us Colette's asleep, and she didn't want to disturb her.

"Probably for the best. You're such an accomplished cook," Diana says, watching Lois plate up the food, including one for Colette for later. "You'll make someone a fine wife one day."

"I'm not sure there's anyone to match up to my standards. Besides, all the best ones are taken." She throws me a brief glance.

"Then just take one."

"Don't encourage her to be a home wrecker," I blast.

"Some homes are already wrecked; she might as well swoop in and procure the man before he's taken by someone else."

I shake my head as the two women titter under their breath. I want Dylan to be older to even out the gender imbalance; otherwise I'll have to get a male dog.

My isolation's soon forgotten when I taste the food. Diana has a smile on her face as she watches me; announcing she'll go soon, to let us relax.

Lois's eyes trace the outline of my face finally settling on my lips, where beads of sweat spring forth. She leans forward to reach for the pepper, brushing her arm against mine. Maybe relaxing with Lois is still possible whilst Colette sleeps. *What am I thinking?*

Colette

I sense someone at the bedroom door, and soon Lois's unmistakable perfume filters in. I concentrate on keeping still, but I don't have to wait long before she retreats.

The smell travelling upstairs is homely and welcoming, yet I feel neither in the house. *House*, not home.

Yet there were times when I was relaxed, happy, hardworking, and loving, in this very house. Then I had Dylan. The nurse said I shouldn't demonise him, but it's so easy to do. I know I've to contend with the looming christening. I'm not sure if I have the mental strength to get through it, so I push it to the attic in my mind.

I hear Diana's voice then the front door closing. I tiptoe to the window to check she's actually leaving, and to my relief I see her climb into her car and melt into the distance.

I move and press my ear to the gap in the doorway to hear Finn and Lois talking. I imagine I'm the topic of conversation and not in a positive way. I'm tempted to go down, but I fear I've lost the ability to be sociable; or perhaps fearful of what I might hear. They're probably more content without me.

The light in my mind is dimming and the blackness is pushing me towards the knife in my jewellery box. Screams are building up in my head, and risk driving me mad if I don't obey the craving. The urge is so strong, and my resolve recedes further from my grasp until I'm holding the knife in my hand and studying the blood-smeared blade.

Lois's laugh trickles into the room. I know that laugh. She does that when flirting with men in pubs and clubs. I try brushing that thought from my mind, but it's intent on staying, not at the forefront of my mind, but by clinging to the rafters to be discovered another time.

Her interruption's allowed the urge to cut to pass, so I quickly replace the knife in the box and return to bed. Sitting up this time rather than cowering under the covers. I try sorting my thoughts into a logical pattern to try viewing them more clearly.

Finn . . . Dylan . . . Lois . . . Diana . . . the black smoke of depression; they all play a part in the mystery of my downfall. I'm determined to climb out of this dingy well to feel the soft green grass under my feet once more.

This illness has given me the time and space to reflect on my life, to assess what makes me happy and what doesn't. All these people contribute to the black smoke in one way or another. I need to sift through them and jettison those who offend me. Who will stay and who will go? I decide.

By the time Lois leaves, it's half past eleven, which is late for a work night for Finn, who usually prefers to go to sleep at ten forty-five. Her car is down the road before the front door closes, as though he's stood there waving her off. Another abnormality for Finn. Distorted images pelt my mind like a relentless snowball fight amongst children. I can't tell what's real or fantasy.

I lie here waiting for Finn to come up, but after twenty minutes I decide to go and find him. Wrapping my dressing gown around me, I creep downstairs and find him lying on the sofa listening to softly playing jazz music.

He looks so peaceful, like the Finn I remember. His crew cut resembles a soft-bristle paintbrush, and his long eyelashes curl so much they almost touch the eyelid. Dylan has the same eyelashes.

"Are you coming in or just stare at me in a creepy fashion?" he asks quietly.

"I didn't want to disturb you." I enter the lounge and sit in the oversized armchair, allowing myself to be swallowed whole.

"Are you feeling better?" he asks.

"The rest has done me good. Having the house to ourselves is also helping."

"You know we can't leave you on your own for long."

"I know, but when you're home—"

"Lois is kind enough to cook for me. I can hardly send her home without sharing the food. I can't be rude."

"I'm not asking you to be, I just find it calmer when we're on our own."

"I can't take any more time off work; they've been good enough as it is."

I exhale, giving me time to consider my words. "You don't seem to be listening to me. I'm just trying to explain how I feel about things."

"These past weeks have only been about your feelings and viewpoint. I want to move on and get on with our lives. Your paranoia and negativity spoil so much."

I feel like he's punched me in the stomach, taking my breath away. Bulbous tears topple from my eyes.

"Please don't bloody cry. I'm close to the edge and I'm struggling to keep a grip on our family. You've got to get stronger."

"I'm trying, truly I am. I've so many negative thoughts, making a positive outlook difficult to envisage." I press my fingernails into my palms to quell the tears. "I haven't heard you play the piano for ages."

"Not in the mood and not enough time."

"I miss it."

"I miss lots of things."

"You're laying the blame firmly at my door, aren't you?"

He doesn't respond, telling me loudly I'm right. Does he think I like what's happened to me, to us?

"Come to bed?" I ask softly.

"I want to listen to a few more tracks. I'll be up in a bit."

I'm crushed, but I don't want to quarrel. I've one more thing to ask. "Who's coming to mind me tomorrow?"

"Diana first thing as Lois has to go to the post office. She said she'd get here mid-morning."

I don't tell him how unhappy I am about Diana coming, I know he knows. But does he care? I don't know?

I stand to leave just as Dylan announces he's hungry, so I offer to make the feed as Finn fetches him down. *See, I can do team work too, Finn.*

He enters the kitchen with Dylan wailing in his arms, just as I'm checking the temperature of the milk. He takes the bottle from me and sits down at the table.

"Would you like me to feed him?"

"I'm fine. Why don't you go to bed; I'll be up after this."

Another knife plunges into my heart as I walk away, listening to Finn talking soothingly to his son.

Morning comes around too soon as I watch Finn straighten his tie, before grabbing a slice of toast.

"You're in court today I see."

"Yes, with yet another failure. This guy can't stay off crack. Prison's his only option."

He looks so handsome in his grey suit and British racing green tie; kind of reminds me of our wedding day. I will never forget his face when he first saw me in my white wedding dress. The image is tattooed on the inside of my eyelids.

He bends down and kisses Dylan and me on the top of our heads. I've forgotten what a proper kiss feels like.

As he opens the front door I hear voices and realise Diana has arrived. I brace myself for the onslaught of malicious comments about my mothering capabilities.

"Oh, you're up," Diana says on entering the kitchen. "How's my little Dylan," she continues, taking him from me.

"Would you like a coffee," I offer in a flat tone.

She eyes me around Dylan's head and mutters yes. I shuffle around slowly waiting for her to belittle me in some way. I don't have to wait for long.

"Lois cooked a fabulous meal last night. Finn thoroughly enjoyed it. You'd imagine your culinary skills would be better than hers seeing as you're the wife."

"Finn's never complained about my food."

"He's too considerate of other people's needs. He's a sensitive soul. I worry about him working with bad people."

"He loves his job."

"That's beside the point. He should have become a barrister as I wanted."

I stop myself from imparting a sarcastic comment; she doesn't need encouraging. I bring both mugs of coffee to the table, and attempt to take Dylan from her.

"I'm not sure he's safe with you."

"I've never harmed him and I never will. My illness turned me against me and no one else." I control my voice even though my heart is pounding wildly.

"I don't trust you. You need to prove yourself to me first. Dylan is so precious; I have to protect him from harm."

I want to scratch her face and rip him from her saggy-skin arms, but decorum prevents me. I don't want to give her a reason to say *I told you so*.

I have to bide my time.

Finn

Court is harrowing as the offender breaks down when he's ordered back to prison. He sobs, saying he doesn't cope there, begging for a second chance. The only thing is, he's had a second and third chance; returning to prison's the only option left. I recommend suicide watch and a mental health assessment to cover all the bases. I'm becoming quite tuned-in to that arena.

Parking my car outside the office, Lois suddenly appears before me.

"Hi, I wonder if we could have lunch together?" she asks in an unmistakably sultry tone.

I glance at my watch and agree to go to the local café, even though a voice in my head is screaming profanities at me.

As she links her arm through mine, I notice colleagues staring at us through the windows.

"I couldn't wait to see you."

I unhook her arm from mine so we can enter the café, then lead us to my usual table in the corner. We sit and study the menu briefly, before Flo walks over and takes our order.

"Why aren't you speaking to me?" Lois demands.

"I'm trying to find the right words to say."

"As long as those words don't include you don't want to be with me anymore."

I lean into her across the table. "I don't want to stop being with you; I just wish I didn't feel so guilty."

"The only way you'd feel free of guilt is if you left her."

"How's that going to make me feel any better?"

"We wouldn't have to hide our true feelings; and you'd get away from Colette's mad world."

"I think she's getting better."

"What makes you say that?"

"She was more her normal self last night."

"But she could have a breakdown at any moment; do you really want to live like that?"

"That's not necessarily the case. You read too much rubbish on the web."

"It's for your own good. I care about you, that's all."

"I know, and I appreciate it, really I do, but I can't abandon her. She'll always be a part of my life along with Dylan. He counts for a lot too."

"Then bring him with you. I'll be his godmother tomorrow. Come and live with me, there's plenty of room."

"I couldn't take Dylan from her; children should stay with their mothers."

"Not if their mother's a crumbling mental mess."

Flo arrives with our food. I take a bite out of my sausage-and-egg sandwich, yoke and red sauce oozes from the edges.

"I'm going to be honest," I whisper, wiping the corner of my mouth. "I love both of you and it's killing me."

She reaches across the table and squeezes my hand.

"You know I love you, too. I've loved you since sixth form, and for you to reciprocate is a dream come true."

"Not quite the dream you imagined, though. Loving you both means things have to stay as they are. Colette will improve and Dylan will grow into a bright little boy. I have to be around to provide for them. You must remember that I love you in the moments we can't be together."

"I'm used to getting my own way, you realise. You'll see eventually."

"See what?"

"That Colette's not the right woman for you."

"You're wrong. Please don't spoil what we have."

"I won't spoil anything, but Colette might, mark my words."

"You sound like Diana."

"We women can see things you men can't. But I'm looking out for you, so don't worry."

"I wasn't worried, but now I'm not so sure. Are you insinuating Colette could harm me in some way?"

"Who knows where her madness could take her?"

The egg in my sandwich has congealed and looks unappetising, so I push the plate to one side and take a gulp of coffee. I don't want to discuss this topic further.

"I've got to get back to work. Are you going to rescue Colette from Diana?"

"Of course, she's still my best friend."

"Not sure how that'll hold out if she discovers the truth about us."

"Let's make sure that doesn't happen, until things change."

I frown at her.

"Until we're finally together. I get what I want, remember?"

I smile a smile that doesn't reach my eyes. Somehow I feel uneasy by her attitude.

"Can't wait to see you at the christening tomorrow," she says, pecking me on the cheek.

Christ, I'm dreading tomorrow.

Diana's already here, two hours early, just to check Dylan's presentable, and Colette's mentally stable.

"I've brought the Forbes' christening gown; we mustn't break with tradition," she says as she drapes it over the back of the sofa. "How is my precious grandson this morning?"

"He's had a good night's sleep, so he should be fine."

"And Colette?"

"Fine too. Why don't you make some coffee, whilst I have some breakfast?"

I follow her to the kitchen, watching her scan the house for signs of disorder and un-cleanliness. I cringe as we enter the kitchen seeing a mound of ironing piled on a chair, threatening to tumble at any given moment. Diana has clearly seen it as she rolls her eyes before filling the kettle.

"Everyone's coming," she says proudly. "The sun's shining and it's going to be a magnificent day. I hope Colette doesn't spoil it. You're sure she's up to coming?"

"Of course. We can hardly stop her, anyway."

"We could if we think she'll ruin the day with her antics."

My head's already throbbing and the day's not yet swung into action. I resist counter-arguing with her as Colette appears with Dylan in her arms.

I pour her a coffee and warm a pre-made bottle for Dylan, who has his fingers entwined in Colette's necklace. He looks fascinated and innocent as he sits on her lap; they look cute together.

"Shall I feed him so you can have a shower?" I offer.

"I'm okay, thanks. Is Lois joining us here or meeting us at church?"

"I don't know exactly. Do you want me to phone her?" I suppose I want a reason to call her to check she's not planning anything nefarious.

"Good grief, you two," Diana chides, "Lois is capable of sorting herself out, whereas neither of you are ready."

"There's still time, don't worry."

It doesn't take long for Dylan to start choking on the milk. His splutters sound distressing, and Diana is quick to show her annoyance with Colette before removing Dylan from her.

Colette looks beseechingly at me, but I'm weak and loathsome, letting Diana take control. Letting her win.

Shortly she'll be in her element at the christening, Colette will be overwhelmed, and I will be keeping my eye on Lois as she becomes Dylan's godmother. I hope I survive.

Colette

The rays of sun entering the bedroom are helping to slowly lift my mood. However, thinking about the day ahead is filling me with trepidation.

I towel dry my hair vigorously before blasting it with the hairdryer. I'm aware of not having Lois's long, sleek hair, nor her slender figure. My stomach still hasn't sprung back enough to accommodate my skinny jeans.

Time passes too quickly, and as I spritz on some perfume I hear Diana calling out that the limousine's here. She's treating this occasion like a wedding, with a limousine, flowers for the church, and a reception in a hotel afterwards. She's even dressed like the mother of the bride, in a white skirt and matching jacket, with a fuchsia peony pinned on the lapel.

Finn has obediently donned his pale grey suit with a small-check powder-blue shirt, and a fuchsia bow tie, and no doubt Lois will look stunning as usual.

As for me, Lois bought me a light-yellow dress, peppered with tiny red flowers and minuscule white bows. She has lent me her white ballet pumps and matching handbag. The outfit is very Lois but the hair and body is very much mine.

Lois is in the kitchen when I descend, looking stunning in a tightly fitting lilac dress, mauve kitten heels and her hair loosely tumbling over her shoulders like a honey-coloured cashmere wrap. She looks ethereal.

"You look stunning, doesn't she, Finn?" Lois proclaims.

"You look beautiful, darling."

Diana bustles in to repeat the news about the limousine. Handing Dylan over to Finn so she can straighten her clothes, she barely acknowledges me.

We all pile in to the limousine, and I end up sitting next to George, who quietly tells me I look lovely, and pats my hand.

A crowd is hanging around outside the church in the dappled sunshine. I recognise most people, and those I don't greet Diana or Finn with a certain amount of familiarity.

People are gazing at Dylan and smiling, but I also sense people staring at me, in awe of seeing a mentally unstable person in the flesh, no doubt. Part of me wants to give them what they want and act up like a woman requiring heavy sedation, but I don't want to give Diana the satisfaction. Besides, I imagine she's hired some undercover bodyguards who are ready to whisk me away if my behaviour deteriorates.

We enter the church before moving to the font at the front. I stand next to Lois and she squeezes my hand, offering me a warm smile; I'd be lost without her.

The ceremony's a blur and before I know it, Dylan's being anointed with holy water and crying at being woken up. His tiny hand gets caught up in the christening gown, and as I move to rescue him, Diana glares at me, so I shrink back.

Dylan's in Finn's arm, and his new godmother is standing by his side and I'm on the other side. George is standing next to me and Diana's hovering around Finn and Lois. I sense the congregation staring at me, and it's disconcerting. Tiny particles of sweat emerge under my armpits and along my back, slowly trickling down my spine.

A photographer's taking pictures, and Lois is glowing with the attention. I love watching her enigmatic persona urging people to admire and love her, defying them to ignore her.

"Ready to go?" Finn whispers in my ear.

I nod and begin walking out as the congregation rises to follow us.

White clouds partially obscure the sun as we step outside. The photographer is busy snapping every movement we make, before announcing the order he wishes people to group themselves in.

Diana's competing with Lois for attention. She links arms with her son, pouts, and throws her head back when she laughs.

"How are you holding up?" Lois enquires, sidling up to me.

"I'm fed up of feeling like a freak show. People I don't even recognise seem to be staring at me, waiting for me to break down in hysterics."

"You worry too much. And the people you don't know are Diana's friends."

"How do you know that?"

"She told me all about her plans for the day. I seem to remember she was a bit like this about your wedding."

I roll my eyes and smile wryly, realising I shouldn't have expected Diana to be any other way.

"By the way, is everything all right with Finn?" she asks me.

"Yes, why?"

"Nothing . . . Well, he seems to be getting home late from work quite regularly."

"And?"

She leans into me, looking around before speaking again. "Well my friend, Sally, her husband was doing the same and it transpired he was seeing a work colleague for three months before she found out."

I put my hand over my throat, sensing a red rash appearing. "You don't think Finn's doing the same, surely?"

"All I'm saying is be mindful of how often he's late, or speaking furtively on the phone, or dropping the same colleague's name into conversations."

I take a deep breath to consolidate her views, but before I can reply, Finn walks up.

"We're ready to move off to the hotel now," he says, smiling at us both. "It's almost over."

The end of the meal has finally arrived and I've managed to see very little of Diana, although George has been rather sweet to me. Maybe he pities me?

Finn carries Dylan to the car, where he promptly falls asleep in his car seat. We all travel back in a weary silence, and I'm trying to picture Finn having an affair. It seems incredulous, but then we've hardly been a couple in the traditional sense since the birth of Dylan; he's been more of a carer than a lover. Perhaps he does have another woman? He works with plenty of dynamic women, who don't have a mental health issue. What could be more tempting?

"I'll have to visit my godson often to impart my wisdom," Lois giggles as we arrive home.

I notice Finn scowling at her, but I am too tired to care right now.

Finn

Lois's request for me to call in after work sounded rather urgent. Even though I said I'd rather go straight home and relieve Diana from carer duty, Lois insisted, saying she has something important to say.

She answers the front door very quickly as though she's been waiting for me on the other side.

"What's so important you couldn't tell me on the phone?" I ask, following her to the lounge and sitting next to her on the sofa like an obedient puppy.

"I just needed a hug, and you can't give me that over the phone."

"You made it sound really important. Why so needy?"

"You don't know the depth of my love for you and Dylan."

"What about Colette? Do you at least care for her as a good friend should?"

"Of course I do. Why do you ask?"

"Because I'll always care for her. I know she's ill, this isn't the real Colette. But I do want the real one back."

"And I thought you wanted me."

"We've been down this road, Lois, I can't say or do any more. I have to get home." I stand to leave.

"Don't I even get a hug?"

She stands up and moves closer, wrapping her arms around me so I have no choice in the matter.

"I need a daily hug from you. I can either grab a secret one in your home, or you can pop in here after work to give me one I can truly enjoy."

"This is really a bad time to have an affair; I don't know what I was thinking."

"You're not thinking of ending it, are you?"

"No, I'm just not thinking straight about anything at the moment." I hug her hard, hoping to pacify her.

"You don't think Colette would harm Dylan, do you? To get back at you for her illness. She does blame you and Dylan for making her ill, I'm sure."

"Why are you filling my head with worries like that? You don't believe she would, do you?"

"Who knows what a woman like that could do if her mind was tormented enough?"

I feel short of breath. "I have to get back, I'm later than I said I'd be." I give her one last hug before heading home with her words ricocheting around my mind.

I'm greeted by the noise of Dylan crying as I arrive home. Blundering into the lounge, I find Diana pacing up and down, bouncing Dylan in her arms.

"What's wrong with him?" I ask.

"He must have colic."

"Where's Colette?"

"Upstairs," she informs me over Dylan's din.

Our bedroom door's closed so I knock before walking straight in.

"You're home late. Busy day at work?"

"Yes, as always. How are you feeling?"

"Better now you're here so Diana can go home."

"Still not getting on with her?"

"What do you think? I was never really accepted as your wife, but since this illness, I'm like a weed on a golf course, I spoil the look of the whole green."

"You're not making sense. Why don't you come downstairs and have some dinner?"

She doesn't move, but grips the quilt more tightly. I sense her reluctance so I leave quietly, only to bump into Diana on the landing.

"He needs changing," she informs me, heading to the nursery.

"I'll do it. Why don't you head home now?"

"What about tomorrow?"

"Lois is coming over."

She smiles her saccharine smile and squeezes my arm before trotting downstairs without saying goodbye to Colette. I enter the nursery to find Dylan's nappy is not a pretty sight and I wonder if I'll ever get used to this.

With a fresh nappy on, he quietens down, allowing me to hold him protectively. Should I really be worried about Colette? The medical team didn't think so.

My mobile rings; the screen tells me it's Lois.

"I'm just phoning to check everything's all right."

"Of course. How are you?"

"You've only just seen me . . . Oh, Colette's there, isn't she?"

"That's right. It would be great to catch up one day. Sorry, I have my son to attend to. Bye."

"Who was that?"

"Just one of the guys from the jazz club. He hasn't seen me since Dylan's birth."

"Do you miss going?"

"Yes, but I'll return there once you get better."

"You think I'll get better then?"

"Of course." I pause to regroup my thoughts. "Do you regret having Dylan?" My mouth's dry, and my palms are sweaty.

"That's a strange question as there's nothing I could do about it now if I did."

Her evasion of answering the question worries me.

"Let's go and see if we can rustle something up for dinner."

She follows me in abject silence, and I wonder whether she regrets how our life has become, as I do.

Colette

Lois's words are stomping around my head, leaving muddy footprints on the lining of my skull. Not only was Finn home late tonight, but he received a strange call. Does he think I believe for one minute it was a guy from the jazz club?

I'm not hungry, so I hold Dylan as Finn rummages around in the fridge. I thought Diana would have prepared something for her precious son, but maybe compassion fatigue's setting in; a family trait, no doubt.

I keep ruminating over his question as to whether I regret having Dylan. Some days I would say a shaky yes, but other days he's more precious to me than anything else. I fluctuate, and that's troubling, as I anticipate life will only get harder as he grows up. Will I end up screaming at him that I wish I'd never given birth to him when he's a teenager full of angst and venom; as I once was?

I didn't think about what being a mother would be like before I fell pregnant. I have a fragile relationship with my own parents, so perhaps I should have thought about it more deeply before agreeing to have a baby. I wanted to make Finn happy; but is he happy now?

All this reflecting over happiness and children has made me think of Chloe, Kerry, and Rachel. Did she ever think about what parenting was about before getting pregnant—twice?

Chloe's depression took any joy away from her, leaving her a husk of a human being living in a dank cave. I lived in that cave with her for a short period and recognised that her only solution was death; but the death of her children still sits uncomfortably in my mind. So, tomorrow I am going to find out where they're buried to pay my respects, they all deserve at least that.

"What are you thinking about?" Finn asks.

"Parenting, children, and the society we raise them in."

"And your conclusion?"

"Society is a mean, self-centred, judgemental, and unforgiving place in which to raise children. I worry about Dylan's future."

"He may be someone who changes society for the better, we don't know the future. Maybe you should just focus on getting better."

"I *am* getting better."

"I haven't noticed that much."

"Perhaps you don't want to notice. Perhaps other things have become more important?"

"There you go again with your paranoia. I am always here for you."

I feel the tension rising between us, and I don't want it to sap what little energy I have, so I put Dylan in his bouncy chair and head upstairs. Finn doesn't stop me. I wish he would.

Throwing myself on the bed so the springs squeak, I turn my attention to my suicide note. Has Finn received it and thrown it away, pretending it never happened? Perhaps he's secreted it away ready to use it against me in the future.

I deeply regret writing it, but it was my only option at the time. It was cathartic to see my words in black ink on white paper; it made them tangible, but now I'm recovering, it doesn't have the same meaning. *I'm recovering, yes I am.*

Finn's strange conversations on the phone bother me. I often hear him speaking in the evenings when I'm up here. I need to find a way to discover who he's talking to.

I open my laptop to research where Chloe's buried when it occurs to me to look for spyware, something I'd seen on a TV programme. I'm amazed at the plethora of businesses selling and installing spy equipment. This is my answer; I won't be defeated by Finn.

The smell of bacon has dissipated, and I hear Finn talking on the phone. Intrigued with the dark edges of paranoia simpering away at the periphery of my mind, I creep halfway down the stairs. He's whispering so I can't catch his words. Moving further down, I spy him in the kitchen.

I'm distracted from hearing what he's saying by the fact he's emptying the night feeds I made up, and replacing them with fresh bottles. I'm perplexed by his actions, and wonder whether he doesn't trust me to make them up properly?

I retreat to the bedroom feeling a bad mother. If I were brave like Chloe I would put everyone out of their misery and use the knife in my jewellery box. But mistrust wanders yet again into my mind, demanding I discover whether Finn is being unfaithful or not.

I hear Lois's voice downstairs, it must be her turn to watch over me whilst Finn's at work today. I need to be alone.

I wait for him to come up and say goodbye, but when he doesn't, it strengthens my resolve to see what's going on with him. I open the laptop and hesitate over the keys before requesting details on installing spyware. With the e-mail sent, I descend to find Lois in the kitchen.

"I was just making some coffee to bring up to you," she says cheerily.

"Thanks, but I'll sit here with you instead."

"How are you feeling today?"

"Troubled about Finn."

"Oh? Do you want to talk about it?" she asks, putting a coffee in front of me.

"What happened to your friend, the one whose husband was having an affair at work?"

"She threw him out. He went to live with the other woman and I understand they're getting married soon."

Her words push my shoulders down as though each letter's made of solid steel. "I think Finn's having an affair."

"Why on earth do you think that?"

"He's coming home late, quite frequently, and he has furtive conversations on his mobile."

"Have you confronted him about it?"

"If I ever make the slightest comment, he calls me paranoid."

"That doesn't sound good." Lois pauses and blows on the coffee, sending plumes of steam around her lips. "Do you know his female work colleagues?"

"I met some at the summer barbeque. I seem to remember some very pretty ones, but I would have thought them too young for Finn."

"Men can be very tempted by the younger ones; it draws them back to their own youth. What are you going to do about it?"

"I'm not sure. I want to concentrate on getting better first." I hide my blushes behind my coffee cup. I hate lying to her, but the spyware option may sound foolish if I say it aloud.

"Has he mentioned anything to you?" I ask at last.

"Of course not; he knows I'd have to tell you. Maybe it's something totally innocent."

"I caught him throwing away the bottles I made last night. He made fresh ones. What's that about do you think?"

"I've no idea. Perhaps he thought they were old ones?"

She has an answer for everything, and I don't like any of them. I don't think she really understands, but then how could she?

I tell her I'm off for a shower, before secreting myself in the bedroom and checking my e-mails. The spyware company's replied, so I set up an appointment for tomorrow. I tell them this is a covert operation as I do not want the fictional nanny to know. They will find a key under a flower pot.

I return downstairs with my wet hair wrapped in a towel. Lois is playing with Dylan who's sitting on her lap.

"I'd like to go out with Dylan tomorrow. Perhaps we could go to the Italian café for lunch?" I suggest.

"It's nice to hear you so positive and adventurous, it'll be lovely."

I feel satisfied I've managed to manipulate the situation to suit me. Now I have to steel myself to waiting and learning about things I may wish to know nothing about. Sigh.

Finn

I can't decide whether to drive straight home or call in and see Lois first. A voice in my head is shrieking for me to go home, but the adrenaline rush I feel when I think about seeing Lois is addictive. I not only crave her company, I also feel she really understands me, especially where Colette is concerned. Lois is my ally in my newly darkened world.

When Lois opens the front door, she leaps into my arms. I love this feeling of being wanted, and not just for a bottle or nappy change.

"This is a lovely surprise," she gasps, pulling me inside.

"I need a reassuring hug."

She pulls away from me. "Is that what I have become to you? Surely you can get that from Diana."

"You know hugs are lowdown on her priority; she never was a very tactile mother."

"I'm sorry, let's not waste precious time quibbling over small matters. What excuse have you told Colette for your lateness?"

"Nothing yet; I'll make something up on the way home."

All the while I embrace her, niggling feelings of guilt bubble in my gut. Colette always said men were weak where women were concerned. If sex were handed on a plate, she'd say, men could not help but devour the treats even if they were already satiated.

"You're thinking about her, aren't you?"

Lois is looking at me intently and I consider lying to her. "Cheating still feels wrong."

"Then leave her. I can give you so much more." She strokes my cheek.

Our faces are so close together I can see the thin trail of eyeliner giving her eyes a feline quality. I don't know how to answer her question, so I do something else Colette says men do, I ignore her question and kiss her hard on the lips before telling her what's troubling me.

"After what you said about Colette, I threw away the bottles she'd made and made fresh ones. I can't keep doing that though."

"I thought more about it too, and I must have it wrong. You know how dangerous the Internet can be; type in symptoms and come up with numerous possible and scary illnesses. Forget it, I was being silly."

There, that's what I need, reassurance Colette isn't trying to kill our son. Lois always hits the mark in knowing what to say.

I get lost in her body and lose all track of time until my mobile rings. I grab it from my jacket pocket and hold it to my ear with my shoulder as I pull on my trousers.

"I'm checking you're okay," Colette asks.

"Sorry, got caught up with the guys. I'm on my way home now," I reply, shoving my feet into my shoes.

I hang up and finish getting dressed, all the while being watched by Lois who's draped across the bed.

"You'd better run home, you bad boy," she teases.

Dylan's asleep in his cot by the time I get in, and Colette's ensconced in the armchair watching TV.

"I'd say your dinner's in the dog, if we had one," she says without taking her eyes off the screen. "As it is, I wasn't hungry, so I made you a pasta dish, which will need reheating."

I apologise, but hang back in case Lois's signature scent has imbued my skin. I need a shower. Will that make me look guilty? *The answer is yes, my friend.*

The reheated pasta is more of a congealed mass of gloop, and I only manage to swallow it with the assistance of a cup of tea. Colette's watching me which is disconcerting; my guilty conscience is running visual images of her stabbing me with the bread knife.

"I'm going out with Lois and Dylan tomorrow for lunch," she says quietly.

"That's great news."

"Do you have a busy day tomorrow?"

"The usual list of offenders to see."

I can't read her facial expression, and an irrational fear swells in my gut. Does she know? Will she kill me in my sleep? Curse Lois for putting such ideas in my head. However, I do sense a change in her, but whether it's for the better I can't yet say.

Before jumping in the shower, I change Dylan's nappy and study his body for abnormal swelling. He just looks like a chubby cherub to me, so I settle him down before washing off the remnants of Lois from my body.

Colette is already in bed when I enter the room, and I feel self-conscious putting on my pyjamas in front of her, as though my body has morphed into something different since sleeping with Lois.

I turn to look at her but she's already asleep. However, I'm not ready to sleep as my mind's racing with shadows of unwanted thoughts. Where did Colette go when she disappeared? Will she ever return to being the woman I married? What do I do about Lois? Where does my heart and fidelity lie? I have to choose soon before everything explodes in my face, permanently scarring me forever.

Colette

I grip the buggy handles tightly as we step outside. My heart's pulsating so hard I fear it may burst and pepper my ribs.

"It's such a lovely day," declares Lois, locking the door behind me.

Determined to make this day successful I agree with her, before taking a deep breath, helping my dizziness subside.

The pavement seems narrower with a buggy, and negotiating other pedestrians, buggies, and dogs requires a certain amount of skill which I don't possess. I sense Lois monitoring me, ready to report back to Finn or Diana about my incompetence. But she's also my friend.

The Italian café is moderately busy, and we manage to find a table with enough room for the buggy to sit next to us.

"How are things with Finn?" Lois asks whilst perusing the menu.

"He was late again last night, but he always has a plausible excuse."

"What kind of mood was he in? Perhaps you can glean something from that."

I had to think for a minute; transport myself back to being in his company. "Slightly distant and preoccupied. But my own dark clouds can obscure my view of others, so my perception may be off tangent."

"He probably had a hard day at work. Have you got to be somewhere else soon?"

I frown at her.

"You keep checking your watch."

"Probably just my insecurities about being out."

She's a good observer, I'd better up my game. I consider telling her about the spyware man currently in my house, but decide against it for the time being as a tiny part of me wonders whether I can trust her not to tell Finn or Diana.

"Are you going to ask Finn about his changed behaviour and tardiness?" she asks me as Dylan stirs in the buggy.

"Not yet . . ."

Dylan lets out a hearty cry, interrupting me. I still dread this, not being able to stop him crying in public and have everyone see what a hopeless mother I am.

Leaning into the buggy I hoist him out, sitting him on my lap and jigging him up and down gently. Lois asks the waitress if she can bring a jug of hot water to the table to warm the bottle. What would I do without her?

I don't enjoy my lunch. Dylan's quietly drinking his milk and playing with his feet, and as I gaze at him, I'm desperately wanting to feel that unyielding mother-love the books talk about. I wonder whether I'll ever experience it, or whether my dispassionate regard for him will continue throughout his life.

We finish our lunch and I discreetly check my watch. The man told me he only required a couple of hours, and since we've been out for three, I feel it's safe to return.

The house looks undisturbed as we enter, just as he promised. We wander into the lounge and I can't see where he's put the camera. I'm intrigued. Lois takes Dylan upstairs to change his nappy and I make a pot of tea.

Again I search the room to see where the cameras are, but they're so well hidden I can't see them. If he had not given me a code to watch the films on my laptop, I would suspect he hadn't done the job at all. I long to be alone to check it out.

Lois returns with Dylan and places him in his bouncy chair.

"What have you planned for dinner this evening?" she asks.

"Hadn't really thought about it; food seems so unimportant these days."

"I doubt Finn feels the same way. Shall I see what you have in and put something together?"

"If you want." I love Lois, but I am longing for solitude as conversation and company wearies me after a while. But I fear I may hurt her feelings should I mention it.

Finn arrives home looking older than I remember. His eyes have lost their vitality, and his shoulders are hunched. He seems disconnected from the room.

"How was your day out with Dylan?" he asks me.

"Okay. We went to the Italian café. Lois has stayed to cook dinner."

"Very kind. What are we eating?" He turns to her.

"Lentil and butterbean stew with pancetta, and some wilted watercress. You need to do a food shop; I could go with you, if it's too much for Colette at the moment."

He doesn't seem to be paying attention as he strides over to Dylan and lifts him up. I watch him enviously, interacting with his son in a way only fathers can; boisterous yet nurturing, sincere yet fun. I haven't yet begun to nourish such sentiments. My feelings are still in seed form lying on hardened soil, at risk of shrivelling in the sun before they have the chance to burst into life.

"That would be a good idea; perhaps you could go this evening?" I suggest, seeing an opportunity of solitude.

Whilst the stew is bubbling away, Lois makes Dylan's bottles for the night. Watching her, I wish I had her energy and impetus for life. However, I know it will return, especially when I stop taking the medication which dulls my senses and appetite for living. I will be me again, but until then, I must endure the watchful eye of others as they scrutinise my actions and moods, watching for any signs of madness streaming back into my life.

"Dinner's ready," announces Lois as she places steaming bowels of stew before us. "Dylan's bottles are ready too," she continues, looking at Finn.

Mundane chatter, mainly from Lois, accompanies the meal. I prod the food and push it around the bowl, taking only occasional small forkfuls, unnoticed by the others thankfully.

"I'll wash up whilst you two are out," I offer.

Lois chivvies Finn along until they are both finally out of the house. At last, the tight band around my lungs slackens and I can breathe once more.

I take Dylan upstairs and lay him on the bed next to me whilst I check the cameras on my laptop. The screen is filled with a black and white image of the kitchen, where I can clearly see crockery piling up next to the sink. Rewinding the film, I re-watch Lois cooking dinner and witness the strain on Finn's face. I missed that the first time around.

I turn the sound up louder to hear our voices, and am pleased by the clarity. I should be able to pick up Finn's telephone conversations easily.

The second camera shows a clear image of the lounge, where cushions in need of re-plumping lie carelessly on the sofa. I imagine watching Finn sneaking in there to have furtive conversations on the phone. I can't imagine how I'll cope with the knowledge of his betrayal, I only know ignorance is eating away at my fragile sanity. However, if I challenge his deception, will he attack my duplicity at having the spyware installed? Where does one wrong end and the other one start?

A whiff in the air tells me Dylan's nappy needs changing before his cry does. My sense of self-worth increases slightly as I manage the task alone without a critical eye watching over me. I'm just about to lie back down on the bed when the phone rings.

"It's Diana, can I speak with Finn?"

I am used to the curt way she converses with me. I suppose I even understand it.

"He's at the supermarket with Lois."

"Have they got Dylan?"

"No, he's here with me; they won't be long." I can hear her anxiety reverberating down the line, heating my ear with its force.

"I'm coming right over," she snaps before slamming the phone down on me.

I can't blame her. Only I truly know I wouldn't harm him; I'm more likely to harm myself, but even that urge is dissipating.

Diana must have accelerated all the way here as I hear her enter the house. *Will Finn ever take that spare key from her?*

I leave Dylan upstairs, as he has fallen asleep, but I should have guessed she wouldn't believe me as she pushes past me on the stairs. I decide not to follow her but put the kettle on to make another pot of tea, in the hope that Finn and Lois will soon return.

Diana's shoes clip-clop on the floor as she arrives in the kitchen with a grizzly Dylan in her arms. I want to ask her why she woke him but I guess I already know the answer.

"When is the health visitor next due?" she asks.

"Tomorrow as it happens. Why?"

"I just think his health should be monitored carefully."

"Because I've been ill?"

"Because he hasn't had an auspicious start. No breast milk, for example."

I feel another nail enter my mothering coffin, but I won't let her see me defeated.

Finally, Finn and Lois bluster through the front door, straining with bags bursting with groceries. Lois's voice echoes down the hallway then goes up an octave as she sees Diana, but before they can greet her, Diana launches into a tirade.

"I'm disappointed in you both. Neither one of you thought to get me here before you went out. What were you thinking?"

"We've only been gone forty-five minutes. Colette can survive that long alone," retorts Finn.

"But can my precious Dylan?"

I want to scream that I couldn't kill Dylan like Chloe killed her children, but the fact I was present when she settled them down to wait for death makes me complicit. So I say nothing, and let them talk about me as though I'm not in the room.

Hearing Finn's attempt to defend me makes me wonder whether he did receive my suicide note, and is trying to show his support in his usual gauche way. I watch the sly glances he affords me and wonder whether there is an element of pity or fear hidden within. Maybe he's actually waiting for the day I disappear. Would he be happier without me?

Finn

The sight of Colette and Lois together is bringing me out in a cold sweat. I've no one to blame but myself, but I wish I'd never ventured down the road of infidelity. Not because I regret my actions with Lois, but because I'm in love with both women.

When Colette suggests Lois and I do a grocery shop, it offers me a glimpse into what a life with Lois would be like.

We speed off like a newly-merged couple performing their first mundane task together. Only it's not mundane, it's thrilling. She puts her hand on my knee as I drive, making me want to pull over, but instead, I find a space in the car park then find a trolley, which I push, as is my habit.

"So, Finn Forbes, what would you like to purchase?"

"You're the cook, I'll let you decide."

"So I'm to be cooking for you for a while longer, eh? I should get something in return."

"You already do: me."

She slaps me on the arm for being so conceited, and I laugh, making people around us turn and stare. Joviality in a supermarket is forbidden.

I'm still in a light mood when we return home, only to be floored by Diana's fearsome tirade. She admonishes me for leaving Colette and Dylan alone, but I have to confess silently, it never occurred to me to worry; I just wanted some time with Lois that didn't include sex.

Colette seems to have zoned-out from the situation. Maybe her medication allows her to float in a room without actually being mindful. Probably for the best.

"I'll be at work tomorrow. The health visitor's coming, but Colette doesn't need me here to see her," I say.

"Well someone needs to be here to hear what she has to say. She might say something important, and Colette won't remember," Diana says.

"She's depressed, not forgetful." I turn to Colette, willing her to defend herself, but she's staring out the window, oblivious to the character-battering she's receiving.

Exasperated by the whole scenario, I unpack the bags, shoving the contents in random cupboards, feeling irked at being observed by Diana. Maybe this is how Colette feels?

"You're so helpful," Diana comments to Lois. "I hope Finn's grateful for all your support."

I hold my breath, waiting for Lois's response.

"I wouldn't have it any other way. They're all dear to me, and I have fun with Finn in any case."

Fun? What will Diana glean from that?

The two women confer quietly by the fridge as Lois retrieves a bottle to warm for Dylan. I rustle the carrier bag loudly to insinuate I have no desire to hear their conversation.

Perhaps feeling redundant, Colette rises and takes herself upstairs without uttering a word. A cloud of sadness is left clinging to the air, tinged with globules of my guilt.

"You see how she's still not right, Finn. I'll cancel my hair appointment to be here when the health visitor calls," Diana grumbles.

"No need to do that. It's easier for me to be here," Lois chips in.

Although the thought makes me nervous, I know Lois is the preferable option as Diana would stifle Colette and worry the health visitor unnecessarily. I smile and nod imperceptibly at Lois as she tests the temperature of the milk. She gently removes Dylan from Diana's arms and balances him in the crook of her arm to feed him. She acts so naturally; a stranger would be forgiven for thinking she's his mother. How different would my life have been had that been the case? *Don't go there, Finn.*

But what if Lois decides to divulge our affair to Colette? How would that pan out? Would Dylan live with me or Colette? *Again, stop.*

I drop a block of cheese on my foot, making me yell and nudging me from my train of preposterous thoughts.

"I'll be off. It's getting late and fog is setting in. Now remember to ring me if a sitter's required," Diana says wagging her finger at me.

Cringing, I watch her leave and hesitate about turning back to Lois, but invariably I do.

"I don't like driving in the fog. Could I stay over please?" Lois whispers to me, the light catching the gloss on her lips.

I fear if I open my mouth to speak, all that will come out is the sound of my palpitating heartbeat, so I just nod and she smiles, kissing Dylan on the top of his head.

"I can do the night feeds to give you both a break, if you wish," she offers.

"That's very tempting . . ." I begin.

"Then say yes."

I grin at her, blowing her a kiss before checking Colette's not watching me from the hallway.

"It'll be hard lying in the next room from you," she muses. "Perhaps you'll get up to Dylan once, forgetting I am here, and meet me in the nursery."

"That's rather risky."

"I thought you said she's hard to rouse thanks to her meds."

"She is, but . . ."

"But nothing. Embrace the excitement, and surrender to your desires."

Dylan pushes the teat out of his mouth and spits out a mouthful of milk onto her blouse. As she wipes it off it turns the fabric translucent. That's all I need.

"Here, I believe your son's satiated," she says, handing him over to me, her cheeks glowing like gala apples.

Creeping upstairs, I peer into the bedroom to check on Colette. I'm surprised to find her awake.

"Has Diana gone?" she asks.

"Yes, but Lois is still here. Why don't you come and join us?"

"I'm sure you're having more fun without me."

I blush. "What do you mean?"

"Everyone, except Diana, treads on eggshells when around me; that must be wearing."

"Not at all . . . At times, perhaps, but only because we don't want to inadvertently upset you."

"Upset is an internal phenomenon. I have to work through it; you can't do it for me."

I see what she's saying makes sense, yet I know what I'm doing now would upset her, even damage her. It's too late to undo what I've done; there's no erasing my infidelity.

I retreat downstairs to find Lois in the lounge with Dylan lying on the sofa next to her.

"Aren't babies amazing?" she says.

"In what way?"

"They trust us to protect and care for them in their vulnerable state. They've a calm aura that transcends the room."

"Not when they're hollering they don't."

"Come here and kiss me." She looks up at me expectantly.

I instinctively turn towards the door.

"She isn't there. Now come here."

I've become like a trusting baby in her presence, trusting her with our passion and keeping me safe and protected. Her kiss is warm and makes me want more, but that's out of the question for now.

Movement from upstairs draws me away from her, licking my lips to remove her taste and smell. I move to the bottom of the stairs and look up towards the dimly lit landing, but the shadows aren't shifting.

Lois slides up behind me and brushes my thigh, saying she looks forward to seeing me later. I have a hunch she will.

Colette

Lois is scurrying around, tidying an already ordered lounge before the health visitor arrives. I, on the other hand, have no such desire to please.

"Do you want to go upstairs and put some makeup on?" she asks.

"I don't feel the need to glam up, she really comes to see Dylan."

"And you. She needs to check you're okay so Dylan's okay."

I look at her and shrug; I don't know what their okay means anymore.

When the doorbell rings, Lois hurries out and lets Katie Daly, the health visitor, in.

Her cheerful tone and sweeping mannerisms fill the lounge. When she asks me questions about Dylan, Lois answers for me as I sink down further into the sofa.

"He's lost a few pounds, is he taking his feeds properly?" Katie asks.

I nod but Lois mentions his periodic diarrhoea. Katie picks him up and checks him over, saying if the problem persists he should be taken to see the doctor. I've no desire to go anywhere near a doctor, so I acquiesce with a smile.

"So, you think he's all right then?" Lois queries.

"He seems alert, doesn't appear distressed, and is taking his feeds," replies Katie, rummaging around in her handbag. "And how's Mummy doing?"

I force a smile and utter the blandest word I can think of: fine. Lois tells her I seem to be getting better on a daily basis, making Katie smile as she jots down some notes. She then puts her coat back on, ready to leave.

Lois accompanies her to the door before returning.

"Don't you need to go home?" I ask.

"I'll go once Finn's home. Would you like me to make the next batch of bottles?"

"I can manage; you've done enough already." I push myself up and shuffle to the kitchen, eager to be alone.

After switching the kettle on I open my laptop on the kitchen table and search for articles on Chloe, Kerry, and Rachel. I shift through the newspaper article giving accounts from people pertaining to know the family, annoyed with the petty views towards single, young mums. I want to write a counter-argument, but that would mean publicly acknowledging I knew them. No one would understand why I stood back and let it all happen; I barely comprehend it myself, especially now the fog is clearing.

I search on the Internet and discover that the local authority pays for the funeral of a person with no family and no money. They take any possessions or property to defray the costs. I store the authority's phone number in my mobile, ready to use at the first available quiet moment.

I turn my attention to making Dylan's bottles, then decide to tell Lois I'm going for a walk. The quiet moment can't wait.

"What a great idea, I'll get Dylan ready."

I falter; missing the moment to say that I want to go alone. The call will have to wait.

"Finn's in a strange mood these days," Lois says, as we head off towards the local park.

"I hadn't noticed."

"That's not a surprise. Your senses are dampened to the world around you."

"He's always talking to you, has he said what's wrong?"

"Not as such, but I think he's finding being a father harder than he anticipated."

"You really think so? I thought he really wanted to be a father."

"I don't think he counted on all of this."

"By 'this' I presume you mean me."

"I don't want to sound cruel; you feel like a sister to me. But you must admit your illness has made things rather difficult for everyone."

"Do you think he'll leave me?"

"I couldn't say. But if he does have another woman and she gives him more than you, well, who knows?"

My heart plummets towards my stomach, leaving a black cavern in its place. Nausea rolls across my body, knocking me sideways until I teeter and sway. Lois guides me quickly to a bench where we both sit with the buggy in front of us.

"I don't know how I'd cope if he left me. He's been in my life since forever, or so it seems."

"Of course you'd cope. You'd have Dylan to care for."

"I'm not doing a tremendously good job at that currently, am I?"

"You're doing the best you can."

Somehow her words don't comfort me. I'm a failure, an abject failure. I watch other mothers playing with their decorous toddlers, looking every part the proverbial yummy-mummy. The connection between them and their offspring looks effortless, seamless, and it's filling me with envy. I imagine they're flawless wives, who have their husbands' meals ready when they arrive home from work, their homes are spotless, and they probably have obedient pets to complete the scenario.

Observing the women brings Chloe's sad life to my mind. She should have felt more sun on her skin and revelled in the joy of her children. Kerry would have loved the swing and the elephant slide. I let out a long sigh.

"What are you thinking about?" Lois asks.

"Closure."

"To what?"

"To certain aspects of life in my personal universe."

"What *are* you on about?"

"Things I've witnessed. You wouldn't understand."

"Try me."

I shake my head; I wouldn't know where to start. And if I spoke the words out loud, that would make the images in my head concrete.

"It's nothing, I'm just being silly."

Dylan whines from his buggy, clearly discontented about something.

I rock the buggy in the hopes of appeasing him, disconnected from his subtle needs as only a mother with dulled senses can be. Lois is more alert, picking him up and talking soothingly to him.

"I never took you to be the mothering type," I say.

She peers at me and shrugs. "Neither did I. He brings it out in me somehow."

Again, a boulder of pain hits me in the stomach and expels any air my lungs have. Panic of not being able to breathe rocks me.

"Are you all right?" she asks.

"I want to go back," is all I can say as I stand up and take hold of the buggy handle forgetting Dylan isn't in it.

We head back at a fast pace, as I'm desperate to hide my failings from the world. I want to get away from the playground full of accomplished mothers.

Once home, I take myself upstairs and phone the council.

After speaking to several different departments, I discover Chloe's, Kerry's, and Rachel's ashes have been scattered in the rose garden in the local crematorium. At last I have found their resting place and I can go and pay my respects and ask forgiveness from them all. Perhaps Chloe's spirit will insist I join them; I owe it to them after all.

This is a private and painful matter than no one can know about, but I do wonder whether this secret will be the end of me, one way or another?

Perhaps my suicide note will turn up when I am gone.

Finn

Lois corners me in the kitchen when I return home.

"I want more time with you, can you make that happen?" she asks.

I don't want to discuss this now. I just want to hold my son to re-inforce the fact there's more to life than just work and heartache. But seeing Dylan doesn't comfort me; something looks wrong.

"He looks limp and lifeless. How long has he been like this?"

"He was all right earlier. I'm sure you're panicking over nothing."

But I'm seeing a different version of my son than she is. His eyes have lost their sparkle and keen interest. I lift him out of his bouncy chair and place him over my shoulder. His head lolls heavily on my shoulder and his hands are lifeless like stone instead of grasping at my shirt. Something's wrong.

Retrieving my mobile from my pocket I dial the doctor's surgery and arrange an emergency appointment. I take him upstairs and tell Colette.

"I don't know if I have the energy to go with you," she says from the bed.

"This is about our son. Get a grip and bloody get up," I say in a deeper voice than usual, trying not to upset Dylan. "I've had enough of your self-fucking-pity. Our son needs us now."

Instead of rising to the challenge, she rolls over so her back is facing me. If I wasn't holding Dylan I would have forcibly rolled her over and shaken her by her shoulders, instead I force air down my nostrils and walk away. I haven't time for her dramas.

"Do you want me to come with you?" Lois queries.

I nod and ask her to hold him whilst I put my coat on. We leave together and I don't bother shouting up to Colette. She can be damned for all I care.

I hadn't realised how much planning's involved in taking a baby somewhere. It feels like I am trudging through treacle just getting into the car, thank goodness for Lois and her level-headedness.

My hands slip on the steering wheel as I navigate my way through the traffic; maybe a cab would have been quicker as they can use the bus lanes. My anxiety increases as Dylan starts crying.

"I'm looking after him, you concentrate on the traffic," Lois commands.

I manage to squeeze into a space in the surgery car park before rushing in with a distressed sounding Dylan. His cries work wonders with the receptionist as we only wait three minutes before seeing the doctor.

The doctor places Dylan on the couch whilst listening to my concerns. I'm jumbling my words and phrases, caught up in the disquiet emanating from the doctor.

Dylan suddenly starts convulsing; his little body contorting and shaking. *I'm frightened.* The doctor tells me to watch over him as he calls an ambulance. It's all happening so fast.

I go with Dylan in the ambulance and Lois follows behind in my car. I don't hear the siren above my own machinations, as I hold his delicate little hand in mine. I couldn't bear to lose him. The paramedic waves a small oxygen tube under his nose to assist him with his breathing which has become laboured.

Once in the hospital, a nurse brings Lois to me and her face blanches as she sees Dylan.

"Could you phone Colette, she should be here," I ask her as Dylan's body goes limp.

"The fit has passed," the nurse informs me as I gaze at her in a state of confusion.

I stare at him as the nurse prepares to take blood from his dough-like arm. He flinches as the needle pierces his skin, and he lets out a pitiful cry. It should be me lying there; I want to suffer on his behalf.

"She's not at home, and she's not answering her mobile," Lois informs me.

Momentarily I wonder who she's talking about. All I can think about is Dylan.

"Mr Forbes," a pasty-faced doctor says on entering the cubicle. "Your son has high blood pressure, lethargy, watery bowel movements and has suffered a seizure. These are all symptoms of hypernatremia, which is a condition where too much sodium is found in a child's bloodstream. The test will confirm my suspicions. In the meantime, I'm putting up a drip to replace lost fluids."

"How can he have too much sodium? He's only on bottles of milk," I reply, looking at Lois and remembering a distant conversation.

"There can be several causes, such as inadequate water intake, diabetes insipidus, or gastrointestinal conditions. As far as you are aware, have any of these factors been an issue?"

I clamp my lips together as scenarios pass through my mind like a train tunnel in a haunted house; leaving scary images etched on my eyeballs. Has Colette been harming him surreptitiously, and I haven't noticed? I shake my head then feel Lois's hand touch my arm.

"Perhaps you should mention Colette's recent illness," she whispers.

The doctor looks at me expectantly, tilting his head to one side.

"I can check Dylan's notes or you can speed things up by telling me now."

"Colette had postpartum psychosis. She's home now and a bit depressed. But she would never harm him." I am aware of wringing my hands so tightly I am crushing my wedding ring into my finger.

"She hasn't really bonded with him though," chips in Lois.

I give her a sideways glance, wondering why she's saying this.

"We've been rallying around her since she came out from the psychiatric ward."

"She's not mad though."

"No one is saying that, Mr Forbes, I just need to know whether this is an organic or care issue."

I surreptitiously slide away from Lois leaving enough room for a wall to build between us. The doctor glances between us and I wonder if he suspects something. Fortunately, the arrival of a nurse with the blood results distracts him. He stares at them before addressing me.

"Normal sodium level in the blood's serum is between 136 to 145 milliequivalents per litre. Dylan's reading is 163, which is a grave concern. He needs to stay in hospital and have his fluids replaced via an IV drip." He looks at me with his dark brown eyes, waiting to see my response. "I may have to contact children's social services to interview you and your wife."

"Oh God. How long will he have to stay in?" I ask rapidly, swallowing hard.

"His fluids will need to be restored and the sodium level must drop. His levels will be monitored. It should only be a short stay. But I can't speak for social services."

I should feel reassured, but I don't. My wife's ill, and now so is my son. I'm the common denominator in this triangle, so is this my fault?

A nurse is now instructing us to follow her and Dylan to the children's unit. I'm watching myself undertake the task as though I'm in a medical documentary. I'm one of the subjects, and the audience is berating me for being an inept father, who's clearly cheating on his poor depressed wife. No wonder she's depressed, they shriek at the screen.

Dylan's placed on a ward with five other children; three beds or cots on either side of the room. Other parents watch from under hooded eyes to see who has the sickest child. They barely acknowledge me except for a subtle nod and twitch of a downturned mouth.

The air smells of disinfectant and baby sick, and is a touch too hot to be comfortable when fully clothed.

"Go and try Colette again please. She needs to be here," I say.

"Maybe she's disappeared again? Look, I wanted to protect you from this, but I think you should see it now." Lois delves in her handbag and retrieves a piece of dog-eared paper which she hands to me.

I recognise Colette's handwriting straight away, but I don't recognise the sentiments scrawled in blue biro. I read the words too quickly to take in the full impact of what I'm reading, but after a second run through clarity hits me like a bowling ball rumbling down the alley.

"Where did you get this?"

"It was on the kitchen floor. She must have dropped it."

"Why didn't you give this to me sooner?"

"I could see you were struggling with returning to work and home life. When I read this I thought no good would come of you reading it, and she obviously didn't kill herself, so . . ."

"You still should have told me," I snap. "I would have realised how serious her depression had become."

"And what difference would that have made? Would you have given up your career to be with her twenty-four-seven, and scrape by on benefits?"

"It would have been up to me to decide, as her husband, not you."

"Your lover," she hisses.

I glance around quickly, relieved to see the other parents preoccupied with their offspring.

"Just go and phone her. *Please.*"

As she disappears I turn my attention to Dylan who's lying flaccid in a cot with high metal sides, like prison bars. The drip looks incongruous next to him, and I want to scoop him up and rush him home to safety, away from this horrid, sterile, and terrifying world.

Where *is* Colette?

Colette

I don't know why I've brought flowers with me when there's no grave to place them at. What was I thinking? As it is, the cemetery gates close in fifteen minutes, so I hurry towards the rose garden.

I'm thinking about Chloe so hard, I swear I hear her whispering to me through the trees. I can't tell if she's welcoming me, or berating me for abandoning her to her lonely exile. Her children are here but are protected by a circle of angels; after all, she did kill them. What right does she have to hold them in the afterlife?

My erratic thoughts twist my mind into seeing their faces contorted by death. Chloe is angry with me, and the children don't comprehend why I just stood back and let her do it.

I walk faster to outrun the visions, until I feel pearls of sweat gathering on my face. I stop and close my eyes, praying to a god I don't believe in to make them go away. I throw the flowers in a bin I pass along the path.

"I'm so sorry," I mumble out loud. "I didn't have your courage. I hope you're at peace now."

I'm not sure I believe what I am saying, I just want it to free me from the grip of spiritual fear spiralling around my brain.

It's too early in the year for the roses to be in bloom, making the garden bleak and desolate, a reflection of Chloe's life, and demise.

My mobile is vibrating in my handbag again but I choose to ignore it. I want to dedicate this time to the three souls who touched my life briefly.

Dense silence shrouds the cemetery, muffling the din of the nearby traffic. London doesn't seem to have a quiet spot; it's too noisy and cluttered for me. I've longed to move away for some time, but Finn is a city boy at heart, pushing my desires out of reach. I thought having a baby would change his mind, but then my mind got in the way.

I make my way to the tube station drifting along in a sea of people, where I could possibly be dragged under and drown.

Descending into the dusty underground station, I melt into the crowd of workers going home, and couples who are still enthralled with each other. I'm invisible, with not even the title of mother to paint me into a discernible caricature.

The rush of wind down the tunnel announces the imminent arrival of the train, blowing rank, grimy air in my face, and matting my hair.

Finally, I'm crammed into a carriage, standing with my face perilously close to a stranger's back, with the sound of someone's iPod fizzing in my ear. I sway and stagger as the train moves forward, knocking the elbows of people trying to read on their mobiles. The melange of sweat, fading aftershave, and smoky clothes, lifts a nauseating veil to my nose.

It's much later than I thought, so when I arrive at my station, I climb into a taxi and head home.

I find the house is in darkness which confuses me.

I switch on the lights as I enter and look for a note on the half-moon table, which is where Finn and I agreed to leave messages for one another. Finding no note, I move to the kitchen and put the kettle on.

Standing here, I'm suddenly aware of being filmed by a hidden camera. The thought makes me smile before I think I might see what's happened to everyone on the film. With a steaming mug of tea, I mount the stairs to find my laptop.

I ensconce myself on the bed and settle down to watch the footage, hoping I can fast forward to just before they leave rather than watching endless frames of empty rooms.

I am still taken aback by the clarity of the images and when I see Finn come into view, I smile at the fact he has no idea I can watch him like this. He moves around aimlessly before Lois enters the room and they talk. Only the sound quality is lamentable, or they are whispering? I thought it was better than this and I'm hugely disappointed.

I'm considering phoning the installation man when something catches my eye. A lingering look, a touch, and then, oh God, a kiss.

My throat dries, and my mouth puckers. I rock back and forth, hugging my knees as I watch the two people I love embrace passionately. Finn draws away from her and looks towards the stairs, clearly checking I am not about to materialise and discover their subterfuge.

I want to stop watching them but I'm drawn to monitor every movement they make. They seem comfortable with one another and I sense this is not their first kiss. How long has this been going on?

Tears gather in my eyes and gradually spill over the edge, inching down my cheeks before dripping onto my lap. Finn disappears from view and Lois switches on the kettle. I despise her beauty that threatens and attacks my happiness.

I feel sick watching her ponytail swish from side to side as she fills the bottles with formula. She has her back to the camera and is hunched over the worktop, periodically glancing towards the door, undoubtedly waiting for Finn to join her and wrap his arms around her miniscule waist. Waves of nausea wash over me as the images of them together replay themselves in my mind.

Lois fills the bottles with cooled boiled water and shakes them vigorously before setting them to one side. I start wondering whether Finn will leave me and take Dylan too as I'm an unsuccessful mother thus far. I do love our son, but in my own quiet way. It will hopefully build over time; I just wonder whether he'll allow me the time I need to adjust to my new life and role within it.

The phones rings as something on the footage catches my eye, but doesn't make sense. As I pick up the receiver, I hear Finn's voice saying loudly that he's found me at last.

"Dylan's in hospital. Get a taxi and get down here, right now."

His words bounce around my head, but all I can see is he and Lois kissing, and it blocks my ability to concentrate. I say I'm coming before ringing off abruptly. When the phone rings again I almost decide to ignore it, but I cannot resist its pull. Finn is requesting I bring a bag of clothes and nappies for Dylan. Again, I hang up quickly. How will I be able to concentrate on Dylan when I'll be standing next to Finn and his mistress? I dash to the toilet and vomit the build-up of bile.

I pop a mint into my mouth and grab Dylan's bag just as the taxi pulls up outside and honks his horn. I wonder what my first reaction will be when I see them both.

Finn

Relieved I've finally contacted Colette, I'm suddenly anxious about seeing her now I know about her suicide note. I'm not sure I will ever be able to see her in the same light. And as for Lois, what's happening with her? Her bubbling possessiveness is wearing me down.

A nurse comes by to check Dylan's drip, which she does in a matter of seconds. She doesn't stop for idle chatter or to reassure me he is doing well. In fact, she avoids looking in my direction all together.

Lois has her back to me, looking out the window at the aerial view of London. The dreary buildings looking macabre against the grey-smudged sky.

"It's started to snow," she announces, so everyone looks in her direction.

I hear recognisable footsteps and turn to see Colette heading towards me with Dylan's bag, which she puts down at my feet before leaning over Dylan.

"What's wrong with him? How's he doing?" she asks.

"They're not sure exactly, they're doing tests; he's really poorly, Col. Where the hell were you?"

"I'd gone for a walk to clear my head."

"You were bloody irresponsible and selfish not answering your phone all that time."

I shrug.

"Colette, you made it," Lois says as she joins us and stands a little too close to me.

"Dylan needs me, so here I am."

The atmosphere is frosty, which I put down to everyone worrying about Dylan. I can't bear to look at his lifeless body anymore, but I'm forced to as the paediatrician approaches.

"I'd like to speak to Mr and Mrs Forbes, alone please," he asks as he pulls the curtain around the cot.

"Lois can stay, she's almost family," replies Colette.

I swallow hard and bounce on the balls of my feet. Lois is positively glowing with pride, with not the merest hint of shame. I bear enough for both of us, perhaps.

"I'm going to come straight to the point: Dylan's levels are so high that the only explanation is that he's been ingesting it." He pauses dramatically and looks between Colette and me.

My face instantly reddens, spreading brazen guilt all over my cheeks and the bridge of my nose. I turn to Colette who appears lost in thought, then to Lois who is trying to tell me something with her eyes as she jerks them towards Colette.

"Have either of you got anything to say?" he says firmly.

"There must be a simple explanation," I start. "Perhaps the formula has been tampered with?"

"There's no evidence to support that. I understand you've suffered with postpartum psychosis, Mrs Forbes."

Colette nods but doesn't jump to her defence. Thinking the unthinkable, I consider whether she would have killed Dylan before killing herself like that single mum did in the newspaper.

I turn to her and grab her by the shoulders. "You wouldn't do that, would you? Tell him." I want to shake her but fear I will look like an abusive husband, even though right now I could slap her just to grab her attention.

"Silence speaks louder than words," whispers Lois.

"Shut up, Lois. This isn't the time for platitudes," I bark.

"I'm only saying what everyone's thinking. Colette hasn't been the same since his birth. I'm sorry, Colette, I do love you . . ."

"But not as much as you love Finn," Colette cuts in.

I'm jolted by her words and the doctor clearly looks troubled.

"Let's take this to my office," he commands.

I'd forgotten the other parents on the other side of the flimsy curtain, and they look disappointed not to hear the denouement of our soap opera. I want to stick two fingers up at the lot of them, but thrust my hands in my coat pockets instead.

The doctor strides towards his office, with Colette struggling to keep up. Lois is tagging along close to me.

The doctor beckons us to sit down as he sits opposite us across a cluttered desk.

"My main concern is Dylan's health and wellbeing. Now clearly there are a few issues between you all, which I suggest you work through outside of the hospital. Now does anyone care to enlighten me about what's happened to Dylan?"

He seems to be suggesting that one of us is deliberately harming Dylan. I now notice that both Lois and I are staring in Colette's direction.

"I suppose I am the prime suspect for hurting my son because I'm depressed," Colette says, her words hanging heavily in the room, suspended like a mobile over a child's cot.

"I'm not sure what to think, Mrs Forbes, but I am concerned that something nefarious may be going on. I'm alerting children's social services and the police."

My throat constricts, hampering my ability to breathe, and the back of my neck prickles with sweat. I instinctively rub my temples to alleviate the dull throbbing.

"Just tell me you didn't do it and I'll believe you," I say to Colette, barely looking at her.

The pause pushes against my chest as I wait for her response. I now look at her, urging her to answer.

"I'm saddened I need to deny it for you to believe me. I'd hoped you'd know it wasn't me automatically," she finally replies.

"I knew the old you; I'm not so sure about the person you've become these days—" I stop short, seeing how much I'm hurting her.

"Are you so blinded by Lois's beguiling ways that you've forgotten why you fell in love with me in the first instance, and not with her?"

"I *am* in the room," Lois protests. "But seeing as this is truth time, yes, Finn and I are in love, and have been for some time."

I open my mouth to speak, but Colette's voice fills the void.

"I don't doubt you are, Lois, but I'm not so convinced about Finn. He may have been led astray whilst I've been trapped in my own unforgiving world."

"You doubt he loves me? Well he's very convincing when we make love."

Slumping forward as though I've been punched in the stomach, I inhale sharply. "I'm not going to stand in your way; you're welcome to one another. However, Dylan won't be a part of your lives, which I'm sure delights you, Lois."

"I dote on my godson," she snipes.

"Is that why you've been adding salt to his bottles?"

I look up sharply, unsure of what I have just heard. My hands are tightly clasped in a prayer-like position as I wait for Lois's rebuttal.

"You see how deranged she is, accusing me of such a heinous act. You're the mad one, Colette, it's your way of getting back at Dylan for making you ill." She turns to Finn. "She's trying to get you to change your mind about me."

"No, that's not the case. I barely recognise the pair of you, my once loyal husband and best friend."

Lois is now standing, gesticulating wildly. "You remember the late afternoon I made the night feeds for Dylan before we went to the supermarket. She had time to tamper with them before our return. In fact, I remember every time she feeds him he wriggles and cries. She's deflecting the blame onto me to make you hate me."

"Stop," I say, barely recognising my own strained voice. "This shouldn't be about how we adults have managed to mess things up, but about saving Dylan and getting to the root of his problem."

"Colette's madness is the root of his problem. Why can't you see that?" Lois shrieks.

"My madness is the least of anyone's problem. I've seen you both kissing and I will never be able to forget that."

"You've never seen us kiss. See how her madness tricks her," goads Lois.

Colette sits up straighter. "I was sane enough to think Finn was having an affair, thanks to your suggestive comments, Lois. So, I had some spyware installed and that's how I witnessed you kissing. And that, Lois, is how I saw you tampering with Dylan's bottles."

I jump up and stand in front of Lois. "Why? Tell me why you'd do such a thing?" I grasp her shoulders, shaking her forcefully.

"I only wanted to hurt him a little so Colette would take the blame, then we'd be Dylan's parents, our own little family."

"You'd harm an innocent baby to get what you want? You're unbelievable!" I yell, causing the doctor to rise to his feet.

"I'm calling the police," he begins, quietly but firmly, "and if you have evidence of this, Mrs Forbes, I suggest you hand it over to them to expedite the matter as quickly as possible." He rings through to his secretary asking for security to come, and for her to contact the police.

For the first time, perhaps ever, Lois looks scared and unsure of herself; losing her enigmatic charm that pulls me towards her. She drops into the chair, quietly contemplating her fate.

I turn to Colette, but she's looking right through me, asking the doctor if she can return to Dylan.

"And I don't want you anywhere near me," she tells me on leaving the room.

I can't really blame her.

Colette

I'm still reeling from Lois's arrest, and Finn's infidelity. Although the house feels empty, at last it feels like home.

Dylan sleeps on the sofa next to me, finally recovered after weeks in hospital, and intensive intervention from social services. I had to prove my parenting capabilities, supported by my health visitor and community mental health nurse. But I survived, and so did Dylan. We survived together.

I reach out and touch him tentatively, not wanting to disturb him. He's so precious, and symbolises a turning point in my life, a change I find hard to put into words.

When the phone rings, Dylan twitches, but doesn't wake.

"Please don't hang up again, I really need to talk," Finn pleads.

I hold the receiver by my ear, allowing it to hover there whilst I contemplate cutting him off again. But something makes me continue listening.

"I'm happy to do the talking if you prefer just listening," he gently continues.

He takes my silence as a cue.

"I've no excuse for my behaviour, apart from being a pathetic man led by his pants, and brow-beaten by two dominating women.

"In our marriage vows, I promised to love you in sickness and in health, and I failed miserably. You needed me desperately and I let you down."

He pauses, I suspect, expecting me to berate him. It's my turn to be unpredictable. It feels empowering, yet dangerous; I'm toying with my future, Dylan's future. Dylan.

"Can I see you and Dylan sometime?" he asks.

"To what end?" I finally find my voice.

"To build the bridge I destroyed between us. I want to show my sincerity."

"I'm surprised you haven't regurgitated Diana's words about me denying you access to your son."

"I've learnt my lesson, and so has she. You wouldn't believe she's now spouting praise for you and condemnation towards Lois, calling her a psychopathic marriage-breaker." The heavy silence underlines his realisation at his faux-pas.

"I no longer care what Diana thinks, or you, come to that."

"I always felt guilty when I was with her, if that's any consolation."

"Not really."

I believe he's sensing my reticence at having this conversation. He's floundering in his tumultuous ocean of guilt, and I don't want to throw him a life-line. Have I become so hard that I choose to watch him drown?

I'm sure I hear him gulping back tears, so I hang up and pick up the novel I'm currently reading.

I place Dylan in his highchair for breakfast, before opening my laptop. I warm his milk ready to pour onto his rusk, as I make myself a coffee.

Dylan's gurgling contentedly and playing with his toy elephant, waiting for the morning routine to kick in, whilst I mooch around until I've had my first cup of coffee. Finn would testify how I'm hopeless before then.

Finn. He comes into my thoughts frequently, but I never allow myself to study the thoughts and images too thoroughly, fearing another trip to the land of madness. And yet, I sense an underlying emotion of love beneath the stronger ones of disgust, disappointment, and anger. Yes, I still feel anger at his betrayal and abandonment, but then there's Dylan. Doesn't he deserve a more prominent father-figure in his life?

Messages via my website rack up spaces in my inbox, and I settle down to read them as I feed Dylan and sip my steaming coffee.

My heart breaks reading the words of mothers suffering from postpartum psychosis, or in recovery from the life-crushing illness. Women abandoned by their partners or families, separated from their babies and home-life, and contemplating suicide. This is a safe place to unload the burden of the illness, and discuss their visions of their future.

I don't profess to be an expert, and I tell them so. The only thing I have to offer is empathy, and some ideas that helped me along the way. I bring them all together in the hope that some women will form lasting friendships to carry them along their journey. As for me, I never make friends, not trusting myself to fail them as I did Chloe.

My health visitor and mental health nurse occasionally do guest question and answer threads on the site, which always prove popular, as in this day of austerity, not everyone is lucky enough to have such resources available to them. God bless the NHS.

The post plops onto the doormat, tearing me away from the screen. Ever since childhood, the sound of post arriving always fills me with excitement about some surprise message awaiting me. These days, that's mixed with trepidation about bills.

Straight away, I recognise Finn's handwriting. I pick it up with the junk mail and return to the kitchen. I tear it open and read it rapidly.

Dear Colette,

Seeing as telephone conversations never go well between us, I've decided to pen my thoughts, allowing you to absorb them at your leisure; I understand how speaking to me doesn't give you the time to reflect on what I'm saying. I think my thoughts are more ordered in this way too.

I don't expect forgiveness anytime soon, or ever, come to that, but I feel we need some form of civility for Dylan's sake. Of course, my ideal situation would be for you and me to tentatively get to know one another again, and to rekindle the love we once shared. I miss you so much it hurts.

I know you said you had the locks changed, but I thought you'd be pleased to hear I took the door key back from Diana, more out of symbolism than anything else. She's chagrined by her behaviour one day, then defiant the next. She's exhausting with her mood swings, so I've tempered our contact to once a week by phone currently. I want to concentrate on you and Dylan.

If it's possible, I'd love to meet up on neutral ground, perhaps the café in the park we so loved. Dylan could watch the ducks. Perhaps you could think about this, and let me know in a week or so. I'm happy to wait, no pressure.

All my love, Finn.

Dylan and I have a fun morning at the baby gym, where we both get exercise and bonding time. I'm still reticent to form friendships with other mothers as I don't want to divulge my chequered mummy history. I want to appear normal, whatever that is.

I still suffer with visual images of Chloe and her daughters on a daily basis, and fear I will forever if I don't open up to someone about my connection with them. Shame prevents me from doing this; big, fat, shame.

Dylan falls asleep on the journey home, allowing me to make a coffee in peace and answer e-mails. And there it is, by my laptop, his letter. I have to acknowledge that I do miss him, and love him, which irks me after all he's done to me. Where is my resolve to cast him aside and move on without him?

Finn

I wipe my sweaty palms on my trousers as I sit at the window table in the café. I'm wearing the t-shirt Colette bought for me in Paris, a few years back. It's now faded and vintage looking, much like my face has become over the past few months. Losing weight has hollowed my cheeks, and the beard gives me a tramp-like appearance, as one of the offenders at work told me with glee.

I squint through the window, shielding my eyes from the sunshine, and spy Colette pushing a buggy. My heart races, reddening my cheeks. I long to look calm, but I fear I'm failing.

"Hello, Finn," she says, expertly positioning the buggy between us.

I smile, anxious my voice will wobble if I dare speak. So I shove the menu in her direction, and she tells me she'll have her usual, without giving me eye contact. I miss her beautiful eyes.

After the waitress puts our drinks before us, I take a sip to moisten my mouth.

"How have things been?" I ask.

"Dylan has fully recovered, without any lasting damage, and I'm fine. What about you?"

I had hoped she'd talk for longer, like she used to do. I remember on our first date, years ago, she warned me that she was verbose, which suited me fine as a man with few words in social situations.

"Work's busy; people are always committing crimes. And I'm lonely." There, I've said it, opened myself up to scrutiny and mockery. I hold my breath.

"I'm sorry to hear that, but life hasn't exactly thrown me bouquets over the last few months. You've only yourself to blame; well, you and Lois equally."

"I know, and I flagellate myself daily. Lois is at least being punished in prison."

"Are you keeping in touch with her?"

"She sent me a letter begging for forgiveness, and putting her act down to insanity brought on by overpowering passion."

"Her solicitor tried that one in court, but the jury didn't believe her. Ironic really, she tried to use the mental health card when she damned me for suffering with the same condition."

"She only cared about herself, I see that now. I thought she was supporting me, but she wanted something you had, and would do anything to get it. I was a fool."

"Do you think she only became my best friend back then to hang around you?"

"I can't answer that, I don't know. I think she genuinely likes you, but when your illness struck she saw a way of getting me. Don't hurt yourself by analysing her too closely."

"I can't hurt any more than I do already; you couldn't comprehend."

"You're right, I couldn't." I stretch across the table to take her hand, but she removes it and places it in her lap. What did I expect?

"How long will Graham allow you to camp at his place?"

"As long as I need to. I haven't asked you here to beg for the spare room." That sounded harsher than I intended.

"I wasn't suggesting that. I imagine you want to set up an arrangement for you to see Dylan."

"Sorry, yes, sorry, shit."

"Now you're being hard on yourself."

"I can't forgive myself for being such a prick."

"Will Graham allow you to have Dylan overnight?"

"He's cool with it. Are you?"

"I don't see why not. Lois can't get to him now."

"I wouldn't let her get anywhere near him now."

"Men are foolish where beautiful women are concerned. Correction, men are foolish generally."

"That's a sweeping statement." When will I learn not to bite back, especially when I'm clearly the underdog here?

She stares at me long enough to see the pain and contempt in her eyes. I'm not forgiven.

I watch her finish her drink and peer at Dylan who's slept throughout our meeting, before putting her handbag over her shoulder.

"I'll see you when you collect Dylan on Saturday."

Did I miss part of our conversation? "What time?"

"Ten." And with that, she leaves the café without turning back.

I think I believed up until this moment she was going to be her warm, loving self to me, but now I see our situation for what it is. Over.

I pay the bill before shoving my hands deep into my jean pockets, and stepping outside. The sun's warmth doesn't elate me as it used to; my mood is so low I may as well live in a burrow, with its dank atmosphere burying what little life-force I have left in me. Is this how Colette felt? *Poor cow.*

I wander past a couple feeding the birds with their toddler. She shrieks with laughter as a duck swims towards a piece of bread she's thrown in. Her parents look at each other with pride, before the mother whips out her camera and begins taking photo after photo, which will all look the same when they get home, but they won't have the heart to delete.

I could have been like them. I should *be* them.

Today came sooner than I imagined, and I'm shocked to find I'm anxious about having Dylan for the day. I haven't told Diana, as I want him all to myself for the first time, and I know she'll smoother me with her demands and criticise my every action with him. I feel Dylan needs to get to know me all over again, without her interference.

I'm grateful I was in court with two of my offenders today, to keep my mind occupied. But now looking around the lounge, I see I'll need to clean and tidy the place before I bring Dylan back. More chores, how does a woman do it?

Colette

I hardly slept last night, fretting about letting Dylan go for the day, and anxious about seeing Finn. I want my life to be so different from this.

Dylan wriggles around freely as I change his nappy and dress him in a t-shirt with a green frog on it, and a pair of green shorts. I slather his chubby thighs and arms in sun cream, and find a hat that I hope Finn will think of using, or at least replace each time Dylan takes it off.

My heart rate doubles when the doorbell rings, and I try walking nonchalantly to the door to allow my glowing cheeks to fade.

"Is the little man ready?" he asks. I detect a tremor in his voice.

I smile, pushing the buggy towards him. "There's everything you need in the nappy bag, including feeds and rusks. I'll see you at six." My hands slip from the handle as he takes the buggy from me, and moves down the path chatting away to Dylan.

The house suddenly feels very empty and quiet, in an uncomfortable way. My thoughts race forward to a time when Finn may meet another woman, who'll then play a role in Dylan's life, and it knots my stomach. Bile rises in my throat as I rush to the toilet and vomit up my breakfast.

Returning downstairs, post lies on the doormat. I scoop it up and shuffle to the kitchen to make some herbal tea. Amongst the bills and junk mail, a handwritten envelope catches my attention. Once the tea is made, I sit down and rip open the envelope to find the sender is Lois. Taking a deep breath, I smooth the paper on the table and begin reading.

Dear Colette,

I'm not sure you'll read this letter once you realise it's from me, but I have to give it a go.

You'll be pleased to hear prison is hard; no luxuries, uncomfortable bed, and poor company. But the memories of what I've done haunt me day and night, and my counsellor says I must try and make amends for my mind to move on.

I've always been jealous of you. You were the brainy, quietly beautiful girl who attracted boys without realising. And the seed of envy was planted in my mind.

When I was your bridesmaid, I willed Finn to refuse you as his wife, and turn to me instead. When he didn't, it felt like a light in my world had gone out. When you got pregnant, I was the closest I've ever been to wanting to die.

So, imagine my joy when you became ill after giving birth. I saw it as a sign for me to infiltrate Finn's world as the woman he should have married. And he was so receptive, more than I imagined. I did have Diana's support of course; whispering in his ear her concerns for him and Dylan. I always knew she liked me, or rather my family's money, shall we say.

Perhaps you can forgive me on some level for chasing after your husband, but I don't imagine you can find any forgiveness for what I did to Dylan. And why should you? It was a heinous act, and I can't bear to think what Finn must think of me now. You see, Finn's thoughts about me still matter, and I'm sorry for that, but my counsellor insists I'm truthful to all in this matter.

I imagine when I'm released, you'll want nothing to do with me, and that saddens me. Yes, Finn will be out of bounds, but over the years I've enjoyed your company for girlie chats. Of course, when Finn was around, I only had eyes for him, and you didn't matter. Honesty doesn't look good on paper.

I will probably have to move away, as my crime was reported in the national and local papers. I need to move and start again. I'll also have to start a new business with a new name.

I've made a mess of my life, and all for love. Yes, I love Finn and that will never stop even after all of this.

You're a lucky woman.

Lois

I finish my tea and sit back in the chair. Her words float before my eyes, especially the word *lucky*, as that's how I felt when I was with him. When he was by my side as I gave birth, I felt so special. I still need him in my life, but how can I forget he slept with Lois. Their naked bodies shared a very intimate moment, and I can't forgive or forget that. I'm no longer that lucky woman, she saw to that.

I'm feeling suffocated in the house, so I head for the hairdresser to see if she can fit me in. The salon is buzzing and noisy, but thankfully she has a slot.

A young girl washes my hair vigorously, attempting small talk, but soon giving up as I close my eyes. The jets of water massage my scalp, and the smell of the shampoo tickles my nose briefly, before it's replaced with conditioner, during which time she performs a head massage, but too softly to relax me.

Sitting in front of the full-length mirror, I'm treated to the view of my dilapidated state. I'm wearing skinny jeans, battered brown leather ankle boots, and a Led Zeppelin t-shirt. Minimal makeup compromising of brown lipstick and smudged black eyeliner grace my face. I really need to start wearing blusher.

I've known the hairdresser, Sally, for years, so she's aware that recently I've become uncommunicative, so she deftly chops my hair into an elfin crop in silence, before finally running some wax through it.

Sally smiles, admiring her work as I get up, hand her a tip, then go to pay. I love the way I feel six feet tall after a haircut; I just wish I had someone to admire it. I must stop feeling sorry for myself.

Exactly on six o'clock, the doorbell rings. I check myself in the mirror, then open the door, seeing admiration in Finn's eyes. I smile to myself.

"I took him to the animal park."

"I can see," I say, noticing the new baby elephant toy Dylan's clinging to. "Was it fun?"

"Yeah." He looks like he wants to say more, but stops himself.

"I got a letter from Lois today." I wasn't planning on telling him that.

His face reddens as he scuffs the toes of his shoes on the ground.

"Thank you for bringing him back on time," I say, taking hold of the handles and bringing the buggy inside.

I smile faintly as I shut the door. That was enough contact for now.

Finn

I'd forgotten how ethereal Colette looks with her wispy elfin cut; it was the first thing I noticed about her when we first met. I smile at the memories, before the dark clouds of guilt hide the visions from me.

I'd had a great day with Dylan, but four days back at work hasn't eased my pain of the situation. I know work colleagues are talking about me, as they fall silent when I approach. They're probably saying what an idiot I am to have cheated on such a beautiful wife. They all liked Colette when they met her at a Christmas do once, before Dylan was born.

Colette mentioned getting a letter from Lois, and I can't help wondering what she said. Has she made things worse? How worse could they get? Divorce.

That word strikes fear in my heart, as it signals the end of something I treasure, treasured, still treasure? I don't know how I feel these days.

"When am I going to see my grandson?" Diana says, sitting down opposite me. "Grandparents have rights, you know."

"I think Colette has the right to be distant with you; you were team-Lois after all," I reply.

George arrives at the table carrying two pints and a gin and tonic. He's aged over the past month.

"Why can't we see him when you do?" she presses.

"Next time, I promise. I just wanted some time alone with him; I miss him so."

"Do you think you and Colette will get back together?" asks George.

He normally never gets involved in family affairs, preferring Diana to take the lead, but I'd forgotten how much he likes Colette. I wish he'd spoken up when she was ill; deflected Diana's negative vibes. She'd always been the power-house in the relationship.

"I'm not sure. I hurt her really bad, I don't know if I deserve a second chance."

"It's her fault you were in that situation. If she wasn't ill, you wouldn't have needed Lois's support," chimes-in Diana.

"That's exactly why Colette has distancing herself from us. You blamed her for getting ill, when it wasn't her fault at all."

"Women didn't get ill like that in my day," she quips.

"I imagine they did, but it wasn't recognised or talked about. Everyone's more open and accepting these days, on the whole." I stare at her intensely.

"I think you men have become too soft over the years. You want to be in touch with your feminine side, whatever that means."

I take a large gulp of beer to prevent myself from retorting; this meeting isn't going well, and all I want to do is dash back to my room. I suspect George knows my thoughts, as he winks at me from behind his glass.

"I saw that," she snipes.

George takes another swig of beer, ignoring her comment. So that's how their marriage has lasted.

"Look, of course you'll see Dylan again soon, I just need things to settle between Colette and me. She deserves that respect from you."

Diana glares at me before studying her manicured nails. I want to say more, but George looks at me and shakes his head surreptitiously.

I stare at the letter in my hand from Colette's solicitor, requesting a divorce. Wow, and I thought she'd eventually forgive me enough to push past this. She's cited infidelity, which I can't argue with, and feel hiring a solicitor would cost me unnecessarily. Diana will be apoplectic when she finds out, mindful of the shame on our family.

My work day passed with me barely connecting with the offenders; my heart and mind was fixated on the dismantling of my life. I return to my temporary home, knowing I'm going to need a permanent solution that negates the need for small talk with the owner of the house; I just want to cuddle Dylan.

When another letter arrives a few days later, I'm half-hoping its Colette's solicitor saying she's had a change of heart, and is seeking reconciliation. Disappointment smacks me in the face. Lois.

Dearest Finn,

Writing this letter is the only way I can reach out and caress your face. How I miss the feel of your skin, the contours of your face, and your powerful arms. Do you miss any part of me? I bet below your anger towards me, you have fond memories of our snatched moments. I replay them constantly.

I wonder if you've forgotten how unhappy you were with your life not so long ago. Are you still unhappy now, I wonder? I was only doing what you needed me to do to repair your life, you must know that. With Colette erased, and me as your lover and Dylan's mummy, you'd have had the life you desired and deserved. I know you understand that, even though you can't show it to the world as they wouldn't understand. Only I understand you, and once you realise that, the happier you'll be when I get out of this place.

I won't burden you with how it is in here, I don't want you to worry about me. No need, my love, I have thoughts and memories of us together to keep me safe and warm. Every memory leaves a trace.

Until next time, darling.

Love always,

Your Lois xx

The paper sticks to my sweaty fingers, so I can't put it down instantly. After a couple of flicks, it lands on the table and stares at me; Lois's twisted sentiments grimacing up at me. Bile rises, leaving the stench and acidity of vomit in my mouth.

Thoughts are racing through my mind, and all I can think of is stopping Lois's ability to communicate her deluded thoughts to me. She can't really think I still love her after all she's done. I laugh at myself, what *she's* done, what I did too. I grabbed those moments of love out of the selfish need to feel a man in control of his life once more; I chose to become intimate with her, foisting my ideals of happiness onto her perceived flawlessness. Colette faded into a blot of imperfection on my vision of family life, a life Diana had imprinted on me at an early age. There I go again, blaming a woman for my mistakes. I hope to God Dylan has a more sanguine approach and attitude to life and women. Who knows how Colette may sway him, as Diana swayed me.

I've no appetite for food, and consider calling Colette with my woes about the letter, seeing as she dropped into the conversation that she'd received one already. But I doubt she'll want to hold my hand through the pain and discomfort, as I held hers during her labour. Only alcohol is my friend at times like these.

I retire to my bedroom with a bottle of vodka, pilfered from the drinks cabinet. Three glasses down and the pain still isn't numb. I'll keep going until I feel no more for the night.

I can see in Colette's eyes she's not impressed with my appearance as I wait to collect Dylan. I awoke late, so I'd no time for a shower and shave. I look dishevelled; a shadow of the man I once was.

"Are you well enough to look after him today?" she asks, without an essence of concern for me in her voice.

I consider opening up my box of cluttered emotions on the doorstep, allowing them to spew over our feet.

"I . . . no, I'm fine."

She hands me his bag before placing him in my arms. He wriggles, arms reaching out for her in a semblance of distress. I recognise the look of anguish in her eyes, before they set on me, cement-like in anger.

"Did you get my solicitor's letter? A simple yes or no will do."

I nod before turning away, lest she see my eyes glinting with tears of self-pity and blackmail. I'm grabbed by a soul-stripping urge to step into the house, and close my arms around my family to shield them from harm. I didn't protect them from the harm I caused them, though, did I?

Colette closes the door behind me, adding another nail to my already peppered heart.

Colette

I hand the brass plaque over to the man in the crematorium office, which he then places on the desk.

"When will the bench be ready?"

"A couple of days. The dead ain't in no rush," he replies soberly.

I sense the closeness of Chloe and her daughters as I stroll through the garden, heading for the busy road, where people are unaware of the death cloud hovering above them.

Without the buggy to push, I feel exposed and vulnerable; naked for all to see. I've grown accustom to using it as a shield and to justify my existence. Yet I don't want to bring him to the place of death just yet; he'll encounter it one day as we all have to.

The doorbell wakes me up. It takes me a few seconds to realise I'm on the sofa, and Dylan's returned. I sprint to the front door.

"Did you have a good day?"

"He was whiny to start with, but soon settled down."

The way he inflected the end of his sentence tells me he has more to say, but can't decide whether to take the plunge. I decide to prod him.

"There seems to be something else you want to say."

"Perhaps I could come in for a chat, just a quick one."

I acquiesce with a shrug and allow him to step inside, even though a voice in my head is hissing obscenities at me. He places Dylan on his play mat before sitting in his once usual seat by the window.

"I also received a letter from Lois, and I'm not sure what to do about it. I suppose I was wondering how you responded to yours?"

Her name in his mouth makes me baulk; and his question is a tad insensitive.

"You were closer to her than I ever was, surely you know how best to engage with her. Why do you need my input all of a sudden?"

My bristling has piqued him, and I see him struggling to contain derogative comments from taking flight like a swarm of poisonous arrows in my direction. This is what happens when a relationship breaks down, all the love curdles like milk left in the sun, making a fetid, gloopy mess in the glass.

"I was ruled by my pants once; I want to make sure I take the right course of action this time around."

"Pity you didn't think to ask me the first time."

"I would have, had you not been so mad . . ." His eyes widen. "Oh God, I'm so sorry, I'm so gauche."

"Stop with your platitudes; you deserve one another, both locked in your respective prisons. You may think I hold the key to release you both, but I don't, and even if I did, I wouldn't use it. You both hurt me too badly."

The tightness in his eyes scares me momentarily, until I see his face blanch, and beads of sweat form along his brow, his eyes darting towards Dylan then back at me.

"Is this really the end for us as a family unit? I thought you'd be willing to give us another chance."

"I'm no longer the wife monopolised by paranoia. I'm in control of my life rather than mental illness being in charge of me. You've damaged me beyond repair. Run back to mummy and let her run your life, I no longer need you."

"Dylan needs me."

"Of course you can see him; he's still your son. But don't use him to get to me."

He looks defeated, chagrined even, but it's too late for that now. He can have sorrow swiping his heart, snagging at the muscles, and leaving red-raw claw marks for all I care. I want him out of my house now, and tell him so.

He bends down and kisses Dylan before standing.

"I see you've returned to being the woman I married. Perhaps if I'd stayed around a while longer, I'd have been here to welcome you back."

My heart pinches. "I didn't push you away, my illness did, you just couldn't see it."

"Perhaps if Lois and Diana hadn't been guiding me away, I'd have remained by your side."

"You can't put all the blame on them, you need to take responsibility for your actions. I need to bathe Dylan now."

He leaves reluctantly, but not before leaning forward surreptitiously, then recoiling just as fast. The sensation of wanting to feel his kiss flashes across my mind, as fleeting as a kingfisher darting across a river; there one second and gone the next.

Acknowledgments

I am eternally grateful for the support and advice given to me by Jessica "Goose" Kristie and James Koukis, from WGP, over the years. I would also like to thank the numerous Guide-Dogs-in-training we have boarded, for either sitting next to me, or under my desk, keeping me company whilst writing.

About the Author

Hemmie Martin spent most of her professional life as a Community Nurse for people with learning disabilities, a Family Planning Nurse, and a Forensic Nurse working with young offenders. She spent six years living in the south of France, and currently lives in Essex with her husband. Her eldest daughter, Jessica, is studying veterinary medicine, and her younger daughter, Rosie, is pursuing a degree in computer science.

Lightning Source UK Ltd.
Milton Keynes UK
UKOW05f0412300617

304364UK00003B/104/P